COLLEGE OF ALAMEDA LIBRARY

WITHDRAWN

PZ
1
E49
Sav

Elwood, Roger
    Saving worlds

DATE DUE

MAY 15 74			
MAY 28 75			

LENDING POLICY
IF YOU DAMAGE OR LOSE LIBRARY
MATERIALS, THEN YOU WILL BE
CHARGED FOR REPLACEMENT. FAIL-
URE TO PAY AFFECTS LIBRARY
PRIVILEGES, GRADES, TRANSCRIPTS,
DIPLOMAS, AND REGISTRATION
PRIVILEGES OR ANY COMBINATION
THEREOF.

SAVING WORLDS

SAVING WORLDS

A Collection of Original
Science Fiction Stories

EDITED BY ROGER ELWOOD
& VIRGINIA KIDD

With an Introduction by Frank Herbert

DOUBLEDAY & COMPANY, INC.
GARDEN CITY, NEW YORK
1973

ISBN: 0-385-05409-2
Library of Congress Catalog Card Number: 72–84910
Copyright © 1973 by Roger Elwood & Virginia Kidd
All Rights Reserved
Printed in the United States of America

First Edition

DOUBLY DEDICATED:

For Bessie Freeze, a woman
who did so much to save the worlds of so many
—Roger Elwood

To open windows on the world,
to clear the air, for Beth and Karen, who leave me
breathless
—Virginia Kidd

ACKNOWLEDGMENTS

Ode on the Source of the Clitumnus © 1973 by the Modern Poetry Association; reprinted from the January 1973 issue by kind permission of the editor of the magazine *poetry* and by permission of the poet, Tom Disch.

The Smokey the Bear Sutra reprinted; being, at the author's express request, in the public domain forever.

Dies Irae © 1950 by *Accent;* reprinted by special permission of the poet, James Blish.

Ecommando Tactics columns © 1970, © 1971 by Roger Lovin; all excerpts are reprinted here under his blanket permission, with heartfelt thanks. *Ecommando Tactics* appeared in the Los Angeles *Free Press* regularly while Lovin was an (adoptive) Californian; he is actually an able seaman in the crew of spaceship Earth, with no very fixed abode.

The idea for this book was entirely Roger Elwood's, and since acknowledgments are here being made, each of the editors would direct a mutual gratitude to the other and to the contributors. Responsibility for the editorial choices represented herein is fully shared and was fully enjoyed. However, a mantle of responsibility is hereby assumed by Virginia Kidd for all opinions expressed and for all material cited in the notes introductory to the stories and poems in *Saving Worlds.*

Gratitude (mixed with apologies) should here be offered to Doubleday's second-most-patient editor, Diane Cleaver, and to Larry Ashmead; they have to put up with a lot but they accomplish much. Gratitude is extended to Alan Ravage for his patient encouragement. And warm appreciation to Annette Charlonne, who helped more than she knows.

CONTENTS

INTRODUCTION

One smoggy, eye-smarting day not too long ago, we awoke to find ourselves as a species in something like a tent revival meeting with the hot gospel of ecology blasting at us from all sides. The *preachers* with the loudest voices were saying:

"Come into the fold or you will experience hell on earth followed by a painful extinction."

Right up there with the loudest was our little band of science fiction writers, a hardy, resourceful and imaginative lot, saying:

"Here are a few of the possible hells, a few of the possible ends, and some colorful alternatives."

Our batting average has been frighteningly high.

Big Brother is watching you.

Have you checked the pills in your Malthusian belt lately, madame?

If your ego has been folded, stapled and mutilated, please be patient. Management has not yet developed a computer program to deal with all contingencies.

It makes me feel good all over when I realize that war is peace.

Keep in mind as you read this new collection of ecological projections that what the human imagination can dream, the human flesh can create. This will be true as long as we have a place to stand and the second law of thermodynamics continues in force. There will be stranger things than we foretell here.

When I think of ecology, I often recall the story about the man who was told he had one week to live unless he invested his life savings in a complex treatment which offered him a fifty-fifty chance of extending his life by only one year.

That's the hot gospel and you'd better believe it.

We say it here as we've said it before: the human species has gone beyond the point where a single individual can control enough energy to obliterate us all. We have no assurances that such energy will remain in the hands of individuals whose good sense will steer us away from the bang or the whimper.

We *did* send chemical weed killers to Southeast Asia in tankers of sufficiently large capacity that the destruction of just one of them could have destroyed the oxygen regenerative capacity of the Pacific Ocean. And that's just one example.

The concept of "fail-safe" does not have a fail-safe built into it.

Power is the name of the game. We are in a wild energy time. This power is an odd thing. The militant says, "Power to the people." The governor says, "Send in the National Guard." The tactical squads are alerted. The newspaper editor tells his staff, "Play it cool; we don't want to contribute to the hysteria."

There also are those great bundles of accumulated energy which we call wealth—money. (The United States has almost no research funds invested in studies aimed at a world without war. The implications and consequences of this gap appear obvious.)

All of these power areas are correct in their internal assessments. Power often is what determines the short-term course in a society. And there obviously are many powers influencing humans. This makes it very easy for us to get sucked into the vortices where we are just reacting, where ultimately we feel we must do anything at all to influence others. This is the pot of message which a great many science fiction writers stir when they use the ecological theme. They do have an influence, too.

There's a striking thing about these power vortices, though. You see it time and again. A center of influence appears—a leader. A succession of leaders may make the scene. It's as though they were drawn into a vacuum of genuine concern whose reality cannot be denied. Don't minimize the concerns. They are real and they focus on problems whose solutions are difficult. But the demand is for simple solutions framed in absolute terms. Here's where the demagogue makes his appeal. "Follow me! I have the answer!" And you want to believe because the simple statement of the problem carries the ring of truth.

Thus—the hot gospel. Thus Occam's razor cuts us up once more.

The vacuums of leadership continue to accumulate around the genuine problems, however. People come into the vacuum, exert power and, in the current idiom, they go on their ego trips. Invariably, these leaders run or drift away. They cut out. They go to Cuba or Algeria, to a commune in the country or a ranch on the Pedernales. They do this partly because they have behaved in a fashion best calculated to achieve this end. Since the abandonment of (or expulsion from) the power center is a predictable consequence of the leaders' activities, you can suspect it follows naturally on the use of power.

The leader goes on his trip, leaves and the vacuum remains. But its shape changes. It's as though the leader took the power with him. His movement starts to die of its own political machinations, sickened by lack of understanding and accumulating disorganization—by a choice of goals which don't really fit the situation.

Then it's everybody go on to the next cause.

There are indications that ecology, as a concern for the future of our species, is following this course.

The problems which aroused concern, however, are still with us. It's only the pattern of a "movement" which has beguiled us. The important thing to recognize is that ecology as a phenomenon reflects a genuine underlying malaise. The boil is a symptom of infection. It's when we confine ourselves to the surface symptoms that we guarantee more and more lethal eruptions.

This is the essence of the ecological message.

We are engaged in a planetwide crisis of the human species which is shared by all. We are well beyond the point of no return in technological developments which exert greater and greater influence upon individuals, often with shockingly destructive consequences which are amplified by war.

At this moment of crisis, we are being sold the hot gospel that our survival decisions must be made within the either/or arena of guilt-innocence. The moral cowardice of this insistence is blocked out by most of our species even while the increasingly strident screams which this insistence provokes trap us in ever more destructive confrontations.

It's the old schoolyard routine where someone inevitably demands that you "cry uncle."

In a typical either/or trap, many latter-day ecologists offer us the alternatives of austerity ("Kick the science habit, baby!") and/or poverty (spending our life savings for another year of dubious survival) or of a despairing decline into extinction. This trap is bound around with "cry uncle" walls of guilt-innocence.

"Who made the decisions which got us into this fix? The only thing wrong with this country is its politicians!"

"We'll straighten things out when we get rid of (Nixon, Johnson, Laird, Wallace, etc.)."

Who are the bad guys?

Nowhere is it suggested that lethal decisions may have been products of their contexts.

Richard Nixon did *not* invent the system of consensus reality within which he made his choices.

The same is true of rebels who feel that the only answer is to plant explosives in a bank.

Or of those who insist we must invent a better machine.

People who say, "The only answer is . . ." demonstrate little more than the tightness, the confining restrictions of the either/or arena within which they insist we must make our decisions.

Few focus on the size of the arena or upon the destructive assumptions which form its walls. Few observe that mankind is attuned to this planet and to tidal forces which resonate in and around it. The word "lunacy" did not enter our language by accident. One of those lunatic tidal forces appears to make us prefer small and comforting arenas, places which do not dwarf us by their immensity or by their dangerous unknowns. We prefer the tranquil pond to the perilous rapids.

But the science fiction writers and ecologists keep saying: "You're already into the rapids, buddy. What're you going to do now?"

And the onslaught of science-technology keeps reminding us that even if we accumulate ten billion years of human history, that will remain a microscopic event in the face of infinity.

Such reminders and their echoes of fatalism tend to fill each of us with despairing anger. In the throes of subjective turmoil, itself partly a product of current contexts, we are told we must raise our ecological sights, raise our awareness, attempt new heights of objectivity. We are told we must do this in a relativistic universe where the best operational answers we can achieve are only probable, not absolute, that we can never test the reliability of our system by requiring it to agree with another system.

All of this continues despite the accumulating evidence that no corner of human endeavor escapes the clouding, the fuddlement and mistaken assumptions of previous contexts. And nowhere does this show up more strongly than in the education which we call science.

Psychologist L. Johnson Abercrombie in *The Anatomy of Judgment* tells us how science students, learning to read X-ray plates, demonstrate an inability to distinguish between what is shown on the plate and what they believe to be shown. When confronted with proof of the extent to which preconceptions influence their judgments, the initial reaction of these students tends to be surprise and anger.

Surprise and anger.

Throughout our lives these emotions represent a dominant tendency through which we interpret the brute facts of experience in a relativistic, changing universe. Having been taught from infancy by countless implicit lessons to expect a universe of perfect cause and effect amidst absolute objects, we react predictably when told: "It ain't so, Joe."

Here may be a major area where ecological science fiction raises the reader's hackles. Many people tell me they read such science fiction "with terrified fascination," suggesting the reaction of a chicken confronted by a snake.

One view of history says men will undergo violent contortions, will even die, to prove themselves "right"—to keep their pet beliefs intact. Another view says terror may attract humans like a magnet, drawing them into the very situation they fear most. Science fiction has been playing with these themes at least since Plato's day.

By the questions asked, by the alternatives displayed for your consideration, such science fiction represents a metaphor of history and sometimes becomes a preview of reality.

Those of us who are looking now at contexts, rather than at *blameworthy* individuals, are beginning to ask a new question: How do we deal with lag times for out-of-date contexts when such contexts represent power and identity to entrenched blocs of our fellow humans?

There may be an implicit answer in the very framework of the question, and it's possible you can see this answer in every story between the covers of this book. Here's one way of putting it: We stop condemning our fellow humans. (My God! That sounds like "Judge not, lest ye be judged.")

If we learn one thing from observing the life around us, it's that hierarchies exist and that mistakes occur within the multiplex niches of those hierarchies. To approach the study of these circular relationships only to find the guilty and the innocent represents a form of nonsense, an old context whose assumptions don't work. That context breaks down. It doesn't march.

The lesson of *Infinity* as applied to hierarchies says there always exists another level beyond the ones we can see. There are more niches in heaven and hell than we have dreamed of in our philosophies, even in the philosophies of ecological science fiction.

Survival decisions (and that's at the core of ecological concern) require us to refuse to be confined in the systems which our ancestors gave us. The geneticist observes that we are continually breaking out of the old genetic framework. This appears to be equally true of those abstract frameworks which we call consensus reality.

The mechanic in us argues: If the gear doesn't work, replace it or design a new one.

The ecologist says: "Now you have to learn about systems."

By understanding system relationships, the ways the parts operate together and how those relationships link us to the infinite universe around us, we enter the real realm of science, including the realm of science fiction. One of the things this art form has been saying to us all along is: "Increase your grasp on probabilities."

Look at your own hand. Isn't that a metaphor standing for how we seek to influence our universe? Think of the limits in that flesh and how we construct amplifiers (waldoes) to overcome those limits, only to find new limits beyond those we had perceived.

The message of this metaphor and of ecology is that we need to stop asking why and start asking how. Behavior is observable and can be dealt with operationally. We can analyze behavior for its probabilities. Infinity merely warns us that because one event regularly precedes another we are not necessarily dealing with cause and effect. The crowing rooster does not cause the sun to rise.

The lesson of hierarchies-over-infinity tells us the probabilities are high that any assemblage of specialized data will indicate larger and more fundamental events in our universe.

Any assemblage.

Short-term cause and effect, that ancient illusion of a universe reduced to the hand of god, is out. That's not the current style. Now we are a world-band of humans seeking a perilous course through a relativistic universe where new conditions constantly assault our sense of balance. An enormous amount of evidence has accumulated around the concept that this is an impermanent universe composed of impermanent bits. An intellect educated to demand otherwise tends to make reactive decisions to this evidence in a pattern of surprise and anger followed by despair and rejection.

Herein may be the essential *new thing* with which ecological awareness has armed us. We appear to be reacting within lethal systems of resonance (vibration) which make it highly probable that we soon will destroy this planet and every living thing on it—unless we dampen the system.

We have more than enough data to describe existing conditions. We understand our moment of surprise and anger. The ecologist is telling us to recognize now that we have limited ourselves to microscopic arenas of either/or within which we cannot solve our problems.

The species knows its travail. This shines through every bit of ecological science fiction I have ever read. The implicit observation within this accumulated artistry appears this way to me—that all of the individual cells, sharing the common condition, must share in the solution. A full description of all those defensive, disconnected, short-term responses we have been making to our problems is also a full description of how we maintain our problems. Behavior cannot be separated from biology with any hope of understanding the system they share. You cannot cure the hand and leave the body sick. Indeed, that approach makes the sickness worse.

It's not so much our addiction to science which is killing us, but how we make our connections. War, as the foremost ecological disaster of any age, merely reflects the general state of man's affairs at that time. It represents a choice of how to use our energy. Our problems appear to arise not from the use of energy, but from destructive by-products of how we choose to use our energy. Discarded by-products are polluting both our physical and our psychological environment. Misused human talents and the toxic effluent of unburned fuels—both are choking us.

We know some things about the consequences of not facing such problems—no matter how large the problems may appear. Facing problems represents positive action. It counters the deadly debilitating force which follows our surprise and anger. It counteracts frustration. By this we revitalize decision-making abilities. Facing the probability of species extinction, an implicit message of ecology, has shocked many humans into various forms of despair which appear to be a kind of blind acceptance. They say: "We are caught in the contradictory systems which give us improved means to produce deteriorating life styles."

The signposts on our mutual road to disaster stand tall and unavoidable. The seamless web of our world has come apart at the seams we didn't know it had. And the ecologist and science fiction writer are merely saying: "Hey! Look there!"

In this moment of despair, I'm suggesting we re-examine the road system. Let's look at the dynamics of the energy flow through our system. Let's examine the connections, the seams. I'm not suggesting we abandon any present social system for another. In my view, communism-socialism and capitalism have such similar energy-flow systems that a visitor from Arcturus might find it difficult to tell them apart. The hierarchies are interchangeable. The motives are interchangeable. The methods of self-justification and enforced compliance are overwhelmingly alike.

In each, the individual is the ultimate cog, abandoned in his solitary despair. Yet the species remains at the mercy of this individual. He can decide to distinguish all of us. He is acquiring the use of greater and greater energy with each passing instant. Just as we cannot separate behavior from biology, we cannot separate the individual from the species and hope to learn what is required of us in this moment of crisis.

Our new condition demands that we understand a new and larger arena of either/or, a new set of choices which balance the needs of any individual against the needs of the species. Each must be served. The energy requirements of this arena are enormous. The need to waste nothing is pre-eminent. The responsibility to our descendants that we keep the system working cannot be evaded.

We are surfboard riders on an infinite sea and the waves around us have changed. This is the lesson of ecological science fiction: *Regain our balance and teach our young how to balance.*

—Frank Herbert

SAVING WORLDS

—Just for openers I'd like to clarify something: *"ecology."* Ecology is a word that's bandied about with ping-pong frequency by everybody and his dog, Storm. But I don't hear one person out of fifty using the term correctly. It is applied to concepts ranging from the New Religion to brands of soap. (I actually heard one well-intentioned lass ask a stock boy for *"some ecology soap."* The kid looked at her deadpan and said, *"We're out of it this week."*)

The most common misuse of the term is found among the more aware folk who can toss off point-getters like *"food-chain"* and *"maximum tolerance curve"* at parties. They confuse it with *environmentalism.*

Well, it ain't the same animal. Follow this: Ecology is usually defined as the study of the relationships of an organism to its living and nonliving environment. We already have the well-established word *bionomics* to describe the study of those relationships and the organism's life cycle, but we needed a word to describe the *systems* within which bionomics functions. Ecology, then, is essentially concerned with ecosystems, which include interacting components—bionomics. Within an ecosystem—a lake, for example—the environment disappears, simply dissolving into the system's component parts. Thus, to a student of human bionomics, smog is a harmful material in his environment; to the ecologist, it is a metabolite in the fluids of the metropolitan ecosystem. Perhaps the definitional difference doesn't seem worth the effort to you, but it is. We have become so enamoured of the *"environment"* that we don't understand the ecology. This is like treating the symptoms rather than the disease. Our problems here on spaceship earth are not environmental: they're ecological. So let's shape up, brothers and sisters. We don't *have* any place to ship out to.

Ecommando Tactics (L.A. *Free Press*)

Terry Carr is the author who wrote "The Dance of the Changer and the Three." He is the editor who conceived of and expertly chose the Ace Specials line of paperback books, thereby raising the whole field of speculative fiction noticeable notches. And Terry Carr has "shipped out." He is a bionomic casualty, a chronic bronchitic who finally fled New York City for upper California. That makes a very acute angle if one were to plot his course on a graph, because he was born in the Pacific Northwest (though probably not in a canyon, a datum which can be suppressed as not relevant to our plotted path). "Saving the World" is the first original story (so far as I know) written by Terry Carr in his Oakland canyon.

Terry Carr
SAVING THE WORLD

The Fifth Co-environment Conference was held back during the smog years, and it was there that we turned the corner on the question. I played a pivotal role at that conference, in my own way, so I remember it vividly.

The night before the conference began, a bunch of us were gathered in the bar for drinks and socializing, getting reacquainted because it had been almost a year since the Fourth Conference. I was at a table with Karen Elkin and a kid named Burt Summers, who'd never been at one of these conferences before; Karen was telling him with astonishing seriousness about the protocols of conference existence.

"If you're here as an advisor, you'll have everybody in the hotel trying to buy you drinks," she said. "You have to know who everybody is or you could get into some compromising situations."

"I'm with Dow," he said. "I'm an environmental futurist." And he did look like the sort of bright young man who'd be in that field: slim, earnest, the glint of contacts in his eyes.

Karen said, "Oh, well then just everybody's going to be flocking around you. Now, it's okay to accept a drink from most of the government people, but be careful of the lobbyists, they can demolish your credibility faster than anyone. And of course you know better than to talk with any of the media."

"I have an interview with some CBS people tomorrow," said Burt, and he actually looked anxious about it.

"Oh—well of course you can't back out now," she said, "but be careful not to say anything. Whatever they ask you, refer them to the printed handouts. If you're lucky, they might not even air the interview." She turned to me and said brightly, "Bradford, you're a government person, why don't you buy us all some more drinks?"

So I did. The martinis were poor at that bar—they were using a too recent vermouth that tasted bitter—but the only other drink I could stand was a bloody mary, and the tomato crop was notorious that year. Burt settled for the purity of a gimlet; Karen smothered all taste in an old fashioned.

Suddenly Karen's eyes lit up and she waved a hand at someone who'd come into the bar. "Tom! Tom! Over here!" I looked around and saw a tall, somewhat stoop-shouldered man heading toward us; his hair had some gray in it but I thought it was probably natural.

Karen introduced us: "Burt's the new man up from Dow, and you probably know Bradford, he's with the President's Commission. Tom is just back from Corfu—some sort of water study you were working on, wasn't it?"

Tom shook hands with us and sat down. "Yes, a water study. I was on loan from Coast and Geodetic, working with people over there on thermal flows; they think they're changing. We did a lot of swimming, actually."

Tom ordered scotch on the rocks, then switched that to straight up. "Ice cubes are made out of water, and I don't drink water in New York City when I can help it," he said.

"It comes from upstate," I told him.

"Wouldn't make any difference if it was from Hudson Bay, I wouldn't drink it. The more I know about water these days the more

I drink scotch. How long have you been with the President's Commission?"

"Four years. I was appointed just before the Second Conference."

"Oh, the one in Hawaii," said Karen. "Remember the demonstrators who fell into the pool?"

"Yes," I said, "and the next morning there were still two of their signs floating face-down in the water like dead fish." The four of us laughed, Burt a little self-consciously; we were making him feel like a latecomer.

"Isn't the NSF party supposed to start about now?" Burt asked. I looked at my watch and, sure enough, it was ten o'clock.

"Might be a good idea to get there before all the liquor's gone," I said. "Besides, there's nothing less compromising than NSF booze, right, Karen?"

"Absolutely," she said, draining the last of her old fashioned. Karen didn't eat the fruit any more, I noticed. It wasn't a matter of calories, either; her figure was as sinuous as ever. I wondered if she was interested in taking Burt to bed tonight or if she'd rather have old tried-and-proven me.

We had to wait fifteen minutes for an elevator, but that's typical at conferences and we thought nothing of it. The NSF suite was on the nineteenth floor, and as we came out of the elevator Tom spotted one of those automatic shoe-polishing machines. "Look," he said, "an electric lobbyist!"

The NSF party was still nearly empty when we got there. The bartender made me a martini that was decent and the four of us commandeered the couch. Burt asked, "Is this an open party, or just for people in the field?"

"Depends how you define the field," Tom told him. "No demonstrators were invited, if that's what you mean."

"Oh, we have to have some demonstrators!" Karen exclaimed. "They're essential to any good conference. Bradford, let's make some signs."

We had a number of napkins on the coffee table near us; we used magic marker pens to write slogans on them. I wrote ECOLOGY—LOVE IT OR LEAVE IT. Karen wrote POLLUTION IS A DEAD HERRING *and* ON

A CLEAR DAY YOU CAN SEE. Tom wrote OFF THE PLANKTON. Burt couldn't think of anything to write; he shrugged nervously, grinning.

"We should stick pencils through the backs of these and march up and down the hall," said Karen. "Anybody know the second verse of 'Solidarity Forever'?"

"They'd throw us in the pool," Tom said.

"There is no pool," I said.

"All the worse," he said.

"What's 'Solidarity Forever'?" asked Burt. The rest of us stared at him, then at each other, and then we sang the song for him, loudly. People coming into the party looked curiously at us and we waved our napkins at them.

Joe Morgan came in then, and we called him over to our couch. Joe was on the commission with me that year, and he was already calling it his lean and hungry year: he'd dieted down from two thirty-five to a hundred and ninety and was still working at it. His clothes hung loosely on him.

"Joe, you're fading away!" Karen cried. "You're going to disappear before the year's over!"

"Here, read this booklet from Food and Drug," he said. "It's enough to make anyone stop eating."

"Oh, don't be an old bear," she said. "Give us a sermon, Joe! We *need* a sermon—the conference hasn't even begun and we're drunk already."

"Dissipation has set in early," I said.

"A sermon," said Joe. "Ah yes, my children, but only a thin sermon, for these are thin times." Joe was famous for his sermons. His father had been a tent-show preacher and Joe had run away when he was twelve; he was an atheist, but he could sure preach hellfire.

"Brethren!" he intoned, "and also sistren—hear the Word of God as He speaks through this mortal vessel. Hear the Word, and the Word is—Dissipation!" He was talking only to us, but as soon as he began to orate he shifted his voice into its resonant pitch, and people all around the room could hear him. Several began to drift over to our side of the room, and more were arriving at the party all the time.

"Remember the evil cities Sodom and Gomorrah! Recall Babylon!

Yea, cast back your memory to that first wellspring of sin and degradation, the Garden of Eden. *Destroyed,* all of them, their ashes spread to the four winds. And do you know the reason? It was Dissipation, my friends . . . Dissipation!"

"Amen, amen!" Karen laughed, and raised her glass in a toast.

"What is Dissipation? I hear you asking. Why, brethren, it is a mortal sin. It is *waste,* it is *moral suicide,* it is Man's prideful refusal to accept God's boon!" Joe looked around at his gathering audience, and there was loathing on his face. "Does the mighty lion scorn the gifts of almighty God? Does the thunderous whale, Leviathan of the sea, refuse God's natural comforts? Does the hawk in flight give lie to God's wisdom in ordering His universe? *No* he does not, nor do any of the creatures of the earth, whether great or small. Except for mankind, brethren . . . except for mankind."

"Right on," I said.

"Mankind has fought its way out of the very Garden of Eden, mankind has built a civilization so great that it has produced as its ultimate achievement . . . New York City! Yes, brethren, we have traded the Garden of Eden for the foul, scabrous city in which we find ourselves tonight. Did God destroy Babylon forever? Then why do we rebuild Babylon?"

Joe paused, and the room was dead silent; he could really cast a spell, even in mockery. "I will tell you why we build these towers of concrete and sin," he said softly. "It is because we *hate God,* my children, we *hate God!*

"Only stop and think on this for a moment and you will see that it is true. We try to destroy God. We form governments so that we may work together against Him . . . we pour garbage into the air so that God might not see us . . . we waste His natural resources in the name of conservation and we poison His creatures in the name of agriculture." Joe was breathing heavily, but now he smiled, laugh wrinkles corrugating his face. "Dissipation, my children, is another word for waste, and it is terrible waste that I see around me this evening. Are we not met here for the purpose of setting right God's world? Is this not our purpose?"

"Amen!" called Karen, and several others echoed her: "Amen, amen!"

"*God can set His own world to right!* He need not wait for us! Do we truly believe that God must wait on decisions from the National Park Service? *No!*" Joe raised his arms in a gesture of benediction. "Therefore waste not your time in caucuses, my friends— leave the tasks of God to God. *Cease* this dissipation of energies, and let's get down to the serious business of *drinking!*" Joe grabbed a gin and tonic from Burt and drained it dry.

There was a spattering of applause, and conversations sprang up as people realized that Joe was finished. He sat down in a chair with us, smiling and laughing. Someone tapped him on the shoulder and said, "God grows His own"; Joe nodded and that person went away.

"Your sermons are marvelous," Karen told him. "Really, Joe, I loved it—how do you think up things like that?"

"God speaks through me," said Joe, and we laughed again.

Later that night we wandered the halls of the hotel, glasses in hand, and eventually discovered the sauna. It was automated, open all night; it wasn't supposed to be co-ed, but we changed that. The five of us sat naked in a steaming room, our bodies drenched with perspiration, and every few seconds one of us would say, "Oh my God," as the heat worked its way into us.

"Is this one of those smoke-filled rooms I've been hearing about?" Burt asked.

"No," said Tom; "actually it's a mock-up called Urban Environment 2000, done by the boys in Health Education Welfare."

"It is a foretaste of Hell," pronounced Joe. "Satan shall once more extend his domain to the world of mortal men."

"Sounds to me like they're the same thing," I said.

Karen was uncharacteristically quiet, and I saw her looking appraisingly at Burt. The rest of us joked and groaned about the heat, but Karen seemed to become more and more serious. When we ran out and jumped into the pool, screaming in delicious agony, she started playing little pool games with Burt, and I knew she'd made her choice. Burt would get the full conference experience tonight.

Eventually I went to bed, swallowing a handful of vitamin B for tomorrow's hangover. I woke up with a headache anyway, and went downstairs to the bar for a bloody mary. But I'd forgotten about the vileness of tomatoes this year, so I was still feeling pretty awful when Tom Mildren came in.

He joined me at my table, ordered a beer and sat sipping it in companionable silence. I found myself, as bad as I felt, feeling very warm towards Tom, and before long I managed to say, "What's on the schedule for today?"

"Seminars," he said. "How to Get from Here to 1990. International Waste Agreements. A couple of others."

"The usual stuff," I said.

"Yes. Farberman is talking at three this afternoon."

"Oh God, Farberman. Doesn't he ever shut up?" Farberman had resigned his university job to write books; he'd done one called *The New Apocalypse* that was a best seller.

We moved from the bar to the coffee shop so that I could put some chowder into myself; Tom had already eaten. As we came in I saw Karen and Burt at a corner table; I wondered whether they'd want company, but then Karen saw us and waved, so we joined them.

"We've been up for hours!" Karen said proudly. "This is lunch for us."

Tom said, "That's a terrible thing to say to mortal people."

"Oh, Bradford isn't mortal; I've seen him stay up all night and talk for two hours the next afternoon. He even quoted figures to us. Remember, Brad?"

"That was in Hawaii," I said. "I was immortal that year, but it went away. Today I couldn't even *listen* to someone talk."

"Oh, but Jules Farberman is on this afternoon," said Burt. "We met him this morning, over breakfast. He's very nice, and a very interesting person."

"A nice fellow, yes," I said. "Did you talk with him, Karen?" I knew what she thought of Farberman.

"He and Burt did most of the talking," she said. "I'm not very strong on things like genetic drift in wheat, or whatever it was."

"He's still talking on his usual subjects, then," I said. "Do we really need him to draw the media? What do we want with the media anyway?"

"They watch us and keep us honest," said Tom.

"Sure they do," I said, and then my soup came and I turned my attention to it.

Karen and Burt went off to do his interview with the television people. I finished my soup and Tom and I went back to the bar for the serious business of the conference.

We found George Chester sitting at the bar and persuaded him to join us at a table. George was on the staff of one of our more high-powered Congressmen. He was a little bit crazy, but he was the kind of crazy that sometimes made sense, and I liked him.

He said, "I had to get through a line of Gestapo pickets outside the hotel. They're vicious today. And I saw more and more of them coming from all around; they've got us surrounded."

"Do you think they'll break in?" I asked. George imagined things like this all the time.

"I think they'll peak by tomorrow, and there won't be any stopping them. I saw zip-guns and pipe bombs. They've bought off the police; we can't get any help from them."

"Maybe we'd better do something," said Tom. "What do you suppose they want?"

"I don't think they know themselves. But everybody gets worked up about the environment today; it's like the anti-war demonstrations ten years ago. And it's especially bad now with all the soldiers home and out of work. They've got nothing to do but cause trouble."

"You mean we're being attacked by the U. S. Army?" asked Tom.

"I saw at least three squad leaders giving orders to their men. That's no ordinary mob; they're organized." Then George stopped, and he grinned widely, showing a gap between his two front teeth that lent a wry quality to his face. "You think I'm crazy, don't you?"

"I think you embellish things a little," I told him.

"I'm not crazy," George said. "It's a crazy world. I lead a life of noisy desperation."

He went away to join one of the seminars. Tom and I finished our drinks and I still had my headache, so I went back up to my room to give it some more sleep. I opened the window for fresh air, and over the traffic sounds from the street below I heard a mob chanting "Action now, action now, action now!" I shut the window and went to sleep.

When I got up and alive again it was nearly evening. Farberman must be about finished talking, I figured, so I went down to the meeting hall and found people milling around in the usual conglomerate: government aides, people from industry, media snoops, pressure people representing this or that lobby, specialists in various sciences. A high-powered bunch of people, but they looked like any other motley crowd.

Farberman evidently had finished speaking, and was now taking questions from the audience. A lot of people had come out of the hall to talk about plans for this evening; I spotted Karen and went over to talk with her.

"Where's Burt?" I asked.

"In the hall listening to Farberman. He's impressed by that stuff."

"Was it the same speech?"

She sighed. "Identical. 'Ours is not merely a task, but an opportunity, for how many men in history have had the clear option of saving the world?' Oh, he was inspirational."

"We ought to sic Joe Morgan on him. Are there copies of his speech set out? I'll need it for my report."

She gave me her own copy and I put it in my jacket. Karen didn't have to worry about making detailed reports; she was a troubleshooter for one of the big power companies and she played things fast and loose.

"Listen, if I know Farberman he'll squeeze questions out of the audience for another hour," I said. "How about dinner?"

She smiled: "Fine." If she thought about Burt first, I couldn't tell.

We ate in a steak house in the hotel; it wasn't great food, but I'd heard an announcement over the musak system that New York was suffering an inversion layer, so we weren't about to go outside. Besides, there were the demonstrators. Afterward we made our way up to the Ford Foundation suite, where tonight's big party was being held.

Tom was there, sitting on a windowsill and smoking, flicking his ashes out the window. I said, "Would you like an ashtray?" and he said, "No thanks, I haven't filled this one yet."

It was early in the evening, but the conference was going full steam. A couple of people from Ag Department were down on all fours in the middle of the room, pretending to be dogs and sniffing each other's assholes. A bunch of other people were laughing at that. Marian McCarthy from Texaco had put her nametag in her hair.

Tom said, "How did Burt's interview go this morning?"

"So-so," said Karen. "But Burt's not very good at changing the subject, and he probably said enough so that they'll put together a tape for tonight's news."

"He has a bit to learn yet about this business," I said, and Karen gave me a slow look.

Just then Burt came in the door; Karen saw him and said, "I'll see how much he's learned so far," and she got up to go over to him. They stood in the foyer to the suite, talking rather tensely. Burt seemed angry; Karen was brushing aside everything he said.

Finally they came over to join us, but not before Burt had gone to the bar for a drink. "Vodka straight up," he announced to us as he sat down. "Dr. Farberman ordered it in the bar this evening and I tried it too. What could go wrong with virtually straight alcohol?"

"Alcohol when it oxidizes produces a little-known compound that causes your belly button to turn inside out," said Tom.

"Would you like my belly button more if it were inside out?" Burt asked Karen, but she didn't answer him. We were being joined by several people at once, delegates from the Midwest somewhere who were still growing their hair long.

One of them was a chemical engineer named Grady, and he had a pack of cigarettes with him that were really joints, only they were made with regular cigarette paper and even filters. There was no mistaking the smell when he lit one, though. Grady leaned over close to me and confided, "I've been stoned out of my mind since halfway through Farberman's speech this afternoon. Man, he's really just too much!"

"I didn't go to hear him," I said.

"Oh, it was a lot of shit about our noble purpose as human beings. Man, do you *know* how much it would cost even to *start* on his program? Do you know?"

"Sure," I said.

"It would bankrupt any state in the union. I mean, the Recession is still on; unemployment is up to nine per cent. What do you suppose that means in terms of practical politics?" He took a toke on his joint, holding in a great lungful as he waited for me to answer.

"It means we can't afford to save the world for Farberman," I said.

He exhaled exuberantly. "That's *it!*" he said. "That's *exactly* it! What's the good of clean air if we're all bankrupt?"

Burt had turned to listen to us; he said, "Yes, but what good is a bank account if our children will die of lung diseases?" His voice was a little slurred; he was getting drunk.

"We all gotta go sometime," said Grady. "A short life but a happy one."

So they began to argue, and it was an argument I'd heard a dozen times before at these conferences. I caught Karen's eye and nodded toward the door; we got up and went out into the hall.

"Here's my plan," I said. "We both go back inside just long enough to refill our drinks, then we go to my room. I promise you there'll be no one there who'll talk about natural resources or health hazards, and the phrase 'moral imperatives' will not be used."

So we went to my room and we spent the rest of the night there. Karen could be brittle and calculating in her job, but she was never that way in bed. That night was the high point of the conference for me.

We were up and about fairly early the next morning, beating the rest of the delegates to the coffee shop. George Chester turned up before long, looking tired and elated—the forty-eight-hour pressure cooker of a conference was his favorite environment.

He said, "You missed all the excitement last night, didn't you? A gang of pickets broke in and took over the lobby. They tried to get upstairs, but the hotel shut down the elevators and closed the riot doors leading to the second floor."

"Are you serious?" Karen asked.

George grinned his wry gap-toothed grin. "You think I'm crazy too. Well, it's amazing what phantasms I can conjure up with my paranoia; it was a whole mob of reverse Tinkerbells. Have you been down to the lobby this morning? All the windows are boarded up."

George was serious, and for once I believed him. I'd never trusted those mobs of demonstrators anyway. "How did the police get rid of them?" I asked.

"Mace. There were over twenty casualties, several of them policemen. After the mob was gone they had to bring in those big blowers to clear the gas out of the lobby. But you can still smell it if you go down there."

We didn't care to. After breakfast we went to the main meeting hall and sorted through the gathering crowd for people with news. What we heard agreed with George: an unruly mob, forced entry, the riot squad, Mace. But all was clear today, and delegate after delegate told me they'd be damned if they'd let such a thing influence their actions at the conference.

The program for today had the usual quota of seminars and committee meetings; I had to chair one committee myself. In the afternoon there'd be an open meeting of all the delegates, since this was the concluding day of the conference; any findings or resolutions we might make would be done then.

Burt showed up, saw Karen and me and pointedly ignored our existence. You win some, you lose some, I thought.

I went off with Tom and Karen for a couple of drinks to get me in shape for my committee meeting. Tom had been up all night because of the excitement of the riot, and now he was drinking Irish coffee to stay awake. He spilled a packet of sugar in his lap, but recovered quickly: "It's a tip I picked up from *Playboy* magazine," he said.

The television set over the bar was on, and I noticed they were running the interview with Burt. I couldn't hear what he was saying from across the bar, but his face had that telltale expression of naïve earnestness that separated the boys from the men. Karen watched him impassively, and when they went on to a different news item she said, "I knew they could edit that tape into something usable."

I went to my committee meeting. We met in a small wood-paneled room with air conditioning that made it feel like an igloo. There were seven of us on a committee to gather data on comparative waste products in different types of power plants; everyone had a report to read, even me, and when we finished that we drew up a few pages of analysis and conclusions.

It was deadly dull, of course. Ideally, it seemed to me, we shouldn't have to read all those reports to each other just so the recorder could write them down again; we should have been able to mail them to each other, let our respective staffs handle the comparisons and conclusions, and skip the committee meeting altogether. But that sort of procedure would have eliminated the conference itself, and none of us wanted to do that, so we did things by the book.

It took almost three hours, and by the time we were finished I was ready to climb a wall. I went straight back to the bar, but Karen and Tom had left. No one else I knew was there either, and then I realized that it was almost time for the big general meeting to begin. I thought about it for a minute, then ordered another martini.

I was tired and worn from that committee . . . a group of dull old farts trying to be efficient so they could get it over with. In that room I'd become a dull old fart myself, and I felt the need to recover my joy in living. So here I was, sitting alone in a bar. Christ. I ordered another drink.

Before I knew it I was pretty sloshed, and it occurred to me that the big meeting must be just about to draw to a close. Wouldn't do for me to miss the big meeting; I hadn't missed a big meeting ever. I paid the bill and went up to the meeting hall.

The hall was full, most of the people seated in their contour chairs with signal buttons and lights attached. No one was at the podium, but the meeting didn't seem to be over. I found Karen and Tom, and got a seat next to them. "What's happening?" I asked.

"We're voting on a resolution," said Tom.

"What resolution?"

"His." Tom nodded to the podium, where I saw Burt conferring with several other people over points of procedure. Farberman was on the dais too.

"Burt's resolution?" I asked. "What's it about?"

Karen said, "He'll read it in a second." She seemed withdrawn, almost sullen; her eyes never left Burt.

Several rows behind us Joe Morgan stood up. He opened his mike and said, "I question whether the delegates present can be expected to vote without being influenced by the events of last night—"

Burt cut him off: "We've already argued that point, Dr. Morgan. None of us needs mob threats to tell us how to think—though it is possible that some of us hadn't *started* to think before last night."

"You're overruled," the conference chairman told Joe. "We'll have the resolution read now."

Burt took the mike again. He read from a sheet of paper in his hand: "Resolved: Whereas we the members of the Fifth Co-environment Conference had gathered for the avowed and specific purpose of seeking means to successfully deal with the problems of health, resources and the esthetics of our environment, and whereas these are matters which affect not only the United States of America but every nation and every individual human being on Earth, and whereas it is recognized that these problems cannot be solved without the informed co-operation of all nations and interests—"

"What is this crap?" I asked Tom.

"Smile for the cameras," he said, and then I noticed the television cameras mounted above the meeting hall. We were being broadcast live.

I turned to Karen; she'd sunk back into her seat and was staring at the floor. "How did he get this resolution onto the floor?" I asked her.

"He's made deals with Farberman and several other people who swing weight in the back rooms," she said. "And he's got a lot of drive; he argued through every one of these clauses independently."

". . . Now therefore be it resolved that this conference calls upon every nation on Earth to join in a truly united international effort in this behalf; and to implement this desire of all mankind we hereby declare the present assemblage to be the final meeting of the Co-environment Conference, which is hereby formally dissolved, with the specific proviso that the data and findings of these five conferences shall be made available to the first truly unified world effort which shall be organized, in the judgment of—"

"Does this say what I'm *hearing?*" I cried. "How can we dissolve ourselves?"

"Just like that, evidently," Karen said.

"It can't pass. It may have gotten onto the floor, but it can't pass." I was sure of that.

And I was, of course, absolutely wrong. The resolution passed by a large margin. I sat and watched the count as it grew on the large electronic tally board overhead, and I couldn't believe it. But the margin of yeas over nays continued to grow.

When at last the count was completed, Tom said, "You've just seen a demonstration of what happens to a group of perfectly normal people when conscience combines with hysteria."

Everyone else was talking at the same time, but I did hear the conference chairman say, "In accordance with the resolution just adopted, I declare this conference closed." I looked again at Karen, and found her laughing—a quiet laugh, really amused, not at all hysterical. I looked up at the podium, saw Burt, and saw the expression on his face.

He was staring at Karen with a grim smile on his face. He glanced at me, met my eyes, and his smile slowly broadened.

And then I understood. "Conscience *hell!* That son of a bitch is mad because he got kicked out of bed!"

Karen laughed aloud. "Yes, exactly. Exactly!"

And that was how I did my bit to save the world at the Fifth Co-environment Conference, the one where we turned the corner on Earth's ecological problems. The following month a United Nations commission was set up which served as the successor to our conferences. That commission had its own share of politicking and personalities, but it started with a lot of momentum and over the past twenty years it's been getting the job done.

If Burt was motivated by a desire to put me out of a job, he wasn't successful. I was appointed to the UN commission and worked there for twelve years. I got to like it, too.

But I think Burt's maneuver was really aimed at impressing Karen. And it worked: she married him a year later.

James Joyce speaks of *the cheer of the gratefully oppressed*. George Zebrowski speaks to the same melancholy point. Zebrowski is Polish, English his second language.

George Zebrowski
PARKS OF REST AND CULTURE

The air was foul, barely breathable, acceptable only to those who had no choice. The pool, five hundred feet long and two hundred wide, was almost completely hidden in the predawn darkness.

The pool had once been operational, but now all the pavement was cracked and huge stones sat on the empty bottom; they had rolled down from the cliffs which rose in a semicircle at the west end of the grounds. The single granite and concrete module which had been the administration building sat on its own concrete island in the center of the waterless pool. Inside, the two floors had partially caved in. On its high granite pillar on the roof the old clock was dead at two A.M.—or P.M. The whole area had once been a park, but now the branches on the trees outside the fence were bare and brittle and dry.

Beyond the tall fence, above the dead trees, the lights from the stone city penetrated weakly through the layers of dirt-fog and morning mists. There stood the old apartment buildings which were not serviced by the numerous air filtration plants scattered throughout the city.

Praeger stood in the metal doorway of the main filter house and peered at the soft grained lights beyond the fence through his air filter mask. The faceplate sprouted a spiral hose which ended in the chemical tank strapped to his chest. At his feet he felt the vibrations of the huge pumps below ground which filtered the air, heated or cooled it for those select New York City buildings whose tenants qualified for the utility and preservice modifications under the Human Resources Allocations Act of 1985. Such buildings had no windows, only locks at the front entrance, seldom used; each roof was a copter square.

This morning, when his night shift was over, he would have to take the subway home; the city copter was out of service. He tried to accept the thought and ignore it.

He peered up past the fence and eroded hillside through his face-plate and thought of the eyes which would be watching him as it grew lighter, when he left the grounds through the gate.

He looked to the east, where the orbital space mirror was hastening the dawn by two hours, to light up the city early with its reflected light; an effort to keep crime down. On the Asian mainland, he knew, the Russians were using similar mirrors to light up their battlefields with the Chinese.

The real dawn was more than an hour away. Praeger turned and walked back inside the open doorway. He did not bother taking off his mask inside.

The plant hummed, and after a few moments the humming seemed to become a roar as the vibrating air pressed in on his ears. He walked down the row of pressure gauges, giving each one a glance. Then he went to the log pad on the wall and filled in the data. He could have done it without checking; the figures were always the same.

He went outside again as if hoping for something miraculous to happen. He stood in the open door, leaning against the metal frame and looking toward downtown—mid-Manhattan, where he could just barely see the old trade center towering over the Empire State Building, a pair of titans against the steel-gray sky. Always, he thought, the old and the new, the old never quite dying away, the dream never replacing the reality entirely. When we start for Centauri, there will still be mud huts in Asia, the unclean washing away their sins in the Ganges.

In the eastern sky an eye opened in the morning mists, a white-hot reflecting surface shouting the sun's light earthward.

Praeger waited, and later came the true dawn; incredibly scarlet, a function of all the dirt in earth's atmosphere, it streaked the sky. The planet could still manage its own kind of beauty. Though the wounds of the biosphere were deep, they were healing into scars.

But the thin layer of human consciousness stretched over the surface of the planet—the noösphere—had ruptured; and the human organism in its entirety was being spilled back into the evolutionary past, into the abyss of screams.

In the morning sunlight the concrete surfaces of the pool area were a bright gray-white. Praeger began his walk around the fence on the inside, checking for damage; a human insect moving slowly on the slightly raised walk.

At the west end of the grounds, just below the cliffs, he found a large hole in the chain fence, the largest of six during the week. It led to the small path that ran on the other side of the fence just below the cliff wall. It was not a planned path, but one which had been created by vandals, prowlers and playing children during the years. He smiled, thinking, they have better wire cutters than the city repair crews. The hole was very neatly cut out. He turned away from the fence toward the administration building and walked briskly across.

He stopped in front of the flagpole by the front entrance, noticing that the rope had been cut again during the night. Then he went into the small office, the only usable room in the empty building, and found that the night watchman had vomited all over the floor again.

The place stank, but he forced himself to sign the blotter and punch out on the creaky old machine. The watchman, as usual, had checked out hours ago, knowing that no one would report him, or care.

Praeger went over to the crusty old bulletin board and peered at the new addition. The examination to renew his technician's rating was to be given at 1:00 P.M., May 1, 1998, which was next Wednesday. He was worried about the rising standards and about his wife's reaction if he did not pass. Would she accept living in a non-environmental-control apartment—one open to the air, with perhaps only an air conditioner for the summer? They had adjusted well to seeing each other only in the afternoons, but she would never be—had never been—very close to him. He did not know what she would do.

He left the office and went along the walk by the fence until he came to the north exit gate, his shadow a long darkness to his right. Here once huge crowds of people had stood in line to gain entrance to the pool. He fumbled with the key and opened the rusty old lock; he pushed at the gate, straining, until it creaked open enough for him to pass. He locked it behind him and paused at the top of the stone steps which led to the street below.

Across the street stood red-brick apartment buildings, five stories each, open-windowed, unserviced by the plant in which he worked. A number of the people who lived in these buildings were hired every month during the backblowing operation at the plant—the process by which the huge filters were removed and cleaned. Usually that was done on his shift and he supervised it with the help of two armed policemen.

He heard a clatter on the step pavement near him. A half-dozen stones struck and bounced and rolled around him. He looked up in time to see the kids on the roof of the house directly in front of him duck away from his masked gaze. He went down the steps and walked north along the street toward the Tremont subway station. He felt slightly relieved when he came to the big police cruiser parked next to a fire hydrant. Inside, the uniformed policemen were asleep in air-conditioned comfort. He stopped and rapped with his knuckles on the heavy safety plastic "glass." One of the cops woke up, looked at the dash clock, grinned and waved his thanks as Praeger turned to continue down the street. In a moment the cruiser turned on its engines and air system to high and streaked past him on its way to the precinct. As he watched it disappear ahead of him, he could almost feel the eagerness of the two cops to get to the station to check out. Momentarily he felt a keen resentment because the copter had not come to pick him up. Normally he would have been halfway home by now.

There was an old man staggering toward him down the street with one hand outstretched. "Money?" the old man said, stopping in front of him, blocking his way. The thought of the old man's mouth so near him, the mouth and nose taking in air in greedy gasps, the chest rising and falling in seeming panic, made Praeger sick. The old man's body was shaking; the effort he was exerting to control his stance resulted in a powerful sustained trembling. The eyes were bloodshot;

one was set crookedly in its socket and seemed to be staring at the pavement.

Praeger shook his head. He never carried any money with him. His green city uniform would be enough to admit him to the subway.

"None left? No more—no more money?" the old man rasped in amazement. He coughed. Then his good eye also turned down to look at the pavement and he dragged himself past Praeger, as if resigned to the fact that there was nothing to be gained from this astonishing masked creature.

Praeger continued down the street. He turned the corner and went up the hill to Tremont. At the top of the hill there was a small park. Here, too, the trees were dead. There were no squirrels or birds, but a lone cockroach darted past him into the sewer. He remembered, years ago, sitting in St. James Park—on a bench, looking into the cracked and gullied clay tennis courts—watching the pigeons and squirrels moving around in the meagre grass. There had even been leaves on many of the trees in those days, enough to hide the tall tower of the bank which held the Fordham clock. Then the Jerome Avenue elevated train had come by, noisier every year as the foliage diminished. It had scared the shit out of all the animals. Every year there had been more dead birds and squirrels lying around. Then, one year, there was no spring.

She came into the room and sat down on the bed where he was sleeping. "Did you hear me, Chris?" There was no urgency in her voice. He mumbled and tried to turn over but she was sitting on the covers.

"The milkman brought an extra bottle of water today by mistake, didn't you notice? I'm not going to tell him."

"Betty, let me sleep." He tried to turn over but she was still in the way. She started rubbing his stomach, to arouse him. He had been dreaming of working on a space station. . . .

He opened his eyes and looked at her. She had that usual blank look on her face, the one she wore when she wasn't angry or dreaming. Her long blond hair was combed out and she had nothing on. The daylights were on in the room. The landscape wall showed the mountain valley in Canada where she had been born. He thought of all the power she used keeping the wall on, and how little of her salary as a daycare instructor she used for the apartment.

"Betty, please get out of here and let me sleep."

"When is your exam?"

"Next Wednesday, now get out!"

She smiled and walked out of the room. The daylights and picture wall went out as she closed the door. In a moment he knew she would be dialing someone on the phone. He became drowsy again, wrapping himself in the darkness. The space station was in front of him, a jeweled toy next to a sparkling earth.

He came into the lobby, his air mask under his left arm, and stopped under the huge glass chandelier. There was no point in worrying about the examination, he told himself. It would soon be done and over with. A large sign on the wall to his left caught his eye. He walked up to it and read the print below the huge photograph of the earth in space. The legend urged him to take a job on one of the trans-lunar-earth stations tied in with ecosystem and resource control.

There was a list of openings—weatherwatch, atmospheric engineering, satellite repair, orbital debris clearance. The requirements were: a technical background and aptitude, and the capacity to work alone. Benefits included generous earth leaves, and further opportunities to work in extra-lunar and moon surface positions. Applications here at Central Park West Station. The wall view poster bore the name NASA-EUROSOV.

The NASA-EUROSOV office was just down the hall from the wall view poster. Praeger walked in, picked up an application from the dispenser and filled in his tech identification number. He waited a few minutes, knowing that it was now too late to get to his examination room, and dropped the computer card into the receiving slot on his way out. His tech rating could not expire before he qualified for the NASA-EUROSOV programs, which usually had to go begging for applicants.

In the hallway he thought of the disadvantages of working in space, all the little things which made it impossible for a man to do it for any great time. Physical and mental disadvantages. The moon was better, if a man made up his mind to stay for good. Otherwise he would have to wear special weights during his stay to keep him in shape for earthside. It was easy, they said, to put off wearing them.

He came into the lobby again and looked up at the twenty-four-hour clock on the wall. It was four in the afternoon. He had four hours before he had to be at the air plant. He went to the nearest exit which led to a sub-park shuttle and boarded a car for the museum. There he wandered around the great halls feeling somewhat lost until it was time to leave for work. He waited until the last possible moment, then put on his mask and boarded the elevator which would take him to the street lock.

There was a stillness in the waiting. The moon was a white disk over the empty pool, riding low toward the morning. Praeger stood looking up at it through his faceplate, waiting to go off shift. Around the moon he saw the clouds which would cover it before it set.

On the other side of the moon, he knew, the Russians had built a grand hotel for their scientists and moon personnel, a huge structure with gardens and fountains, where the air was very much like that of Odessa in the 1880s. It was rumored that the Russians were mining the first discovered deposits of moon ice, and bottling some of it as a special mineral water for their more credulous countrymen. The "hotel" was really the living quarters of the large science city located in Tsiolkovsky Crater. He had heard stories of beautiful interiors, filled with red carpets and paintings, grand banquet halls and shiny brass railings, where aging Soviet leaders would go to spend their "longer years" in the one-sixth gravity. The science city itself was devoted to physics and biology and astronomy—generally to the exploitation of conditions which were unique for a variety of research programs. Even the aging bureaucrats could be made useful by entering them as case histories in various medical programs. The educated elite who lived there breathed perfect air; for them the Marxist dream of parks of rest and culture had been fulfilled; for them and those like them, technological men and scientists, would come all the fruits of knowledge, perhaps even immortality. To live on the moon required all the planning a. d care which had been denied to those on earth, and which was being given to the home world very late; but for those who had lived on the moon for many years and would never come back, perhaps raise sons there, the bitter native land which was earth was too beautiful in the sky to be in need of help. The American science city was less stylish, more cool and professional, but essentially the same.

On earth one generation of the overgrown organism which was humanity would have to die off to make the population manageable again. Praeger wondered about the plague proposal made a while ago. A good plague, they had said, would leave everything standing, and mankind would have a chance to get itself back on the right path. Better than a war. Anyway, some would make it, he thought. He wondered about the long-term good of it, and the short-term evil; and the ones who would not understand, the ones who would die to create the compost for the future.

Clouds obscured the moon and he thought, somehow . . . we men . . . were on the way to becoming fully ourselves just a little while ago, getting a grip on ourselves and reality; then we made some horrible mistake which kept us from passing that threshold into becoming something . . . new . . .

He stopped thinking and went back inside the plant to take his readings. Someday, he hoped, children would look back at this time as the great depression of the 90s . . . what year would be the cut-off point?

The apartment was quiet when he woke up that afternoon. He strained to hear Betty in the kitchen, but there was no sound. Maybe she was sitting at the table sipping coffee? He turned over and looked at her bed. It was neatly made and empty, a dark mass in the faint nightlight.

He got up slowly and stretched, went to the door, opened it, and

took three strides to reach the bathroom. He found her note taped
to the medicine cabinet mirror. It read: "I left you a message on the
recorder." It was written in big black letters.

He turned and went out into the living room, turning the daylights
on with his presence. He walked over to the green sofa and sat down,
staring at the recorder on the coffee table. As he turned it on, he
heard the front door open and close. He pushed the play button and
looked at himself in the large mirror sitting in his pajamas. Behind
him Betty came into the room.

"Chris, understand—" her voice on the tape started to say.

"Turn it off," Betty said in the mirror. He watched her in the glass.
She was dressed in a green raincoat cut to look like a jacket and skirt.

"—what I'm going to tell you." He stabbed at the off button.

"I didn't want you sitting around like an orphan listening to a voice
on a tape," she said. "I want to tell you myself—I owe you that
much."

He wasn't going to speak to her, no matter how much he wanted
to.

"I'm leaving, Chris. You're not going to make much more of yourself, you'll start to slip and we'll wind up in open housing. I'll look
great when I'm wheezing and bald. I'm not going to sit around and
wait for it."

He was silent, wishing she would just go.

"You're going to blame me now, aren't you?"

He shook his head suddenly, *no,* hoping that she would say it
and be finished. There was a trembling in his insides. He felt as if
he were in a trance which she would break with her next words.

"There's someone else and he can help me get what I want—everything we'll both ever want . . ."

He looked directly at her for a moment and saw that her lower lip
was shaking. Her face was a frightening thing; it repelled him and he
looked away. He began to rub his eyes with his hands. She turned
and left the room. He heard the front door shut itself automatically
behind her. He felt his face become drawn and he felt a great warmth
surround his consciousness, as if the room were becoming a furnace;

and he heard the sound of his pulse in his ears, the blood pounding behind his eyes.

It began to rain in the late afternoon and continued all night. Toward morning there were huge puddles of water in the empty pool at the air plant. The metal door to the inside jammed and Praeger had to leave it open and wear his mask all night. In the morning he took a chair and sat in the doorway watching the rain come down in the gloom, beating on the pavement. Thousands of hurrying rivulets ran on the concrete and cascaded into the empty pool. The sound of the water relaxed him. He thought of the empty apartment waiting for him, and felt the tiredness creeping into his body. He looked forward to the oblivion of sleep.

Today also the helicopter would not come for him; he was no longer worth the effort, he thought. He was leaving at the end of the week; the copter fuel was more valuable to them.

Just before he had left for work, notification had come from NASA-EUROSOV through the mail readout slot telling him they had a job for him on one of the earth-moon sector stations. He was to settle his affairs and vacate his apartment. There had been a word of congratulations on the print-out, and a note asking him if he would waive minimum earth leave for higher pay.

As a NASA-EUROSOV employee he had regained the right to have children, indirectly, by depositing his sperm; a right which Betty had convinced him to sell. But the sperm bank was a good bet against the future. He had heard of illegal children being readied for a new earth swept clean by deliberate plague; children hidden away throughout the solar system. Somewhere, he was sure, men were preparing for the stars. He dreamed of unspoiled earths around far suns, wondering how long it would be before the stardrive breakthrough changed the world and if he would be part of it.

He went off shift and walked up the hill to the Tremont station. The rain ran down his Pyrex faceplate. He wore no hat and his hair was wet. His clothing was waterproof. He tightened his collar to keep the water from running inside. The rain seemed to be coming down harder than before and he could not see very far ahead. He needed a windshield wiper, like the big blades on the police cruiser. The thought tickled him—sweep, sweep! He couldn't see it but he could feel it: the water was high around his boots as it ran down the hill.

Two men grabbed his arms and twisted them behind his back and a third ripped off his air mask, chest tank and all. They pushed him on his back with his head downhill and in a moment they vanished again in the thick curtain of rain.

He got up breathing hard and coughing. The air was heavy and wet in his lungs and he felt nauseous. His wrists seemed sprained. His face was streaming. Water ran in his eyes, blinding him. He screamed and shook both his fists in the rain; the gesture hurt, and the sound was lost against the rush of water in his ears. His eyes began to hurt and he rubbed them, cursing silently now. Then he walked the remaining half block to the subway entrance, coughing without letup all the way.

The entrance was a gaping black hole leading down into the earth, surrounded by a wilderness of rain. On the platform he took out a handkerchief and tied it around his face.

On the train going uptown he knew the other passengers were all staring at him, secretly pleased that he had lost his mask; but when he confronted their eyes they seemed to lose interest in him. He wondered, did NASA-EUROSOV know about Betty leaving him? Was that why they had mentioned the e-visitation clause, knowing that he would have no immediate ties on earth? If she had started the divorce action, then central information—CENTIN—would have it in his file, which could have been already tapped by NASA-EUROSOV. He could check it, but it didn't really matter. The sperm deposit. That, too. If he had gone in to be sterilized, they would have given him money, just like for blood, just like they had sold their right to have kids. But now they would put his sperm in a bank, with the eventual certainty that it would be used. Someone was making all possible bets against the future, making sure that as many different combinations were at least available as possible. It was being used as a kind of incentive to go along with his new job, he was sure of it.

He thought of the stories he had heard of hidden groups of children belonging to high officials on earth or on the moon, children being readied for a new earth, maybe even the stars? He hoped, perhaps something will happen and we'll get a stardrive in my life-time, and if I'm out there working when it happens maybe I'll get in on it! He felt a wild surge of expectation at the thought, a momentary release from the dark prison of his puny self.

The train reached his station and delivered him into the drenching rain and acrid air, again.

At the end of the week he closed the apartment and took a jet to Nevada, where the whip catapult serving the earth stations was lo-cated. The desert conjured up visions of the sun domes on Mars, green plants growing lush in low gravity, filling the bright space of the dome with oxygen. He did not have to wear a mask here, in Nevada, where the helicopter had left him off. What of Mars, where the desert bloomed . . . what of earthlike planets around far suns, unspoiled! How soon, he wondered, will we make the crucial breakthrough which will save us—tip the balance in favor of our dreams? A gust of wind came up from nowhere and blew some sand in his face and made his eyes water.

The spaceport was surrounded by a city of trailers and cabins. They gave him a cabin with a skylight for the one day before his departure for earth station one. He lay resting, and then dreaming, in the still-ness of half sleep, of sun over treetops, an uncancerous sun, setting; a sliver of daylight moon; sky deep blue; evening star blazing; wind on the tall grass; shadows of clouds; last spring with no sound in the air . . .

The last real spring he had known had been in Central Park, years ago. The water of the small lake had been a green mirror, and the white swan had sailed curve-necked toward where the willows washed their branches in the water . . .

Tomorrow he would be on the shuttle.

The earth was blue-green below as he thought of yesterday's thought of being here now. Acceleration was over and he leaned weightless in his straps toward the porthole, knowing that the stars and moon would look clearer now than from earth, that bottom of a dirty ocean where he had been born. It was a clean break now. Sunlight flooded the shuttlecraft like a shout. He floated back in his seat and tightened the straps, and dreamed of earth as it might still be, one hundred . . . five hundred . . . years hence, free of its billions and the guilty minority responsible for a century of plunder.

He dreamed he saw parks of rest and culture filled with elegant people, full-leafed trees casting broad shadows; and at night stars would be looking down, bright lights in an empty hall above an earth abandoned by most of its people, earth healed.

*. . . scratching when it don't itch and laughing
when it ain't funny—hollering and turning the
amps up at the very beginning . . .*

*. . . and because America has a taste for shit,
that goes over better than the real McCoy.*

—Johnny Otis (interviewed by Pete Welding)
            —*The Rolling Stone*

Kris Neville has been crying in the wilderness
since he began writing. A practicing chemist, he
has known longer than many of his fellow Americans that it IS *a hard rain . . . gonna fall.*

Lil & Kris Neville

THE QUALITY OF THE PRODUCT

Lunsford sat down to write a script about pollution. The characters
were given, the outline was approved and the assignment should flow
freely from the fingertips without much active intervention by the
brain. This time Sam Follander, Pollution Fighter, uncovered a plot
by foreign agents from an unspecified country who had secretly
purchased a large automobile manufacturing operation in the Midwest and were using a new, one-hundred-year paint that was poisoning the production workers, but upon which they hoped to launch
a whirlwind advertising campaign to capture a substantial share of the
existing prestige car market for the profit of European and Asian in-
vestors.

Except that Lunsford didn't feel very good. He hadn't felt very
good for over a month, and whenever he'd dragged himself down to
the typewriter, his thoughts turned into a substance as immobile as
concrete. His wife also wasn't feeling very good.

The symptoms were more akin to a hangover than not. "They
think it's a virus going around," his wife called to him after a telephone exchange with a fellow sufferer.

"Whatever it is, I just can't get with it again today," said Lunsford. "If they're going to depend on me, they may wind up with a rerun."

Knowing full well the answer, his wife said, "Why don't you phone Ray and tell him you just can't do it?"

"You know as well as I do," he called back. "Once you get the reputation of letting producers down, and the reputation is easily acquired, new assignments come with great infrequency. And besides, we need the money."

Oh, god, he thought, turning once more to the typewriter and now beginning to type at last, the words coming in clotted stumbles. It's not going to be any good. This is going to be terrible. I just hope they don't notice!

Three series built around the pollution theme were all doing well this year.

Plump J. R. Martin went down to breakfast without his bow tie because he wasn't certain he felt up to going into the plant. He lingered over the financial section of the morning paper, feeling even worse than before he had eaten. He told his butler, "With the government spending seven billion dollars this year to save the birds, this is the time to buy Consolidated Petrochemicals."

In spite of the headache and the blurred vision, it gave Martin several levels of satisfaction to pass this intelligence on. He imagined George spreading the word among associates and amplifying simultaneously on his employer's wisdom, foresight and generosity. Further, it gave him another subtle hold over the man. "If you would have followed my financial counsel in the last few years, George, you'd be a rich man today."

The more he thought about it, the better he liked the stock, himself. He decided to call his broker and place an order, taking the inevitable short-term gain on it before the word leaked out that Biosphere, their new biodegradable insecticide, was ineffective on mosquitoes. But the effort suddenly seemed out of proportion to the rewards, and he said, "George, I think I'll go back to bed for a little bit. I'm feeling liverish today. Please call Mrs. deWitt and tell her she can reach me at home if there's an emergency."

The faceless man knocked at the door of the apartment.

She admitted him.

"What a nice place you have here, Mrs. Rollins. You've really done wonders with it."

"Thank you," she said, with a trace of annoyance. "The telephone is over there."

"Oh, I'm not the fellow from the telephone company," he said, smiling pleasantly. "I just came over to kill you." He took out a giant meat cleaver.

There seemed to be quite a few absentees today. The professor wasn't feeling well himself and now he wished he'd stayed home. As he moved into his familiar lecture, it seemed to him in that distant recess of himself that was attending his words that he was more disorganized than was appropriate to his station.

He told the class that the Greeks, over two millennia ago, had addressed themselves seriously to the very problems that confront us today. They created and refined democracy and laid its inner workings out for our examination. They seriously examined psychological drives and incestuous relationships and the interaction between men and gods. In eros and agape, they suggested a multiplicity of loves which we have not, to this day, followed up; in fact, we've retrogressed. They wrote brilliant satires. They knew well the tendency of power to overreach itself. Their women were liberated and influential. They created art and philosophy as we know them and laid the foundation for our science. They were perhaps the first people in history to understand the ironical. They provide the ancestorial thoughts which set off the explosion that created our technological civilization. Study of the early Greeks offers us a window into the contemporary world.

"Yes?"

"But what did they have to say about pollution?"

The professor surfaced from his private misery. For a moment, he did not even understand the question. That moment passed, and he began searching his memory for justification of the thesis that the Greeks also invented that.

Jane was seventeen years old. She and her current lover slept in a pallet of blankets on the floor of her unfurnished, fifty-dollar-a-month room. He was forty-five and had dropped out of society eighteen months ago, leaving a middle-class wife and four children to fend for themselves.

Jane said, "They must be spraying some chemical or something on our pot. I feel this morning like a juice head does."

Her lover answered, "Rick was complaining about the same thing last week." He was afraid to admit he also was suffering, lest the subject of his years be brought indirectly to mind. "He constructed the case that you suck in too much smog when you smoke it."

He rose and went to the open window. The smog seemed not quite as bad today as it had yesterday. But the scientific community's consensus was that we really weren't holding our own at all. The stuff you couldn't see and the stuff that didn't sting your eyes was more harmful than the stuff you could see and that did. The problem was buried by invisibility. He breathed a little and his lungs hurt a little and he suddenly felt philosophical.

"You know," he said, "the only problem with smoking pot is that you convince yourself people are far more intelligent than you are, and that the world is in good hands, contrary to surface appearances. And as a consequence, there's no need to exert yourself because everything is going to turn out all right."

"Oh, god, my head hurts," Jane said. "Yogi can get you in that frame of mind without drugs."

"Yes, and look at India."

At the Rand Corporation, Dr. Felix Matheson undertook the job of project director on a top-secret Pentagon survey and assembled his mathematicians for a conference behind locked doors.

"The boys in Washington," he told the assemblage, "want us to investigate the thesis that the accumulated misfortunes which are now

besetting the planet, ecologywise, might at some point become ir-
reversible. If possible, they would like us to predict how many years
in the future this will be. In other words, how much time do we have,
realistically, to arrest environmental deterioration and at what point
will we lack the resources, irrespective of will, to effect a favorable
long-term outcome? This is what the Matheson Report will detail."

"Pollution is not the major problem," the President's economic
advisor insisted. "The problem is too many people. We should get
them out of Washington and back South where they belong with a
National Welfare Program of sufficient magnitude and scope to be
truly meaningful. A properly funded resettlement program would
quarter the population of our large industrial cities practically overnight and halve it when the unemployables were followed back home
by the welfare workers and other bureaucrats who make a living off
of them."

The President cherished warm feelings for the man, but he would
have preferred a positive suggestion on other, and to him at the
moment, more pressing problems, not the least of which was what to
do about the headache. He said, "I've been trying to get ahold of
Dr. Brown all morning. I think I must have eaten something last
night that disagreed with me. But apparently he's indisposed."

"You could pay for the whole program with the savings people who
stay in the cities would realize on rent alone. And no southern Con-
gressman could possibly vote against all that money going South."

The police commissioner of New York City said there had been an
astonishing increase in senseless assaults and murders recently and
he didn't know what to do about it. The remarks were off the record, but the press noted: POLICE HELPLESS TO COPE WITH NEW BREED
OF MURDERERS.

The poet wrote:

Symbiosis
between plant and animal

and little things swimming in the sea
make the whole greater than the sum of the watery
parts they share.
Man buries his dead in vaults to deny his relationship
with nature and refute the endless cycle
of birth and death
and mutual need
that symbiosis is.

"Golly, they had a honey of a pollution story on the tube last night. About foreign elements making up poison paints for our cars, just so they could make more money for the Japanese. They didn't mention Japan by name, but it was plain enough who they meant. I sometimes wonder what's really behind all this pollution, and who really is benefiting by it. And there were some of the best chase and fight scenes I've seen for years."

The junior Senator from Missouri said, "You know, I've not heard from a single constituent in St. Louis for over a month. I still hear from the countryside, but people in the cities just aren't speaking up like they used to."

The senior Senator from New York said, "My constituents are surprisingly apathetic this year, also. Well, since we're not going to have a quorum, we may as well adjourn the hearing."

The evening news reported that a six-year-old boy in Miami Beach, Florida, had eaten Biosphere insecticide and was paralyzed for twenty-four hours.

"I used to know Woodie Guthrie," said the recording studio executive to his secretary. "In our wildest dreams, back then, nobody would have ever thought this would have happened." He looked out the window at the familiar streets of Hollywood, where visibility was about half a mile in the sweltering midafternoon heat.

He hummed under his breath, letting the words to the tune fall unspoken through his mind:

This land is your land.
This land is my land.
From California
To the New York Island.
From the gulf stream waters
To the redwood forests,
This land was made for you and me.

"Who should we get to record it?" asked the secretary.
"I wish everybody would," said the executive.

The statistician for the National Institutes of Health was three months late with his report. His excuse was the difficulty of accumulating the data from the vital statistics bureaus of the various states. That was only partly true. New York City held him up only two months. He'd also been sick quite a bit recently, and while he was on the job most days, his efficiency was minimal.

The statistician felt the report to have confirmed his guts reaction, occurring spontaneously when the project was assigned to him over a year ago. The birth rate was slipping, except among the young kids. Fewer people over twenty-five years old were starting families. He advanced a number of reasons for this, including: lack of faith in the future, economic factors, the increasing use of contraceptives, the declining importance of the family unit, the atrophy of the Church, and perhaps, but not conclusively, some increase in sterility among males.

In his own case, he was not as interested in sex as he used to be, and his wife felt the same way. Most of the time, they just weren't physically up to it.

A man named Ed listlessly turned three-by-five white cards. Names of famous movie personalities, politicians and college presidents did not carry their old magic and none had been added for a full month. Two people for sure had died during that time and he had been too lethargic to remove their cards. It used to anger him when one of the names died, but now he felt strangely indifferent.

The file was a careful accumulation of the names of people he wanted to send to the wall after the Revolution.

He looked over at his package of dynamite and promised himself that tonight he'd plant it in the Federal Building if he had to go there in a wheelchair.

He went back to bed and tried to keep his breakfast on his stomach.

"I think the problem is mental pollution," said the free-lance writer. "What actually happened was that the war went on so long it sapped the will of the country. The number of man years the nation spent thinking about it defies calculation. It was being thought about *at least* five solid hours a week by at least a hundred and fifty million people for nearly ten years. I figured that one out and it's about four hundred trillion man hours. Billions of words were spent in print and on the electronic media. In justifying and attacking the policy, let alone in implementing it, more energy was expended by six orders of magnitude than in getting to the moon. It just drained our brains, rendered them useless for other purposes and entirely exhausted us as a nation."

The editor was not interested in that as an article. She was worried about her husband, who was in the hospital, and the doctors hadn't even made a diagnosis yet. "The problem is actually some kind of metal poisoning," she said. "There's a combination of metals we're putting in the environment that is wracking everyone up in a synergistic fashion. People are mad as hatters any more."

The editor began to warm to her subject, which had become somewhat of an obsession with her in the last year. What articles she couldn't fit in would find a home elsewhere and she never ceased to encourage them. She got suddenly to her feet and unloaded volume after volume from her lower right desk drawer. "Look at this. And this!" She opened volumes at random. "Here's a ninety-seven-page report from Health, Education and Welfare that goes all the way back to 1971. It tells us that there may be no margin of safety left. It says even if these industrial discharges are completely eliminated, existing deposits in sediments will continue to yield highly toxic methyl mercury to waters for decades. And ten years later, 1981, the amount we were dumping was almost double the six million pounds in 1971. In those ten years alone, we discharged a quarter of a pound of mercury into the environment for every man, woman and child inhabitant of this country.

"Do these symptoms sound familiar: headaches, weakness, emotional upset, tremors? And acrodynia in kids: mental disturbance, loss of appetite, diarrhea and disturbances of neurovascular phenomena. Mercury poisoning has been known since Paracelsus described it in 1533.

"Here's an article on metals in alcoholic beverages. Look at this. Methyl mercury in fish. How about this one? Acute toxicity of two organic mercury compounds to the teleost *Oryzias latipes* in different stages of development. Behavioral changes in the pigeon following inhalation of mercury vapor. Distribution of mercurial pesticides in quail. This volume is all on the Minamata fishermen. Look what it does to rabbit livers, here. Look at that picture. Early changes in the proximal convoluted tubule of the rat induced by mercuric chloride intoxication. Poisoning of ferrets by tissues of alkyl-fed chickens. There's mercury in the land and the water and the air.

"And that's just mercury. Take lead. Well, I don't need to bother with that. Everyone knows about lead poisoning. Clear back in the 1920s people were being driven insane and killed by tetraethyl lead in gasoline and New York State outlawed it for a while. But how many people know the importance of other trace metals that can cross the blood-brain barrier in human diseases generally? Do you know abnormal zinc metabolism is associated with dwarfism, hepatosplenomegaly and hypergonadism, not to mention cirrhosis of the liver?"

"Hey, baby, got a buster! Sniff this stuff. You're paralyzed for twenty-four hours!"

"What about smoking it, Tim?"

"No way, dig. You're likely to set the bed on fire and kill yourself when it takes hold."

"Dr. Harbringer, how can you justify continued use of DDT after all these years?"

"Well, ladies and gentlemen, as the kids would say, that's a paralyzing question. You have to make decisions based on trade offs. Biosphere, as many of you know, has little effect on mosquitoes and none on the larvae. In the mosquito belts of the world, we'd literally condemn millions to death from malaria and this new sleeping sickness that is getting out of hand in the underdeveloped countries if it weren't for DDT."

"Dr. Harbringer," asked another of the panelists, "we've had this war on malaria for almost sixty years now, and to a layman, like me, we still don't seem to have won it. Are the mosquitoes smarter than we are, or what?"

"That's the third dog I've had die on me in the last two years. I'm not going to get any more. It breaks the kids up too much. They don't understand, they're too young, and it's not fair to them."

"Well, I think the quality of the dog food is degenerating. Why else would they have the warning on the can, *Caution: Not for human consumption?*"

"I feel like the wrath of god," the actress said, after having blown the scene four times. "I've tried this new synthetic food and I think that's what is upsetting my stomach. My doctor says I ought to adopt a wait and see attitude on it, and he's given me a lot of different pills, which don't seem to work, but I'm really scared to eat most of the canned goods, and you know what they say about fresh meat!"

Frank Ryan, D.D.S., was arrested for common assault after he struck his assistant. The wire services picked up the story. "I told her," Dr. Ryan was quoted as saying, "never to bring a patient with an amalgam filling into this office again. There's mercury in them, and it's poisoning me."

The story triggered a wave of people besieging their dentists to have metallic fillings removed and plastic ones put in their place.

The American Dental Association was quite unhappy, since they resented having patients come in the office and tell the doctor what materials to use in their mouths.

The police reporter did the story he wanted to do. His sources were questionable, if not actually non-existent, and the editor delivered an indignant lecture on think pieces.

The police reporter's article said that law enforcement agencies were of the opinion that the new wave of violence was traceable to some metabolic imbalance. People in the big cities weren't breathing as deeply as they used to, and this, coupled with an overall reduction in the efficiency of hemoglobin in carrying the oxygen, either because of an increase in carbon monoxide or because metals other than iron were being incorporated in erythrocytes preferentially—or for whatever other reason, such as a reduction in kidney function—all this was producing a new form of chemical insanity. Today's killers were completely unhinged from any reality the rest of us recognize and different in kind from previous breeds.

The police reporter, anxious to get the story in print, considered submitting it to one of the national magazines. He conceivably might be able to use it later in his own defense if they ever caught him.

At home that evening, he was suffused with the warmest and most delightful feeling, which he was overly familiar with and which he no longer resented. He knew that the only thing that mattered in this world was hacking to death another child. He began to smile like a beneficent grandfather.

One of the underground newspapers in Atlanta, Georgia, ran a three-thousand-word article on methods for ingesting Biosphere. The article was syndicated by the Revolution Yesterday news service to seven hundred and twenty weeklies.

The major point was that Biosphere should not be taken when standing or sitting, since the onset of paralysis might leave a person in a cramped position for hours and heighten the risk of colds and other diseases. Biosphere should only be taken in bed, preferably early in the morning after a good night's rest for maximum effectiveness.

"Artie McClair, and in fact the whole cast," wrote the critic, "turned in a listless performance last night on 'The Polluted City.'

The direction and camera work were also below the series' previously high standards, as was the cutting, which seemed hasty and somewhat disorganized. The only good thing was the script. This time, Arthur Barnett is involved in salvaging the reputation of a physicist at MIT who committed suicide when the bureaucracy hounded him from his post with ridicule and sustained denunciations because he claimed to have invented a catalyst for gasoline which produced polymerized combustion products—polyethylene-like plastics—which did not foul the atmosphere and actually had commercial value. The program left us with the tantalizing question: Did the MIT professor really have the solution to smog, and what are the economic interests that resulted in his destruction? We need more programs like this to alert the American people to the very serious problems the country is facing in the field of pollution."

"Well, say what you will, developing new insecticides requires great intelligence. No other species on the planet can do it."

On the golf course, Hampton, who was owner of an electronics firm, said to his companion, a cardiovascular anesthesiologist, "I thought I wasn't going to make it out this morning. Wife's been feeling poorly, and I've not been doing so good myself. Something's going around, eh?"

The cardiovascular anesthesiologist nodded, wondering irrelevantly why he wasn't seeing as many aortic aneurysms as he used to.

"Not many people out today," Hampton said. "Staying home and taking care of business. I'm glad to see that. Tell you the truth, I didn't get into the plant all yesterday. It's such a mess in there, I'd almost as soon stay out of it entirely. You know what our absentee rate was last month? It was nearly twenty per cent, that's what it was!"

The cardiovascular anesthesiologist wondered why there were so many of the young kids presenting with septal defects. He didn't particularly like to work with little children, it took too much out of him, seeing them as merely extensions of his own frightened and helpless little son. More and more he found himself picking up the assignments. It was about a five-hour job, with scrub-up, and he'd almost blown one last week while the girl was on the pump. He still hadn't finished chewing himself out for it. He'd felt just miserable that day, but his palms began to sweat still when he thought about it.

"I don't know what's wrong with the American worker any more," Hampton continued. "We're just coddling them too much, what with the unions and all. The ones that do show up—I'll tell you, fully half of them might as well have stayed home. My little firm is falling apart because of it. I don't know how long I'll be able to meet the payroll and stay in business. I'm just at wit's end to figure out what to do."

He teed up for the first hole and sliced the ball far to his left. The only thing you could say about the shot was that it had distance.

"The only way to take that shit is shoot it with a needle. Take my word for it. You're gone, zap! Baby, I've been paralyzed twenty times in the last thirty days that way, and it's really off!"

"You're losing a lot of weight, Roger."

"Yeah, baby. But it's good for you, know what I mean? I don't feel so bad any more. And getting bread isn't nearly the hassle it used to be, because I only eat less than half the time."

The National Association of Licensed Morticians (NALM) announced a technological breakthrough: offshoot of biochemical research in the fixation of cells for a new microdissecting procedure used in the investigation of mutagens. They could now impregnate corpses with an aliphatic thermosetting acrylate and a special catalyst/activator combination. The resultant product was as hard as a rock and said to be equally as durable.

It need no longer be dust unto dust for cherished loved ones.

"The Free Health Underground claimed credit for the assassination of two physicians in the Detroit area over this weekend. In a letter received by this station, they gave as their reason the indifference of the medical profession to the nation's health. There was a lot more, which we need not go into. Dr. Foley, as a spokesman for the AMA, here in Chicago, what do you make of this bizarre development? Are we in for a wave of this sort of thing?"

"I certainly hope not," Dr. Foley said.

"I resent the implication, Mr. Moderator, that because I am a Jehovah's Witness that I am insensitive to these developments. This is the fulfillment of the word of God. It is an organic process. It doesn't give me any personal satisfaction. These events we see around us today are the pangs that are issuing in God's reign on earth. They are as necessary as the pain of any childbirth. We are witnessing the birth of the Universal Child, which God has promised us, and if I rejoice, I'm still just as upset about all the suffering as you are, and I resent any other implication."

One evening, the bus driver, after dinner, said, "There's been an awful rise in traffic deaths. I heard today that a hundred and fifty thousand of them got split off the earth just this year."

His wife said, "Be careful, because I do worry about you, because of the accidents, but also because so many of those people are going insane, and one of them might get on your bus. I wonder if a lot of the accidents are at night? I don't see as well as I used to and my night vision is really not good. In fact, I went down to Safeways today and thought I'd get us some nice carrots for dinner, but they didn't have a single carrot in the whole store, and the manager said he hadn't seen any for a couple of weeks.

"I really hate to go shopping. The clerks just aren't stocking the shelves and they're half empty, and you have to wait in line fifteen or twenty minutes. Every time I go down there, I try to lay in a big stock, but there's a lot of things they just don't have any more, like carrots. And then I get thinking, well, I've heard don't buy this and don't buy that, to the point I just don't know. Since you've been feeling so bad recently, I wonder if I should continue to give you liver and kidneys, even though I know you like them. I think we'd be better off without the kind of integrating those people have been passing around lately."

"I don't think it's vitamin A deficiency," said her husband, "that's ruining your night vision. I think they have taken the formaldehyde out of the dead and put it in the living. Our whole metabolism is screwed up by those people. We're probably making methanol out of sugar and breaking it down to formaldehyde, and this is cross-linking our proteins."

To hear him talk like that made her want to cry. It was so unfair for him to have to drive a bus with a Ph.D. degree in chemistry, just because the government couldn't find work for chemists in the last few years. You would think there would be some way to use his training.

At a party, the host got drunk, waved his cigar and said, "When you talk about polluted rivers, you don't know what you're talking about! The most polluted rivers on this planet are our blood streams. We've got every imaginable chemical in them, some intentionally, and most not. Do you know they don't even know all the stuff which is dissolved in our blood any more?"

He bumped into an old girl friend and felt a sudden wave of contrition at not having called her in more than three months.

"I just go home at night, Marge, and sit there exhausted and stare at the tube."

"It's like summer all year around with the reruns," she said.

"And with them canceling out at the last minute like that, but I really don't mind, it takes less energy and concentration if you've already seen it a couple of times."

The obstetrician came out and said, "I'm terribly sorry, Mr. Jones. The baby was born badly, badly deformed. I don't know whether we can save it or not."

Without waiting for the father's anguished questions, the obstetrician hurried off. There was just too much of this happening. He didn't want to talk about it to anybody.

"I've never heard of a soul having a bad trip with good, pure Biosphere. On the other hand, now, the kids are getting into something else again. The stuff they're buying on the street for a buck a hit also contains cocaine and mescaline and a little THC, and some dealers even put speed in it, for Christ's sake!"

"That ain't mescaline, Barry. That stuff's too hard to come by. It's actually acid laced with strychnine."

"You can talk all you want to, but I don't care if all the birds die off. You can't even eat eggs according to what I heard today. Listen, we've got lots of problems, believe me, and let's use that seven billion trying to solve them, not to save the birds that just crap on everything anyway.

"Do you know what the average American, the Joe like me, is most worried about? Let me tell you, mister, and don't make any mistake about it. I read a poll today taken by the Gallup people, and it said that nearly eighty per cent of Americans said they were most worried about their own health. And that's the way it is, and the government is spending all these billions on the birds. Now, if you ask me, that really is for the birds!"

The Chairman of the Board sat in on a plant conference for the first time since his departure from active management. The bear had come out of his cave, and the President knew he was under the gun.

"Let's turn from these distribution problems for a minute," the President said. "What are the consumers buying these days, Marvin? For some strange reason, nobody seems to be eating green beans any more, and that's always been a leader with us."

"John, my wife said she heard they were supposed to be radioactive."

The President stifled a groan that complicated his headache. "There's a lot of distrust about the way foods are grown, and these little guys putting out the synthetic meals, which are supposed to be a hundred per cent certified pure, although I seriously doubt that, are beginning to cut into us."

"We're working on it, John. I've got my people on it, but there's a virus going around, and productivity is down. One of my best people has been off nearly a month."

The President glanced at the Chairman of the Board and concluded that he had no choice but to move and move energetically.

"You've been saying that for the last four months. It's time now for some hard decisions."

He waited for an approving nod from the Chairman for this uncharacteristic display of vigor, but the Chairman gave no sign. The President felt perspiration on his palms, definitely a bad sign.

"There's still a lot of quality control problems to work out on the process, John. I'm just not entirely satisfied with the product, either. These things take time."

"That's the trouble with you scientific people. You're too negative. I want to see some positive attitudes around here. We're going to announce that new line in exactly two weeks from now, and if you can't get the bugs worked out and the quality control set up before that time, I'll find people who can."

For the first time, the Chairman of the Board spoke. "Gentlemen," he said, rising to his feet. "You'll have to excuse me. I'm afraid I'm not feeling well right this minute. I'm sure you can carry on without me."

"A case can be constructed for cats thinking. After all, they have brains, and they respond differently from individual to individual, unlike ants. Now that I am a cat, I begin to appreciate this more than I did before I was a cat. But we cats are not very smart, Doctor, and humans are a queer kind of cat god we have to debase ourselves in front of. You should be ashamed of yourself for making us have to scream and cry sometimes just to get you to feed us. We cats have no real conception of your world, and you have no conception of ours. You don't know what it feels like to have lost the fight with the cat down the street yesterday. You don't know the difficulty of finding birds to catch. You can't imagine what a job it is accomplishing sexual release if you're a cat, and how restless and evil it makes you while looking. And you don't know how grass tastes or you'd eat more of it, and how the wind really feels, or you wouldn't wear clothes in summer. You have no idea of what it feels like to feel really good. You can't even smell the bouquet of odors in this room. I could name a hundred! But, Doctor, we cats have a problem that I want to discuss with you. We think you humans are trying to poison us. Why would you want to do something like that?"

After witnessing an acrimonious debate on a new bone glue from the floor, a group of the younger physicians met in the bar. The debate would be fully reported in the literature. But the iceberg of the profession would never be reported at all, as circumspect sentences dropped almost casually amid discussions of stocks and bonds and boats and planes and nymphomaniacal nurses.

"What do you suppose we'll do with all these monsters we've been saving recently? Twenty years from now there won't be enough institutions to hold them."

An answering shrug. "Not much hospital space now. But I'll be retired by then. I hope."

"You know, I've been getting a lot of old-timers referred to me recently. They're overflowing the office, and there's just one thing after another wrong with them. I've had one alive by keeping her sitting up in a chair for nearly a year. I've got one going on nine months and six operations, and his kidneys are going and the family now demands hemodialysis."

"I just refer them on. What gets me is the non-specific illnesses I'm seeing in the twenty- or thirty-year-olds, people in the prime of life."

"That's maybe what I ought to do, refer them on. To tell you the truth, my energy's drained at the end of the day, and I've got to think about cutting back anyway."

The science fiction writer, feeling fairly decent for the first time in the last week, perhaps because the weather had turned cooler and the rain had refreshed the air—or perhaps just a part of the ups and downs people seemed to be going through anymore, like symptoms of a terminal illness—thought he would do a novel on how the various poisons, organic and inorganic, combined in the body with various drugs, synthetic and natural, and with medicinals and psychotropics and unknown and unsuspected substances and new metabolic by-products to produce grossly varied effects and ultimately, over the course of ten generations, a resistant species of lower and lower intelligence. The lower the intelligence gets, the better the environment becomes. By the time the environment is halfway decent again, the race is too dumb to co-operate enough for any project necessary to its survival and dies off.

The American Communist Party was secretly much encouraged by recent developments, no matter how loudly they lamented them in their media, although somewhat alarmed that their membership, being mostly in their sixties, was dying at an alarming rate of respiratory, kidney and cardiovascular diseases.

Soon the workers' call for action would be irresistible and some predestined leader would arise to crystallize the sentiment for Revolution. Of all the volunteers in the Party for this role of leadership, one must surely guess correctly what the future required and become an immortal hero of the Movement and be revered endlessly and eternally by true believers everywhere.

Much attention was devoted to the Party line.

The President of the United States awoke one night with tachycardia. The attack lasted for several minutes, allowing him to time his heartbeat at 160.

Afterwards, his thoughts turned as restlessly as his body. Somewhere there was the smartest person in the world, and the odds were somewhat better than one in 4.5 billion against it being him.

The President used to daydream about the subject. First, you would establish some criterion for intelligence. Then appropriate tests would be given. The process would continue with additional testing as necessary. In the end, all but one would be eliminated. This man or woman would then be available to world leaders for advice and consultation.

But inevitably the President's thoughts arrived at an unwanted destination. One instinctively mistrusts intelligence. How could you be sure of the motives behind the advice. Would the giver be a father or mother figure or a person alien to humanity at large pursuing devious ends that none could anticipate? Think how long it takes to trust one's own parents completely, if that can ever be done!

And finally, the President inevitably decided, nobody wants to follow advice, and we can prove it by the example of our children. No, what each man wants is the right to make his own mistakes and learn from them and enjoy the triumph of his own successes, and learn also from them.

Still, a month ago, the subject slipped from his lips in a conversation with his science advisor, his reservations forgotten in the desperation of his need.

But the science advisor said, "In my opinion, man thinks like a computer of some sort, and what you're asking for is someone who is better than anyone else at organizing the garbage. Now a man might make a living selling organized garbage, Mr. President, but he would starve to death trying to improve the quality of the product."

The analogy was unfortunate.

Thoughts of garbage drifted through the President's mind. It was getting harder and harder to have it collected. Why was the absentee rate so much higher among sanitation engineers? Was it really that pollution seeped in through their skins? He didn't believe it.

And then his thoughts turned to the Postal Service. The backlog had built up to where you couldn't be sure of getting a letter from Boston to San Diego in under two months. The only hope was in the reported reduction in the volume of junk mail. If it continued to tail off, maybe they'd get caught up before the Christmas rush. Please let us get caught up before then, he prayed desperately to something he really didn't believe in in spite of his regular attendance at church for the benefit of the example it set.

In the area occupied by Los Angeles County-City, the summer fires, before the white man came, occurred only every generation or so, and the floods which followed them, with the same infrequency.

The black smoke that hung in the air of downtown Los Angeles from the conflagrations in Griffith and Elysian parks occupied the news for several days.

The mayor of Los Angeles County-City wanted to cut down every tree and announced solemnly that if his advice were not followed, someday there was going to be a really big fire and most of the north side, including several very expensive residential areas, would go up in flames.

The Sierra Club, strangely lethargic of late, countered that we needed more trees, not fewer. One group of youth said the oxygen was being consumed too fast and the people would smother to death, while others chanted mantras for rain in Southern California in the summer.

The mayor finally telephoned the governor of Southern California and said, "My men are just too sick and too exhausted, and the situation is rapidly getting out of hand. Can you send me a couple of thousand fire fighters?"

The psychoanalyst said, "I think we can get to the root of your problem nicely. I've seen other cases not too different and they all responded very well."

At the same time, he was telling himself that he wasn't feeling up to it. But he'd missed a number of appointments recently. Imported food was getting more and more expensive—if you really wanted the good stuff that was coming out of western Canada, Denmark and northeastern China. And Greenland water from thawed glacial ice. That cost an arm and a leg and a testicle. But you knew it was at least five thousand years old and untouched by any by-product of civilization.

The trick, of course, was not to listen. And he had been feeling better under his new regime of self-medication. He closed his eyes and let the queasy feeling carry away his thoughts. Was it the beginning of withdrawal symptoms? Maybe he better excuse himself for a minute. The needle was right in there. This would be—

Good god! his third fix today! He better try to make it through the hour.

"I have the feeling, Doctor, that the whole world is falling apart. I can't sleep at night because I keep worrying about the sun not going to come up tomorrow. But I do know this, and it's not my imagination, Doctor. I can prove it to you. No matter how hard they try to keep it from us, it slips out. You see hints of it in newspaper stories. THE SALT CONTENT OF THE OCEAN IS CHANGING DAILY!"

"Yes, of course," said the psychoanalyst. "But that isn't your problem, now, is it, really? We have found that the things which really upset a person go a long way back, to things they've forgotten, and it's our job to bring these things out so people can look at them and see them for what they are."

"But the sons-of-bitching Martians have got these machines to dump salt in the ocean one day, Doctor, and pull it out the next."

"There's an interesting article in the newspaper," said the girl friend. "It's a theory about why so many pilot whales have been committing suicide. They have a highly developed social order and a strong leader. The leader goes insane and takes all the other whales with him in an assault on the beach. They're mammals, after all, and they are trying to recapitulate evolution. There's an impulse in all sea creatures, it says here, no matter how buried it is, to come out on the land, just like there's an impulse in all of us to go back to the sea. What do you think of that?"

"I think it's just because the ocean is becoming uninhabitable."

The TV stations carried a public service announcement telling parents not to be alarmed if they found their teen-agers immobile and apparently paralyzed. It was merely because they had taken a little dose of Biosphere. The children should be put to bed, if they weren't already there, and kept warm and they would recover completely within twenty-four hours.

Parents were requested please not to phone their family physicians unless the child were under ten years old, because the physicians were already overworked and their services were desperately needed elsewhere.

The absentee rate continued to go up. Congress adjourned without having accomplished very much except adoption of "This Land Is Your Land" as the new National Anthem, replacing the unsingable "The Star-Spangled Banner." Spokesmen promised renewed vigor when they came back from their vacation. Commentators said a lot of needed legislation would get passed quickly during the second session.

"Frankly, Mrs. Delano, if I were you, I'd get off this diet of yours, because I think that's part of what's making you feel badly. You see, there's a lot of things that get stored in human fat, and when you go on a diet, and the fat starts to dissolve, these things all return to your circulatory system. I think we'll get the liver back to normal if you just put on a little weight again."

"But, Doctor, I'm still a hundred and eighty-seven pounds!"

The junior Senator from Missouri returned home to find out what the cities and the countryside were thinking about since he had not heard from either recently. There was much sickness in even the small towns, and he was distressed to see a general decline in the appearance of nearly every building because of poor maintenance practices. If he hadn't felt so bad physically, the situation would have distressed him even more than it did.

"There's a period of disorientation that comes when you run into a cloud bank or are on Instrument Flight Rules, and for about five seconds, you can't tell up from down. It's a weird feeling, and, you know, that's just exactly the way I felt when I woke up this morning and couldn't see a thing for a minute. I called my doctor, and he said there were a lot of people feeling that way and it was probably a virus going around."

The medical profession announced that fully 35 per cent of the nation's health problems were genetic in origin, up 10 per cent from thirty years ago, and that there was an increasing number of serious illnesses among the young.

A comedian on the late night talk show, looking wan and pale, began his monologue:

"*Science* magazine reported an astronomer at Jodrell Banks believes these black holes we've been reading about are actually an indication that the universe is being slowly digested. Mankind is safe, though. Human beings are now so contaminated that they're unfit for consumption. I heard about a cannibal that lives on Fire Island—" At this point, he broke off. "I'm sorry, ladies and gentlemen. I feel a little weak tonight. I think I better skip the rest of the monologue and go to our first guest, Miss Hildegaard Winters! who—oh, Miss Winters isn't here yet, so we'll hear a number from the orchestra, after this message about a new detergent that is absolutely safe to use."

The Journal of the American Medical Association carried a small announcement, which was little noted elsewhere, that the number of physicians in active practice had declined sharply in the last eighteen months. In another section, the *Journal* noted that many members of the organization were now reported to be arming themselves with hand guns.

There was an article in the Los Angeles *Times* about the death of whole forests in the lumber country.

The Matheson Report for the Pentagon was completed by the Rand Corporation nearly on schedule. It concluded the point of no return had actually occurred some six years previously. The Armed Services, without bothering to notify anyone else, began contingency planning.

Finally there came a day when fewer than 20 per cent of the nation's workers reported to their jobs. Their being there, half sick, lethargic, and some actually disoriented, probably made the situation worse, and the next day, most of them, too, stayed home.

In a couple of weeks, the smog began to clear, but there were little pockets of it remaining here and there a full year later.

Back in the stone age (environmental awareness time) a U. S. Public Health Service official said some interesting things. This was March, 1969, and the occasion was a seminar sponsored by the American Water Works Association and Water Pollution Control Federation. The speaker was Charles C. Johnson, head of the PHS Consumer Protection and Environmental Health Service.

Said official spoke thus: 33 percent of all public water supplies serving some 50 million people don't meet PHS standards—which are admittedly archaic and inadequate to protect human health. And thus: There were 26,000 reported cases of illness from unsafe water between 1946 and 1960; and estimated figures for unreported illnesses run a hundred times that figure. And thus: "This country cannot afford to be apathetic about the safety and purity of its water." And thus: "If we don't take action now, we are flirting with disaster."

. . . The problem [is] twofold. Most of our water systems were built more than a quarter of a century ago when all we had to worry about was removing bacteria from relatively unpolluted water. But since then, surface and ground water supplies have become increasingly polluted with an incredible variety of wastes, including many that are simply not affected by present-day water treatment procedures. So all this crap ends up glugging out of your tap . . .

[These] doomsday facts [were] published in a July, 1970, HEW report which was called the "Community Water Supply Study" . . . a survey of 969 public water supply systems serving eighteen million people in nine states. And it said:

1. 41 percent of the 969 systems surveyed were delivering water of inferior quality to 2.5 million citizens. 360,000 people were being supplied with potentially dangerous or dangerous water.

2. 36 percent of 2,600 individual tap water samples contained one or more bacteriological or chemical constituents exceeding the limits in the recommended *PHS Drinking Water Standards.* (*You remember those? The archaic, quarter-century-old standards?*)

3. *9 percent of the 2,600 samples contained bacteriological contaminization at the consumer's tap in potentially dangerous quantities.*

4. *30 percent of the 2,600 samples contained at least one of the chemical limits indicating dangerously inferior water.*

5. *11 percent of the samples drawn from 94 systems using surface waters as a source of supply exceeded the recommended organic chemical limit of 200 parts per million.*

6. *77 percent of water plant operators were inadequately trained in fundamental water microbiology; and 46 percent were deficient in chemical knowledge pertaining to plant operation.*

Now, the real *hidden duck here is this: 79 percent of the water systems in the nine states involved were* not even inspected! *In over half the cases, plant officials didn't even remember when— if ever—a state or local health department had last surveyed the water supply!*

Ecommando Tactics (L.A. *Free Press*)

Tom Disch is the poet. (Wearing another hat, he is Thomas M. Disch the novelist, best known for *Camp Concentration.*) He has been ill—probably from drinking the local water—in great style, all over Europe, and first encountered the Clitumnus while spending a truncated year in Rome. Wherever he is and whatever he does, he celebrates his occasions in poems: sometimes deceptively sly, sometimes quite formal.

The Union League Civic & Arts Foundation Prize for 1972 has been awarded Tom Disch for his poem *Clouds*—which, like *Ode on the Source of the Clitumnus,* also appeared in the magazine *poetry.*

Tom Disch

TWO POEMS

Ode on the Source of the Clitumnus

There you are, waiting for me,
Or someone, to praise you. Propertius praised you,
Carducci praised you—it isn't enough.
There you are, still, bubbling away,
Filled with more fish than Nature unassisted
Could possibly contrive, and not three yards
From the highway—in short, a perfect sight.
Walden Pond, which I have never visited,
Is said to be in the same fix—clogged
With cans and candy wrappers, alive with the jokes
Of tourists who drive there with no good
Idea of who this Thoreau
Might have been or why he settled in of all places
This, but who all certainly must have expected
Something a little nicer.

But wasn't the world always a mess—especially
Just off, like this, Via Flaminia?
Without wanting to lay asphalt
On the last living blade of grass, one may suggest
That any beauty, over-advertised,
Inevitably perishes. Mont Blanc has not survived
Unscathed till now: then could
The Source of the Clitumnus?
No. You will grow uglier year after year
Until no one will stop to look at you,
No guidebook will mention your name, and poets
Will have ceased to read

Propertius and Carducci; the Fiats and Peugeots
Will whiz by you in their haste to see St. Mark's
        Subsiding into the lagoon.

        But still you will persist to rise
Miraculously from the earth, and while you do
You must be praised. Every day the world
        Grows poorer as the population
Soars. There doesn't seem to be much time
        Until the likeliest holocaust prevails.
        Billions of us, at least,
Will die, and this fact already begins to seem
A little tiresome. So we are dying—haven't others
        Died before? Yes—and that's exactly why
We must praise the Source of the Clitumnus.
        Not that you are beautiful, not at all—
        But because you have outlived
Temples, highways, and religions, and because
        You are there, waiting for us.

The Politics of Darkness

Everyone waiting for the assassination pretends
Not to notice the accordion player, who storms
Up and down the long long line (it stretches east
As far as Second Avenue), growing angrier and

Angrier, until you'd like to hurl handfuls of dimes
At the wretch, *sharp* dimes, and the girl who had been
So hostile until now agrees, adding: "If it weren't for
People like him the blue whale would be alive today."

—And so you move to California, or lacking that you both
Take classes in relaxation and a better way to breathe;
You fission like an amoeba and spread through the inner city
Like rumors of new products and shortages. And you wait

For the right person to come along who'll understand
The love you feel, and the hate, and the tides of fear.

There is a record album consisting of the songs
of the humpback whale; recorded on the spot, un-
derwater, without any Disneyesque touches to mar
it anywhere. It is a moot question whether these
songs are cetacean works of art, or partly conver-
sations and only partly works of art—but I think
it must be impossible to listen to them without
experiencing some kind of thrill. People with re-
ceptive ears—those who are willing to be communi-
cated with, and who know communication when
they hear it—surely experience the aesthetic thrill
while listening.

Katherine MacLean is nobody's aesthete. She
invented logic in the cradle and has been instruct-
ing her teachers ever since; except that now she
is a teacher at a university and is wisely letting
her students instruct her.

Katherine MacLean

SMALL WAR

Humming smoothly, a giant ship designed to kill, dismember, cook
and can whales moved toward a society of whales: bulls and their
harems and playfully sporting pups.

An Audubon Society submarine followed the giant ship, swerving
nervously as the people inside grew more excited.

"They mustn't do it! I can't let them do it!" Tears streaked Mrs.
Appleton's cheeks. She was fat and rich, and she had put up half
her personal fortune for the submarine study of the social life of
whales. Her crew consisted of a mechanic, a field naturalist, a
specialist in dolphin language, and a xenobiologist and universal
linguist. They were surprised by her tears but they all shared the same
anger and dismay as they saw the commercial ship prepare to destroy
the herd they had been studying. Fury struggled with caution.

"Maybe we can stop them." "Let's ram them." "Maybe the submarine could . . . could . . ."

The mechanic made a gesture demanding attention. "We can ram a hole . . ."

Mrs. Appleton brightened and wiped her eyes, restraining sniffles. "If we crash into them, will it make a hole?"

"It will go through four feet of pack ice to get to the air, ma'am. It's built for ramming. The front end is pointed. We could make a hole below their waterline that would let in water."

Mrs. Appleton shoved the throttle forward and they took up the chase after the whale-killing ship. The fat woman handled the control with skill and determination. She fastened safety straps. "Everyone strap in for the crash."

"Strike amidship," said the mechanic. "Strike just aft the center bulge."

They strapped in. The xenobiologist brought Mrs. Appleton a large foam pillow and stuffed it between her and the instrument panel.

He was a specialist in the study of totally alien species from other planets, and he wanted to live long enough to meet an alien intelligent species someday when the spaceships made contact. To live so long requires caution. He fastened his safety straps and said, "Are you sure this is safe?"

"No," said the mechanic.

"Whales help their friends," said the dolphin expert.

"We can't let them kill Horace and Aimee," Mrs. Appleton said, gripping the wheel tightly and hardening her double chin with determination. She was referring to two whales. She said, "They'd help us. So we have to help them. Hang on. Hang on everybody."

They watched the huge side of the whale-killer ship loom over them, growing bigger and closer, and gripped handholds.

A harpoon with an explosive charge struck and exploded against the hull of the submarine, veering it sideways. Therefore, they struck the whaling ship at a slant. Striking armor plate was not in any case the same as striking pack ice. The impact was shattering.

Badly dented, leaking, with controls shattered, the submarine sank slowly, tilting at odd angles as it went deeper. The big factory ship hummed on its way with a rent in its side below the waterline.

Presently four survivers of the submarine bobbed to the surface, their scuba suits inflated like balloons.

Three miles away, nearer the coast, seal hunters in powerboats were circling a seal island, looking hungrily at the seals, using binoculars to search their view of the rocks for signs of the assassin who protected the seals, the hunterhunter, a fanatical conservationist who was rumored to be responsible for the death of five missing seal hunters. His action had been declared and filed as a small war between voluntary organizations. He was registered as an agent of the SPCA. He was legalized. They could not ask for help from the Coast Guard. Their only defense was to fire first, and the Small Wars Agreement limited their weapons to an ineffective, single-shot, hand-loading rifle. Circling the rock island they stared, looking for a man disguised as a seal, exchanging curses against hunterhunters over their CB radios.

One of them heard the whale ship sending a distress call to the Coast Guard and reporting the sinking of the Audubon submarine. He told the others. They cheered, and turned their radios to the distress band and heard the feeble signals of the survivors' safety suits. Turning the powerboats and roaring the engines, the seal hunters raced toward the signals, readying their rifles, happy to have a chance to pick off members of the hated Audubon Society.

From HANDY LEGAL ADVISER FOR HOME AND BUSINESS, 16th revised edition:

Any voluntary organization can legally declare war on any other voluntary organization engaged in any activity which the first organization considers objectionable or harmful to its own or the general welfare. Such a declaration of war must be given two months in advance of any overt act. Certain professions and activities which may be considered harmful to other groups are classified as membership in a voluntary organization. Listings of these are available from the UN Committee on Regulation of Small Wars. Nations, states, or any organization founded on place of residence, or political or religious beliefs or racial differences, cannot declare war, or have war declared upon them, because such attack would involve injury to persons whose membership had not been entered into as a matter of easy, adult, reversible choice.

The Society for the Prevention of Cruelty to Animals had long ago declared war on any commercial organization or individual entrepreneur attacking or killing endangered or intelligent species of animals.

On the rocky seal island, the young SPCA member straightened up from his crouch inside the reflective gray and black fabric that had surrounded him with the outward appearance of a gray and black rock. He watched the seal boats go, then went to his disguised motorboat and followed at a brisk twenty knots, a startling speed for an object that looked like floating, dirty ice.

As he went he stripped off the boat's disguise and tried to arrange it like a seal hunter's powerboat. His name was Joseph. He was seventeen and felt a deep conviction that all animals were people, and therefore all hunters were murderers.

After twenty minutes of driving across the choppy, cold waves Joseph saw the seal hunters' powerboats circling small floating objects in the sea that he knew were the Audubon Society survivors.

He closed in and joined the circle, hoping that they would not wonder how such a small craft could be a seal hunter's boat, hoping they would not hail him.

In Small Voluntary Wars, only single-shot, hand-loading firearms shall be authorized.

The boats circled the floating survivors at high speed, the white lines of their wake intersecting and jolting the starfishlike floating safety suits. The seal hunters stood on deck taking turns with a single shot each, jeering at each other with gestures for being poor shots.

Two of the survivors were losing air from their punctured suits and began swimming frantically in the choppy waves, trying to hold their heads up.

Joseph had a perfect opportunity to riddle every one of the hunters, but he did not have a machine gun. Wishing for a better weapon he raised his authorized single-shot rifle, cradled it as though he were picking off one of the swimmers and shot the man standing on the boat at the opposite side of the circle of boats. It was a good shot, from one heaving deck to another heaving deck at a distance of over a hundred feet. The hunter dropped his rifle and fell backward. Hastily Joseph reloaded and tried to pick off another before the other hunters realized something had happened.

He missed ten shots and then became impatient and swung the rifle toward a near boat and dropped another. One of the loudest of the jeering hunters stopped in the middle of a yell and fell forward off the side of his boat.

Seal hunters yelled to each other and pointed to the boat that was too small and the man who pointed his rifle in the wrong direction. Bullets began to smack into Joseph's boat and bounce off with a clang and a high ping. He set the controls for slow forward circles and hastily scrambled into a solid steel barrel with a rotating platform and a slit opening that fastened down its lid. He continued shooting, through the slit. He saw blinking blue lights flashing to one side, rotated the barrel and saw a Coast Guard cutter coming at full speed, violently flashing and blinking warning lights, thundering air and radio commands.

His boat tilted and settled to extra weight as it was boarded from behind by hunters who hated SPCA hunterhunters of Joseph's kind with an intensity greatly exceeding their hatred of Audubon Society members. Among big game hunters it was rumored that SPCA members collected a bounty from the SPCA for each human left ear they delivered. One of them carried a bottle of gasoline, intent on painful murder of the steersman of the boat.

Joseph watched as the Coast Guard cutter nosed into the middle of the circle bellowing orders from an amplifier. All of the Audubon Society members had their suits deflated and were swimming feebly in the freezing water, presumably wounded. One gave up and sank.

Through his concern about the helpless swimmers, Joseph became aware that his boat was tilted to extra weight. He cranked his barrel around, and the slit spun across the field of view, showing the sky, the rear storage section and then four faces and four rifles pointing at him. One of the rifle muzzles entered the slit.

He slammed a sliding piece of armor plate over the slit and heard the rifle discharge outside with a deafening clang. He was safe inside the steel barrel but he could not see out.

The Coast Guard ship broadcast orders to cease fire and noted down boat numbers while crewmen pulled in the three remaining survivors of the submarine, including a numb and dripping fat woman. They then turned their attention to peculiar activity on the small boat that looked different from the others. Puzzled, they drifted the big ship close and watched as the seal hunters finished unbolting the steel barrel from its rotating support, and rolled it over the side and into the waves.

"That's a registered SPCA game protector number," announced one who had been consulting an index. "What do you bet there's a man inside?"

"CEASE AND DESIST!" called the amplified Coast Guardsman voice. "THIS IS DECLARED AN ILLEGAL RIOT. FURTHER AGGRESSIVE ACTS WILL NOT BE PERMITTED." The barrel floated for an instant, settling, then turned over and sank. The Coast Guard crew caught it in a rescue net, hoisted it on deck and puzzled at the lock until a shuddering, dripping, blue young man managed to open it from the inside. Everyone present was given a summons for rioting without a Small War license. The wet people were taken back to the mainland.

Three miles away the giant whaler sank slowly, small lifeboats being lowered and circling it.

Ten miles away the whale tribe: bulls, cows and babes, alarmed by the shooting, were on their way, swimming deep and fast, to safer waters.

The Small Wars weren't over; the Small Wars had only recently begun.

But this engagement had come to an end.

The penis of the great sperm whale is nearly nine feet long. It is the mightiest organ in the history of the earth. Divers who have witnessed the mating of Leviathan speak of it in tones of awe. Big Earl Carruthers, in the Seven Seas bar in New Orleans, vowed that after seeing the gentle giants make love, he couldn't get it up himself for two weeks. I once watched a courtship while standing watch on the U.S.S. Opportune *in the arctic. For two hours an eighty-foot cow teased a bull a few tons larger than herself. She would roll over and over on the surface, then dive into the green depths with him a fluke's length behind. We would stand breathless, our mouths unconsciously open in the bitter air, trying to guess where they would breach next. No sound but the sharp cry of an occasional tern and the groan of icebergs rolling over in their sleep.*

Then the cry: "There! There! Off to starboard!"

And out of the deeps, like birthing mountains, the great gray shapes exploded, arching completely clear of the water in leaps so graceful it made the soul ache, sinking back in fountains of spray.

The bull got so frustrated that he came over and rubbed himself back and forth along the length of the ship, his crusted hide causing sandpaper sounds to boom through our hull.

Then the cow, having decided she was ready, lured him away and they sank together, bodies spiraling around one another, into the privacy of the Greenland whale fisheries.

—Roger Lovin

André Norton lives quietly in rural Florida and writes sword-and-sorcery for young adults, compelling fantasies of witches and witchworlds. She must also grieve for the rivers and lakes, in Florida as elsewhere, going down to eco-death. Witness her story: set in the *here* and not-very-far-from-*now*.

I went to the river
to drown all my sorrow
But the river was more
to be pitied than I . . .

—Scots ballad

André Norton

DESIRABLE LAKESIDE RESIDENCE

Her face felt queer and light without her respirator on—almost like being out here without any clothes. Jill thumbed the worn cords of her breather, crinkling them, smoothing them out again, without paying attention to what her hands were doing, her eyes were so busy surveying this new, strange and sometimes terrifying outer world.

Back home had been the apartment, sealed, of course, and the school, with the sealed bus in between. Sometimes there had been a visit to the shopping center. But she could hardly really remember now. Even the trip to this place was rather like a dream.

Movement in the long ragged grass beyond the end of the concrete block on which Jill sat. She tensed—

A black head, a small furred head with two startling blue eyes—

Jill hardly dared to breathe even though there was no smog at all. Those eyes were watching her measuringly. Then a sinuous black body flowed into full view. One minute it had not been there, the next—it just was!

This was—she remembered the old books—a cat!

Dogs and cats, people had had them once, living in their houses. Before the air quotient got so low no one was allowed to keep a pet in housing centers. But there was no air quotient here yet—a cat could live—

Jill studied the cat, sitting up on its haunches, its tail laid straight out on the ground behind it, just the very tip of that twitching a little now and then. Except for that one small movement it might have been a pretend cat, like the old pretend bear she had when she was little. Very suddenly it yawned wide, showing sharp white teeth, a curling pink tongue, bright in color, against the black which was all the rest of it.

"Hello, cat—" Jill said in that quiet voice which the bigness of Outside caused her to use.

Black ears twitched as if her words had tickled them a little. The cat blinked.

"Do you live here—Outside?" she asked. Because here things did dare to live Outside. She had seen a bird that very morning, and in the grass were all kinds of hoppers and crawlers. "It's nice"—Jill was gaining confidence—"to live Outside—but sometimes," she ended truthfully, "scary, too. Like at night."

"Ulysses, where are you, cat?"

Jill jumped. The cat blinked again, turned its head to look back over one shoulder. Then it uttered a small sound.

"I heard you, Ulysses. Now where are you?"

There was a swishing in grass and bush. Jill gathered her feet under her for a quick takeoff. Yet she had no intention of retreat until that was entirely necessary.

The bushes parted and Jill saw another girl no bigger than she was. She settled back on her chosen seat. The cat arose and went to rub back and forth against the newcomer's scratched and sandy legs.

"Hello," Jill ventured.

"You're Colonel Baylor's niece." The other made that sound almost like an accusation. She stood with her hands bunched into fists resting on her hips. As Jill, she wore a one-piece shorts-tunic, but hers was a rusty green which seemed to melt into the coloring of the bushes. Jill had an odd feeling that if the other chose she could be unseen while still standing right there. Her skin was brown and her hair fluffed out around her face in an upstanding black puff.

"He's my uncle Shaw," Jill offered. "Do—do you live Outside, too?"

"Outside," the other repeated as if the word were strange. "Sure, I live here. Me—I'm Marcy Scholar. I live over there." She pivoted to point to her left. "The other way's the lake—or what used to be the lake. My dad—when I was just a little old baby—he used to go fishing there. You believe me?"

She eyed Jill challengingly as if expecting a denial.

Jill nodded. She could believe anything of Outside. It had already shown her so many wonders which before had existed only in books, or on the screen of the school TV they used when Double Smog was so bad you couldn't even use the sealed buses.

"You come from up North, the bad country—" Marcy took a step forward. "The colonel, he has a big pull with the government or you couldn't get here at all. We don't allow people coming into a Clear. It might make it bad, too, if too many came. Bad enough with the lakes all dead, and the rest of it."

Jill's eyes suddenly smarted as badly as they did once when she was caught in a room where the breather failed. She did not want to remember why she was here.

"Uncle Shaw walked on the moon! The President of the whole United States gave him a medal for it. He's in the history books—" she countered. "I guess what Uncle Shaw wants, he gets."

Marcy did not protest as Jill half expected. Instead she nodded. "That's right. My father—he worked on the Project, too, that's how come we live here. When they closed down the big base and said no more space flights, well, we moved here with the colonel, and Dr. Wilson, and the Pierces. Look here—"

She pushed past Jill and swept away some of the foliage. Behind those trailing, yellowish leaves, was a board planted on a firm stake in the ground; on it, very faint lettering.

"You read that?" Marcy stabbed a finger at the words.

"Sure I can read!" Jill studied the almost lost lines. "It says, 'Desirable Lakeside Residence.'"

"And that's what all this was!" Marcy answered. "Once—years and years ago—people paid lots of money for this land—land beside a lake. Of course, that was before all the fish, and turtles and alligators and things died off, and the water was all full of weeds. You can hardly tell where the lake was any more—come on—I'll show you!"

Jill eyed the mass of rusty green doubtfully. But Marcy hooked back an armful to show an opening beyond. And, at that moment, Ulysses came to life in flowing movement and disappeared through it. Fastening her respirator to her belt, Jill followed.

It was like going through a tunnel, but the walls of this tunnel were alive, not concrete. She put out a hand timidly now and then to touch fingertips to leaves, springy branches, all the parts of Outside. Then they were out of the tunnel, before them what seemed to be a smooth green surface some distance below where they now stood. However, as she studied it, Jill could see there were brown patches which the green did not cover and which looked liquid.

This was very different from any lake in a picture, but then everything was different now from pictures. Old people kept talking about how it was when they were young, saying, yes, the pictures were right. But sometimes Jill wondered if they were not just trying to remember it and getting the pictures mixed up with what they wanted to believe. Perhaps the pictures were stories which were never true, even long ago.

Marcy shaded her eyes with her hand, stared out across the green-brown surface.

"That's funny—"

"What's funny?"

"Seems like there is more water showing today—like the weeds are gone. Maybe it's so poisoned now even the old weeds can't live in it." She picked up a stick from the ground by her feet, and then lay full length to reach over and plunge the end of it into the thick mass below, dragging it back and forth.

Ulysses appeared again. Not up with them, but below. Jill could see him crouched on a slime-edged stone. His head was forward as he stared into the weeds, as if he could see something the girls could not.

"Hey!" Marcy braced herself up on her elbows. "Did you see that?"

"What?"

"When I poked this old stick in right here"—she leaned forward to demonstrate—"something moved away—along there!" She used the stick as a pointer. "Watch Ulysses, he must have seen it too!"

The cat's tail swept back and forth; he was clearly gazing in the direction Marcy indicated.

"You said all the fish, the turtles and things are dead." Jill edged back. Once there had been snakes, too. Were the snakes dead?

"Sure are. My dad says nothing could live in this old lake! But something did move away. Let's see—" She wormed her way along, striking at the leaves below, cutting swaths through them, leaving the growth tattered. But, though they both watched intently, there were no more signs of anything which might or might not be fleeing the lashing branch.

"Bug—a big bug?" suggested Jill as Marcy rolled back, dropping the stick.

"Sure would be a *big* one." Marcy sounded unconvinced. "You going to live here—all the time?"

Jill began to twist at her respirator again. "I guess so."

"What's it like up North, in the bad country?"

Jill looked about her a little desperately. Outside was so different, how could she tell Marcy about Inside? She did not even want to remember those last black days.

"They—they cut down on our block quota," she said in a rush. "Two of the big breathers burned out. People were all jammed together in the part where the conditioners still worked. But there were too many. They—they took old Mr. Evans away and Mrs. Evans, too. Daddy—somehow he got a message to Uncle Shaw, and he sent for me. But Daddy couldn't come. He is one of the maintainers, and they aren't allowed even to leave their own sections for fear something will happen and the breathers break down."

Marcy was watching her narrowly.

"I bet you're glad to be here."

"I don't know—it's all so different, it's Outside." Now Jill looked around her wildly. That stone where she had sat, from it she could turn around and see the house. From here—now all she could see were bushes. Where was the house—?

She got to her feet, shaking with the cold inside her.

"Please"—somehow she got out that plea—"where's the house? Which way did we come to get here?" Inside was safe—

"You frightened? Nothing to be frightened of. Just trees and things. And Ulysses, but he's a friend. He's a smart cat, understands a lot you say. If he could only talk now—" Marcy leaned over and called:

"Ulysses, you come on up. Nothing to catch down there, no use your pretending there is."

Jill was still shaking a little. But Marcy's relaxation was soothing. And she wanted to see the cat close again. Perhaps he would let her pet him.

Again that black head pushed through the brush and Ulysses, stopping once to lick at his shoulder, came to join them.

"He's half Siamese," Marcy announced as if that made him even more special. "His mother is Min-Hoy. My mother had her since a little kitten. She's old now and doesn't go out much. Listen, you got a cat?"

Jill shook her head. "They don't allow them—nothing that uses up air, people have to have it all. I never saw one before, except in pictures."

"Well, suppose I let you have half of Ulysses—"

"Half?"

"Sure, like you take him some days, and me some. Ulysses"—she looked to the cat. "This is Jill Baylor, she never had a cat. You can be with her sometimes, can't you?"

Ulysses had been inspecting one paw intently. Now he looked first at Marcy as if he understood every word, and then turned his head to apply the same searching stare to Jill. She knelt and held out her hand.

"Ulysses—"

He came to her with the grave dignity of his species, sniffed at her fingers, then rubbed his head back and forth against her flesh, his silky soft fur like a caress.

"He likes you." Marcy nodded briskly. "He'll give you half his time, just wait and see!"

"*Jill!*" a voice called from nearby.

Marcy stood up. "That's your aunt, you'd better go. Miss Abby's a great one for people being prompt."

"I know. How—how do I go?"

Marcy guided her back through the green tunnel. Ulysses disappeared again. But Marcy stayed to where Aunt Abby stood under the roof overhang. Jill was already sure that her aunt liked that house a great deal better before Jill came to stay in it.

"Where have you been—? Oh, hello, Marcy. You can tell your mother the colonel got the jeep fixed and I'm going in to town later this afternoon, if she wants a shopping lift."

"Yes, Mrs. Baylor." Marcy was polite but she did not linger. There was no sign of Ulysses.

Nobody asked Jill concerning her adventures of the morning and she did not volunteer. She was uneasy with Aunt Abby; as for Uncle Shaw, she thought most of the time he did not even know she was there. Sometimes he seemed to come back from some far distance and talk to her as if she were a baby. But most of the time he was shut up at the other end of the house in a room Aunt Abby had warned her not to enter. What it contained she had no idea.

There were only four families now living by the lake, she was to discover. Marcy's, the Haddams, who were older and seemed to spend most of their time working in a garden trying to raise things. Though Marcy reported most of the stuff died off before it ever got big or ripe enough to eat, but they kept on trying. Then there were the Williamses and they—Marcy warned her to stay away from them, even though Jill had no desire to explore Outside alone. The Williamses, Marcy reported, were dirt-mean, dirt-dirty and wrong in the head. Which was enough to frighten Jill away from any contact.

But it was the Williamses who caused all the rumpus the night of the full moon.

Jill awakened out of sleep and sat up in her bed, her heart thumping, her body beginning to shake as she heard that awful screaming.

It came from Outside, awakening all the suspicions her days with Marcy had lulled. Then she heard sounds in the house, Uncle Shaw's heavy tread, Aunt Abby's voice.

The generator was off again and they had had only lamps for a week. But she saw through the window the broad beam of a flashlight cut the night. Then she heard Marcy's father call from the road and saw a second flashlight.

There was another shriek and Jill cried out, too, in echo. The door opened on Aunt Abby, who went swiftly to the window, pulling it closed in spite of the heat.

"It's all right." She sat down on the bed and took Jill's hands in hers. "Just some animal—"

But Jill knew better. There weren't many animals—Ulysses, Min-Hoy, the old mule the Haddams kept. Marcy had told her all the wild animals were gone.

There was no more screaming and Aunt Abby took her into bed with her so after a while Jill did sleep. When she went for breakfast, Uncle Shaw was in his usual place. Nobody said anything about what had happened in the night and she felt she must not ask. It was not until she met Marcy that she heard the story.

"Beeny Williams," Marcy reported, "clean out of his head and running down the road yelling demons were going to get him. My father had to knock him out. They're taking him in town to a doctor." She stopped and looked sidewise at Jill in an odd kind of way as if she were in two minds whether to say something or not. Then she asked abruptly:

"Jill, do you ever dream about—well, some queer things?"

"What kind of things?" Everyone had scary dreams.

"Well, like being in a green place and moving around—not like walking, but sort of flying. Or being away from that green place and wanting a lot to get back."

Jill shook her head. "You dream like that?"

"Sometimes—only usually you never remember the dreams plain when you wake up, but these you do. It seems to be important. Oh, stuff!" She threw up her hands. "Dad says to stay away from the lake. Seems Beeny went wading in a piece of it last night, might be he got some sort of poison. But all those Williamses are crazy. I don't see how wading in the lake could do anything to him. Dad didn't say we couldn't walk around it, let's go see—"

They took the familiar way through the tunnel. Jill blinked in the very bright sun. Then she blinked again.

"Marcy, there's a lot more water showing! See—there and there! Perhaps your dad is right, could be something killing off the weeds."

"Sure true. Ulysses," she called to the cat crouched on the stone below, "you come away from there, could be you might catch something bad."

However Ulysses did not so much as twitch an ear this time in response—nor did he come. Marcy threatened to climb down and get him, but Jill pointed out that the bank was crumbling and she might land in the forbidden lake.

They left the cat and worked their way along the shore, coming close to a derelict house well embowered in the skeletons of dead creepers and feebler shoots of new ones.

"Spooky," Marcy commented. "Looks like a place where things could hide and jump out—"

"Who used to live there, I wonder?"

"Dr. Wilson. He was at the Cape, too. And he walked on the moon—"

"Dr. Morgan Wilson." Jill nodded. "I remember."

"He was the worst upset when they closed down the Project 'cause he was right in the middle of an experiment. Tried to bring his stuff along here and work on it, but he didn't have any more money from the government and nobody would listen to him. He never got over feeling bad about it. One night he just up and walked out into the lake—just like that!" Marcy waved a hand. "They never found him until the next morning. And you know what—he took a treasure with him—and it was never found."

"A treasure—what?"

"Well, he had these moon rocks he was using in his experiment. He'd picked them up himself. My dad said they used to keep them in cases where people could go and see them. But after New York and Chicago and Los Angeles all went dead in the Breakdown and there was no going to the moon any more—nor money to spend except for breathers and fighting the poison and all—nobody cared what became of a lot of old rocks. So these were lost in the lake."

"What did they look like?"

"Oh, I guess like any old rock. They were just treasures because they came from another world."

They turned back then for they were faced with a palmetto thicket which they could not penetrate. It was a lot hotter and Jill began to think of indoors and the slight cool one could find by just getting out of the sun.

"Come on home with me," she urged. "We can have some lemonade and Aunt Abby gave me a big old catalogue—we can pick out what we'd like to buy if they still had the store and we had any money."

Wish buying was usually a way to spend a rainy day, but it might also fill up a hot one.

"Okay."

So they were installed on Jill's bed shortly, turning the limp pages of the catalogue and rather listlessly making choices, when there was a scratching at the outside door just beyond the entrance to Jill's bedroom.

"Hey"—Marcy sat up—"it's Ulysses—and he's carrying something—I'll let him in."

She was away before Jill could move and the black cat flashed into the room and under Jill's bed as if he feared his find would be taken from him. They could hear him growling softly and both girls hung over the side trying to look, finally rolling off on the floor.

"What you got, cat?" demanded Marcy. "Let's see now—"

But though Ulysses was crouched growling, and he had certainly had something in his mouth when Marcy let him in, there was nothing at all except his own black form now to be seen.

"What did he do with it?"

"I don't know." Marcy was as surprised as Jill. "What was it anyhow?"

But when they compared notes they discovered that neither of them had seen it clearly enough to guess. Jill went for the big flashlight always kept on the table in the hall. She flashed the beam back and forth under, where it shone on Ulysses' sleek person, but showed nothing else at all.

"Got away," Marcy said.

"But if it's in the room somewhere, whatever it is—" Jill did not like the thought of a released something here—especially a something which she could not identify.

"We'll keep Ulysses here. If it comes out, he'll get it. He's just waiting. You shut the door so it can't get out in the hall, and he'll catch it again."

But it was not long before Ulysses apparently gave up all thoughts of hunting and jumped up to sprawl at sleepy ease on the bed. When it came time for Marcy to leave Jill had a plea.

"Marcy, you said Ulysses is half mine, let him stay here tonight. If that—that thing is loose in here, I don't want it on me. Maybe he can catch it again."

"Okay, if he'll stay. Will you, Ulysses?"

He raised his head, yawned and settled back.

"Looks like he chooses so. But if he makes a fuss in the night, you'll have to let him out quick. He yells if you don't—real loud."

Ulysses showed no desire to go out in the early evening. Jill brought in some of his food, which Marcy had delivered, and a tin pie plate full of water. He opened his eyes sleepily, looked at her offering and yawned again. Flashlight in hand, she once more made the rounds of the room, forcing herself to lie on her stomach and look under the bed. But she could see nothing at all. What *had* Ulysses brought in? Or had they been mistaken and only thought he had something?

A little reluctantly Jill crawled into bed, dropping the edge of the sheet over Ulysses. She did not know how Aunt Abby would accept this addition to the household, even if it were temporary, and she did not want to explain. Aunt Abby certainly would not accept with anything but alarm the fact that Ulysses had brought in something and loosed it in Jill's room.

Aunt Abby came and took away the lamp and Ulysses co-operated nicely by not announcing his presence by either voice or movement under the end of sheet. But Jill fought sleep. She had a fear which slowly became real horror, of waking to find *something* perhaps right on her pillow.

Ulysses was stretched beside her. Now he laid one paw across her leg as if he knew exactly how she felt and wanted to reassure her, both of his presence and the fact he was on guard. She began to relax.

She—she was not in bed at all! She was back in a sealed apartment but the breather had failed, she could not breathe—her respirator—the door—she must get out—away where she could breathe! She must! Jill threw herself at the wall. There were no doors—no vents! If she pounded would some one hear?

Then it was dark and she was back in the room, sitting up in bed. A small throaty sound—that was Ulysses. He had moved to the edge of the bed, was crouched there—looking down at the floor. Jill was sweating, shaking with the fear of that dream, it must have been a dream—

But she was awake and still she felt it—that she could hardly breathe, that she must get out—back—back to—

It was as if she could see it right before her like a picture on the wall—the lake—the almost dead lake!

But she did not want—she did—she must—

Thoroughly frightened, Jill rocked back and forth. She did not want to go to the lake, not now. Of course, she didn't! What was the matter with her?

But all she could see was the lake. And, fast conquering her resistance, was the knowledge that she must get up—yes, right now—and go to the lake.

She was crying, so afraid of this thing which had taken over her will, was making her do what she shrank from, that she was shivering uncontrollably as she slid from the bed.

It was then that she saw the eyes!

At first they seemed only pricks of yellow down at floor level, where she had put the pan of water for Ulysses. But when they moved—!

Jill grabbed for the flashlight. Her hands were so slippery with sweat that she almost dropped it. Somehow she got it focused on the pan, pushed the button.

There was something squatting in the pan, slopping the water out on the floor as it flopped back and forth, its movements growing wilder. But save for general outlines—she could hardly see it.

"Breathe—I can't breathe!" Jill's hoarse whisper brought another small growl from Ulysses. But she could breathe, there was no smog here. This was a Clear Outside. What was the matter—?

It was not her—some door in her own mind seemed to open—it was the thing over there flopping in the pan—it couldn't breathe—had to have water—

Jill scuttled for the door, giving the pan and the flopper a wide berth. She laid the flashlight on the floor, slipped around the door and padded towards the kitchen. The cupboard was on the right, that was where she had seen the big kettle when Aunt Abby had talked about canning.

There was moonlight in the kitchen, enough to let her find the cupboard, bring out the kettle. Then—fill it—she worked as noiselessly as she could. Not too full or it would be too heavy for her to carry—

As it was, she slopped water over the edge all the way back to the bedroom. Now—

The floppings in the pan had almost stopped. Jill caught her breath at the feeling inside her—the thing was dying. Fighting her fear and repulsion, Jill somehow got across the room, snatched up the pan before she could let her horror of what it held affect her and tipped all its contents into the kettle. There was an alien touch against her fingers as it splashed in. But—she could hardly see it now!

She knelt by the kettle, took the torch and shone it into the depths.

It—it was like something made of glass! She could see the bulbous eyes, they were solid, and some other parts, but the rest seemed to melt right into the water.

Jill gave a small sound of relief. That compulsion which had held her to the creature's need was lifted. She was free.

She sat back on her heels by the kettle, still shining the torch at the thing. It had flopped about some at first, but now it was settled quietly at the bottom.

A sound out of the dark, Ulysses poked his head over the other side of the kettle to survey its inhabitant. He did not growl, and he stood so for only a moment or two before going to jump back on the bed with the air of one willing to return to sleep now that all the excitement was over.

For a time the thing was all right, Jill decided. She was more puzzled than alarmed now. Her acquaintance with things living Outside was so small, only through reading and what she had learned from Marcy and observation these past days. But how had the thing made her wake up, know what it had to have to live? She could not remember ever having known that things which were not people could think you into doing what they wanted.

When she was very little—the old fairy tale book which had been her mother's—a story about a frog who was really a prince. But that was only a story. Certainly this almost transparent thing would never have been a person!

It came from the lake, she was sure of that from the first picture in her mind after she woke up. And it wanted to go back there.

Tonight?

Almost as if she had somehow involuntarily asked a question! A kind of urgency swept into her mind in answer. Yes—now—now! It was answering her as truly as if it had come to the surface of the water and shouted back at her.

To go out in the night? Jill cringed. She did not dare, she simply could not. Yet now the thing—it was doing as it had before—pushing her into taking it back.

Jill fought with all the strength of will she had. She could *not* go down to the lake now—

But she was gasping—the thing—it was making her feel again something of what it felt—its earlier agony had been only a little relieved by the bringing of the kettle. It had to be returned to the lake and soon.

Slowly Jill got up and began to dress. She was not even sure she could find the way by night. But the thing would give her no peace. At last, lugging the kettle with one hand, holding the flash in the other, she edged out into the night.

There were so many small sounds—different kinds of bugs maybe, and some birds. Before the bad times there had been animals—before the Cleanup when most everything requiring air men could use had been killed. Maybe—here in the Outside there were animals left.

Better not think of that! Water sloshing over the rim of the kettle at every step, Jill started on the straightest line possible for the lake. When she got behind the first screen of bushes she turned on the flash and found the now familiar way. But she could not run as she wished, she had to go slowly to avoid a fall on this rough ground.

So she reached the bank of the lake. The moon shone so brightly she snapped off the flash. Then she was aware of movement—the edges of the thick banks of vegetation which had grown from the lake bottom to close over the water were in constant motion, a rippling. Portions of leaf and stem were torn away, floating out into the clear patches, where they went into violent agitation and were pulled completely under. But there was no sign of what was doing this.

In—in! The thought was like a shout in her mind. Jill set down the torch, took the kettle in both hands, dumped its contents down the bank.

Then, fully released from the task the thing had laid upon her, she grabbed for the flash and ran for the house, the empty kettle banging against her legs. Nor did her heart stop its pounding until she was back in bed, Ulysses once more warm and heavy along her leg, purring a little when she reached down to smooth his fur.

Marcy had news in the morning.

"Those Williameses are going to try to blow up the lake, they're afraid something poisonous is out there. Beeny is clear out of his head and all the Williamses went into town to get a dynamite permit."

"They—they can't do that!" Though Jill did not understand at first her reason for that swift denial.

Marcy was eyeing her. "What do you know about it?"

Jill told her of the night's adventure.

"Let's go see—right now!" was Marcy's answer.

Then Jill discovered curiosity overran the traces of last night's fear.

"Look at that, just look at that!" Marcy stared at the lake. The stretches of open water were well marked this morning. All that activity last night must have brought this about.

"If those invisible things are cutting out all the weeds," Marcy observed, "then they sure are doing good. It was those old weeds which started a lot of the trouble. Dad says they got in so thick they took out

the oxygen and then the fish and things died but the weeds kept right
on. Towards the last, some of the men who had big houses on the
other side of the lake tried all sorts of things. They even got new kinds
of fish they thought would eat the weeds and dumped those in—
brought them from Africa and South America and places like that.
But it didn't do any good. Most of the fish couldn't live here and just
died—and others—I guess there weren't enough of them."

"Invisible fish?" If there was a rational explanation for last night,
Jill was only too eager to have it.

Marcy shook her head. "Never heard of any like those. But they'd
better make the most of their time. When the Williamses bomb the
lake—"

"Bomb it?"

"Use the dynamite—like bombing."

"But they can't!" Jill wanted to scream that loud enough so that
the Williamses 'way off in their mucky old house could hear every
word. "I'm going to tell Uncle Shaw—right now!"

Marcy trailed behind her to the house. It was going to take almost
as much courage to go into Uncle Shaw's forbidden quarters as it
did to transport the kettle to the lake. But just as that had to be done,
so did this.

She paused outside the kitchen. Aunt Abby was busy there, and if
they went in, she would prevent Jill's reaching Uncle Shaw. They had
better go around the house to the big window.

To think that was easier than to do so, the bushes were so thick.
But Jill persisted with strength she did not know she had until she
came to use it. Then she was looking into the long room. There were
books, some crowded on shelves, but others in untidy piles on the
floor, and a long table with all kinds of things on it.

But in a big chair Uncle Shaw was sitting, just sitting—staring
straight at the window. There was no change in his expression, it was
as if he did not see Jill.

She leaned forward and rapped on the pane, and his head jerked
as if she had awakened him. Then he frowned and motioned her to
go away. But Jill did as she would not have dared to do a day earlier,
stood her ground, and pointed to the window, made motions to open
it.

After a long moment Uncle Shaw got up, moving very slowly as if it were an effort. He came and opened the long window, which had once been a door onto the overgrown patio.

"Go away," he said flatly.

Jill heard a rustle behind her as if Marcy were obeying. But she stood her ground, though her heart was beating fast again.

"You've got to stop them," she said in a rush.

"Stop them—stop who—from doing what?" He talked slowly as he had moved.

"Stop them from bombing the lake. They'll kill all the invisibles—"

Now his eyes really saw her, not just looked at something which was annoying him.

"Jill—Marcy—" he said their names. "What are you talking about?"

"The Williamses, they're going to bomb the lake on account of what happened to Beeny," Jill said as quickly as she could, determined to make him hear this while he seemed to be listening to her. "That'll kill all the invisibles. And they're eating off the weeds—or at least they break them off and pull them out and sink them or something. There's a lot more clear water this morning."

"Clear water?" He came out, breaking a way through the bush before the window. "Show me—and then tell me just what you are talking about."

It was when Uncle Shaw stood on the lake bank and they pointed out the clear water that Jill told of Ulysses' hunting and its results in detail. He stopped her from time to time to make her repeat parts, but she finally came to the end.

"You see—if they bomb the lake—then the invisibles—they'll all be dead!" she ended.

"You say it talked to you—in your mind—" For the third time he returned to that part of her story. She was beginning to be impatient. The important thing was to stop the Williamses, not worry over what happened last night.

"Not talked exactly, it made me feel bad just like it was feeling, just as if I were caught where a breather broke down. It was horrible!"

"Needed water— Yet by your account it had been quite a long time out of it."

She nodded. "Yes, it needed water awfully bad. It was flopping around in the pan I put down for Ulysses. Then I got the kettle for it, but that wasn't enough either—it needed the lake. When I brought it down—there was all that tearing at the weeds—big patches pulled loose and sunk. But if the Williamses—"

He had been looking over her head at the water. Then he turned abruptly. "Come on!" was the curt order he threw at them and they had to trot fast to keep at his heels.

It was Marcy's house they went to, Marcy's Dad she was told to retell her story to. When she had done, Uncle Shaw looked at Major Scholar.

"What do you think, Price?"

"There were those imports Jacques Brazan bought—"

"Something invisible in water, but something which can live out of it for fairly long stretches of time. Something that can 'think' a distress call. That sound like any of Brazan's pets?"

"Come to think of it, no. But what do you have then, Shaw? Nothing of the old native wildlife fits that description either."

"A wild, very wild guess." Uncle Shaw rubbed his hands together. "So wild you might well drag me in with Beeny, so I won't even say it yet. What did Brazan put in?"

"Ought to be in the records." Major Scholar got a notebook out of his desk. "Here it is—" He ran his finger down a list. "Nothing with any remote resemblance. But remember Arthur Pierce? He went berserk that day and dumped his collection in the lake."

"He had some strange things in that! No listing though—"

"Dad," Marcy spoke up. "I remember Dr. Pierce's big aquarium. There was a fish that walked on its fins out of water, it could jump, too. He showed me once when I was little, just after we came here."

"Mudskipper!" Her father nodded. "Wait—" He went to a big bookcase and started running his finger along under the titles of the books. "Here—now—" He pulled out a book and slapped it open on the desk.

"Mudskipper—but—wait a minute! Listen here, Shaw!" He began to read, skipping a lot. " 'Pigmy goby—colorless except for eyes—practically transparent in water'—No, this is only three-eighths of an inch long—"

"It was a lot bigger," protested Jill. "Too big for the pie pan I had for Ulysses. It flopped all over in that trying to get under the water."

"Mutant—just maybe," Uncle Shaw said. "Which would fit in with that idea of mine." But he did not continue to explain, saying instead:

"Tonight, Price, we're going fishing!"

He was almost a different person, Jill decided. Just as if the Uncle Shaw she had known since she arrived had been asleep and was now fully awake.

"But the Williamses are going to bomb—" she reminded him.

"Not now—at least not yet. This is important enough to pull a few strings, Price. Do you think we can still pull them?"

Major Scholar laughed. "One can always try, Shaw. I'm laying the smart money all on you."

After dark they gathered at the lake edge. Uncle Shaw and Major Scholar had not said Jill and Marcy could not go too, so they were very much there, and also Aunt Abby and Mrs. Scholar.

But along the beds of vegetation there was no whirling tonight. Had—had she dreamed it, Jill began to wonder apprehensively. And what would Uncle Shaw, Major Scholar, say when no invisibles came?

Then—just as it had shot into her mind last night from the despairing captive in the pan—she knew!

"They won't come," she said with conviction. "Because they know that you have that—that you want to *catch* them!" She pointed to the net, the big kettle of water they had waiting. "They are afraid to come!"

"How do they know?" Uncle Shaw asked quietly. He did not say he didn't believe her, as she expected him to.

"They—somehow they know when there's danger."

"All right." He had been kneeling on the bank, now he stood up. But he stooped again and threw the net behind him, kicked out and sent the water cascading out of the kettle. "We're not going to try to take them."

"But—" Major Scholar began to protest and then said in another tone, "I see—see what you mean—we reacted in the old way—making the same old mistake."

They were all standing now and the moon was beginning to silver the lake. Suddenly there was movement along the edge of the beds, the water rippled, churned. The invisibles were back.

Uncle Shaw held out his hands. One of them caught Jill's in a warm grip, with the other he held Aunt Abby's.

"I think, Price, perhaps—just perhaps we have been given another chance. If we can step out of the old ways enough to take it—no more mistakes—"

"Perhaps so, Shaw."

"You won't let the Williamses—" began Jill.

"No!" That word was as sharp and clear as a shout. It even seemed to echo over the moon-drenched water, where there was that abundant rippling life. "Not now, not ever—I promise you that!" But Jill thought he was not answering her but what was in the water.

"The moon is very bright tonight—" Aunt Abby spoke a little hesitatingly.

"Perhaps it calls to its own. Pierce's creatures may have provided the seed, but remember," Uncle Shaw said slowly, "there was something else down there—"

"Those moon rocks!" Marcy cried.

"Shaw, surely you don't think—!" Major Scholar sounded incredulous.

"Price, I'm not going to think right now, the time has come to accept. If Wilson's suspicions were the truth and those bits of rock from the last pickup had some germ of life locked into them—a germ which reacted on this—then think, man, what the rest of the lunar harvest might mean to this world now!"

"And we know just where—"

Uncle Shaw laughed. "Yes, Price. Since they are now dusty and largely forgotten why shouldn't we make a little intelligent use of them right here. Then watch what happens in a world we befouled! It could be our answer is right up there and we were too blind to see it!"

On the lake the moonlight was shivered into a thousand fragments where the invisibles were at work.

A letter from the National Resources Defense Council, Inc., which arrived among the junk mail, bears the genuinely reassuring notation that it is printed upon 100 per cent Reclaimed Waste Paper. On the Board of Trustees of this organization appear the names of Dr. René J. Dubos, Dr. Gifford B. Pinchot, Charles A. Reich, Esq.—these are three among a score of prominent workers listed there in the cause of conservation. The letter is signed by Trustee Laurance Rockefeller, and it brings bad news.

What would you think of a forester who cut down the trees faster than they could grow? who scarred the land by stripping vast tracts bare? who hastily logged areas proposed by conservationists for preservation as wilderness?

That "forester" is the U. S. Forest Service. The forests are your National Forests. Spanning 40 states, with 187 million acres, they are the last great remnants of our once limitless frontier.

What happened, we may ask, to the Good Forester who cared for the forest as a natural whole, of soil and water, trees, animals, and birds; who selected only the mature timber and replanted what he cut; who was conscious of generations to come? The Good Forester has nearly gone; he is being replaced by the Sales Agent. The Sales Agent listens to the timber industry, which has found it more profitable to cut down our forests than to replant its own. The result is that twice as much timber was cut in the National Forests last year as was cut twenty years ago. The impact on the land, however, was far more than twice as severe, because today the principal logging method is clear-cutting—where every tree is bulldozed down and the land laid waste, as if by strip-mining. The future looks worse, for the Administration has approved Forest Service plans to increase cutting another 60% by 1978.

Gary Snyder

THE SMOKEY THE BEAR SUTRA

Once in the Jurassic, about 150 million years ago, the Great Sun Buddha in this corner of the Infinite Void gave a great Discourse to all the assembled elements and energies: to the standing beings, the walking beings, the flying beings, and the sitting beings—even grasses, seed, were assembled there: a Discourse concerning Enlightenment on the planet Earth.

"In some future time, there will be a continent called America. It will have great centers of power called such as Pyramid Lake, Walden Pond, Mt. Rainier, Big Sur, Everglades, and so forth; and power nerves and channels such as Columbia River, Mississippi River, and Grand Canyon. The human race in that era will get into troubles all over its head, and practically wreck everything in spite of its own strong intelligent Buddha-nature.

"The twisting strata of the great mountains and the pulsings of great volcanoes are my love burning deep in the earth. My obstinate compassion is schist and basalt and granite, to be mountains, to bring down the rain. In that future American Era I shall enter a new form: to cure the world of loveless knowledge that seeks with blind hunger; and mindless rage eating food that will not fill it."

And he showed himself in his true form of

SMOKEY THE BEAR.

A handsome smokey-colored brown bear standing on his hind legs, showing that he is aroused and watchful.

Bearing in his right paw the Shovel that digs to the truth behind appearances; cuts the roots of useless attachments, and flings damp sand on the fires of greed and war;

His left paw in the Mudra of Comradely Display indicating that all creatures have the full right to live to their limits and that deer, rabbits, chipmunks, snakes, dandelions, and lizards all grow in the realm of the Dharma. . . . .

Wrathful but Calm, Austere but Comic, Smokey the Bear will illuminate those who would help him; but for those who would hinder or slander him,

HE WILL PUT THEM OUT.

. . . And he will protect those who love woods and rivers, Gods and animals, hoboes and madmen, prisoners and sick people, musicians, playful women, and hopeful children;

And if anyone is threatened by advertising, air pollution, or the police, they should chant *SMOKEY THE BEAR'S WAR SPELL:*

DROWN THEIR BUTTS
CRUSH THEIR BUTTS
DROWN THEIR BUTTS
CRUSH THEIR BUTTS

And SMOKEY THE BEAR will surely appear to put the enemy out with his vajra-shovel.

Now those who recite this Sutra and then try to put it in practice will accumulate merit as countless as the sands of Arizona and Nevada,

Will help save the planet Earth from total oil slick,

Will enter the age of harmony of man and nature,

Will win the tender love and caresses of men, women and beasts,

Will always have ripe blackberries to eat and a sunny spot under a pine tree to sit at,

AND IN THE END WILL WIN HIGHEST
PERFECT ENLIGHTENMENT.

thus have we heard.

(May be reproduced free forever)

The Smokey the Bear Sutra, with a Kama changed or deleted here and there, is Ripped Off from the COSMEP *Newsletter*'s Rip-Off Editor, who ripped it off from various publications.

Gary Snyder is a well-known trustee of the counterculture, and a much-published poet, besides. The Establishment thanks him for his generous contribution.

*Let us take heart. There are those concerned that
the arts of Field and Stream should not die. . . .
I am not fully convinced that Gene Wolfe is one
of them.*

Gene Wolfe is a mild man who carries a long
stiletto. His *The Fifth Head of Cerberus* is a tour
de force: three *Novellen* which add up to considerably more than a novel, demonstrating his
mastery of form. It seems fitting that "An Article
About Hunting" is not an article, but a story—
a very *sic* story. All of his spellings are intentional.

Gene Wolfe
AN ARTICLE ABOUT HUNTING

As we had arranged earlier by vidphone, I met Mr. Roman Cowly
in the lobby of the administration building of Federal Farm_____.
Mr. Cowly, who has held the office of District Commissioner of Ecology since his appointment in 1982, is a tall, robust man of about
fifty. He shook my hand cordially when I introduced myself. "Glad
you could make it. So you feel that your readers will be interested in
a closeup look at the science of wildlife management, do you?"

I assured him I did.

"Well, I think you'll find our modern, scientific methods quite a
revelation if you're not already 'up on them' as we say. You understand," he led me through the building as he spoke, having already
introduced me to the Farm Manager, Mr. Swint, "we are not simply
going to hunt *any* bear tomorrow. We will be 'thinning out' a particular one who has been doing a great deal of damage."

I assured him that I understood this, and ventured to ask him the
purpose of the numerous low white-painted buildings I saw behind
the farm's main structure.

"Those are poultry houses," Mr. Swint, the farm manager, informed us. "Poultry and apples are the principal products of our farm here. We also raise a little corn for poultry feed—that's what's known as diversified farming."

I said, "Has the bear been killing the poultry?"

"No," said Mr. Swint, "he's been after the apples." He took us into the orchard and showed us several spots where the bear had been feeding on rotten apples that had dropped to the ground, and even in some cases biting at ripe apples while they still hung on the tree. "You wouldn't think he could reach up that high and get them, would you?" Mr. Swint said, pulling down the remains of an apple for me to examine. "He's a regular monster, this one."

The tracks, or "spore", of the bear were considerably confused, but Commissioner Cowly was able to show me several clear prints and two places where the animal had vomited meals composed largely of half digested apples. "It's the spray that does that," Mr. Swint said. "Of course nobody ought to eat so many apples at one time, but you can't tell a bear that."

I asked if he thought it was a grizzly bear.

"No," Commissioner Cowly explained, "we're fairly certain this is simply the common black bear," (Euarctos americanus) "and not a Grizzly." (Ursus horribilis.) "Of course it could be the brown or 'cinnamon' color phase." (Also E. americanus. Color distinctions are not ridgidly enforced among American bears.)

Mr. Swint explained that the grizzly bear was no longer found in this area, and I asked why this was so.

They had to be controled because they killed sheep," he explained. "Fortunately that could be done pretty easily because they went back to a dead sheep again and again until they had eaten the entire carcass. If you couldn't find a sheep a bear had killed but knew bears were in the vicinity you could shoot a couple yourself and put the poison in them." He added that sheep had never done well in this locality and that he had none on the farm.

In a section of the orchard close to the surrounding woods I was shown two pits being dug. One would hold the "marker"—as the man charged with the duty of "marking" the offending bear with an indelible luminous orange dye sprayed from an aerosol can is called

—and the other myself. Because of the necessity of sawing and chopping through a number of large roots the work was proceeding slowly, but I was assured that it would be complete before nightfall. It had been my understanding that Commissioner Cowly himself was to be the "marker", that night, but he informed me that due to unexpected business he would be unable to join the hunt proper until next morning, and that Mr. Swint would take his place.

While this was still under discussion we were interrupted by the sound of a truck stopping in front of the main building. This proved to be Mr. Alexander ("Sandy") Banks, a Preditor Control Agent of Commissioner Cowly's, and the truck contained six of the commission's best trained hunting dogs. These were "domiciled" in the back, which had been transformed into a sort of kennel with chickenwire. Mr. Banks had not been scheduled to put in an appearance until the next day, but had become confused about the nature of his orders— for which he was subjected to a bit of good natured joshing from Commissioner Cowly, who was inclined to treat the error humorously no matter how often Banks explained it.

Later I was shown the dogs Mr. Banks had brought, and Commissioner Cowly explained that such a pack was not simply flung together fortuitously. "Every animal you see there," he explained, "is an expert, with his own particular function to perform in the pack. Sandy will show them to you if you like."

I was eager to see them, and "Sandy" accordingly pulled the dogs one by one from the truck so that I could examine them at close range.

"This here is 'Wanderer'," he said as he led out the first animal, a sad and very dignified looking hound of more than ordinary stature. "You notice how I led him out first? That's because he's what we call the head dog or 'boss' dog. He's part foxhound and a quarter coon dog and half bloodhound on his mother's side." When I stepped cautiously away from "Wanderer" Commissioner Cowly added, "You don't have to be afraid of him; Wanderer's a very gentle dog. If he were to catch this bear he'd just lick his face, wouldn't he, 'Sandy'?"

"Sandy" nodded. "People don't know it, but bloodhound blood's the gentlest blood there is. We got Wanderer to hunt for kids that gets lost, and when he finds them he don't do no more than lick their faces. He's so gentle, is what we say, he squats to pee." Sandy tied Wanderer to the bumper of the truck and drew out two hounds together. "These here's 'Nip' and 'Tuck', the twins," he informed me. "Nip's a bluetick, and 'Tuck', he's a redbone hound." Nip and Tuck were duely tied to separate trees, where they howled softly until Mr. Swint quieted them with a rock.

"This here is 'Sweet Sue'," Mr. Banks informed me, drawing another hound from the truck. "Sweet Sue" was diminutive in size, possessed of a melting glance, and indubitably female and the recent mother of puppies. The three male dogs seemed at least mildly intrigued at her appearance, despite the hours of her company in the back of the truck. Sandy didn't bother to tie up "Sweet Sue", and she frisked around his feet as he extracted the last dog, a white bull terrier with a torn ear, from its confines. "My catch dog," he explained. " 'Lance' 'll tree anything that won't tree for the hounds or fight it 'til I come." The bull terrier grinned in that peculiarly unprincipled way bull terriers have. His teeth would have done credit to a small shark.

"You see," Commissioner Cowly said, "as I told you, each of these animals is a specialist. Fascinating, isn't it?"

On the way back to the pits, which he wished to examine (Commissioner Cowly having decided that although Mr. Banks had not been instructed to appear until the day following he should, since he was now available for duty here, remain to "mark the bear") I asked "Sandy" what part Sweet Sue would be expected to play in the hunt.

"Sweet Sue is just a general all around good hound dog," Sandy said. "But I mostly bring her to encourage the others and make them braver; of course when she's in heat I got to keep her locked up. Now, like you see, she's just whelped—I drowned them—and that's because a while ago I let her go too long. It was a fruit case, just like this here one, except that it was a possum doin' it. I put the dogs after him and waited for them to yell 'treed', which they never did, and along about sunup I give up myself and went back to the truck figuring they had about run that rascal into the next county. But the joke was on me because that night the possum was back again and took some more, but them dogs didn't come draggin' back for a week and when I saw the look that was on their faces I knowed but by then it was too late. Also that 'Sweet Sue' is a good dog for rabbits."

That night after Commissioner Cowly had returned to his office Mr. Banks and I established ourselves in the pits. It was necessary that this be done early, since the bear might well "spy out" the orchard before deserting the safety of the woods, so six o'clock found us in position, our locations artfully concealed beneath screens or "blinds" of leafy branches from the apple trees. A gentle rain was falling.

I had taken the precaution of filling a thermos with hot coffee from the kitchen, but I resolved to limit myself to a single cup an hour. My other equipment consisted of my camera, flashgun, and bulbs; and an extra can of the florescent spray paint—this last for emergency use only, since I was not the official marker and there could conceivably be legle difficulties about hunting a bear marked by someone not directly associated with the Bureau of Wildlife Management. "Sandy" Banks (in the other pit, not fifteen feet from where I crouched, but in the rain and the darkness how far it seemed!) I knew, had a paint can like mine (save that his was full), and a Kap-Tscher gun which fired (by means of a powerful latex spring) "hypodermic darts", each consisting of a four inch needle about as thick as a knitting needle, a "mainbody" or syringe containing a carefully calculated dose of powerful tranquilizing drug (a tricky business this, since too small a quantity would fail to quiet the bear, while an overdose of even a few milligrams would be fatal), plastic quidance feathers, and a small siren with a blinking light (battery powered) to assist the huntsman in locating the immobilized animal. In addition, although this was somewhat against instructions (Commissioner Cowly wished to donate the animal to a National Park) Banks had, I knew, an old military assult rifle; he had showed me this weapon in strictest confidence after I had assured him repeatedly that I would not mention its existance in this article, since exposure would almost certainly mean the loss of his position.

After the first four or five hours the wait grew monotonous. The rain that had been falling all afternoon turned somewhat heavier, and it occurred to me that our blinds—that is, the mats of apple tree limbs that covered our holes—would have been much more effective in shedding water if they had been made with a pitch in the center, such as is found in the roof of a small house or a tent. It might even be possible (I intend to experiment with this idea at the next opportunity) to actually *use* a small tent, erecting it over one's pit and covering the canvas with branches; it would not, of course, be possible then to part the leaves from inside to look out, but this might be taken care of by cutting holes in the walls of the tent as needed. If the wait were to be of long duration I might even have a stove or a little fire.

I had been crouched under the blind about six hours when I discovered that there were apples still clinging to the limbs that made up my shelter. I picked one and, recalling what Mr. Swint had told us about the sprays used on them, washed it with what was left of my coffee, which was cold by this time anyway. Since it was now completely dark this was a tricky operation, but I discovered that each apple had a little recessed area (I call this a "well") surrounding the stem, and I contrived to fill this with the cold coffee and wash the remainder of the surface by dabbling my fingers in this natural "reservoir".

I had treated a second apple in this same way and was groping through the leafy "blind" for a third when my fingers stumbled on something which, at first contact, I might almost have taken for a raw oyster. I raised myself to a sort of half crouch (I had been sitting) and thrust aside the leaves to see what it was, and found myself staring at what at first seemed—before I had found my mental focus, so to speak—to be the face of a man suffering from a gross deformity of the nose and jaws, so that the lower part of his face protruded in a way that was grotesque and pathetic in the extreme. An instant later I realized that I was "eyeball to eyeball" with the bear, and with what I still feel to have been considerable presence of mind I yelled to inform "Sandy" Banks of my discovery and threw myself backward (that is, back down into the pit) as forcefully as I could, thus putting an additional eighteen or twenty inches between myself and the animal, should he choose to attack.

The bear, who must have understood that he was to be hunted as soon as he heard me call to Banks, at once displayed the extreme agility which renders all his kind such formidable antagonists. With a peculiar cry I can only describe as approximating the note of a large dog kicked unexpectedly while asleep he flung his head and shoulders in the direction opposite me so vigorously that he was able to continue in a sort of rolling motion until his hind feet were high in the air, and, following through, bring them down *behind* his head so that he had, in the twinkling of an eye, revolved his entire body, which must have weighed several hundred pounds, through a full three hundred and sixty degrees of arc.

He then showed (all this took place, as you must realized, in less than a few seconds) yet another of the remarkable abilities with which nature has armed his tribe: the ability to "charge" or sprint at an exceedingly high speed from what is called a "standing start" —or even, as in this case, beginning from a movement already in progress with considerable celerity in the opposite direction. Fortunately for me this charge was directed not toward myself but at Sandy Banks' position. Lying flat, as I was, in my own, I was unable to see just what occurred, but I distincly heard the crash as Banks' "blind" gave way beneath the weight of the bear. I ran to get help.

By this time it was pitch dark, and the rain, which was increasing in force, had rendered the footing extremely trecherous, so that the first four or five persons I encountered were apple trees. I could hear shouting in the distance however, and I assumed from this that Mr. Swint (the farm Manager) had been appraised of the bear's presence and was coming to our assistance. In the hope of encountering him on the way I decided to dash straight for the main farm building, but had taken only a few strides when I fell into a hole filled with water and brush.

After a few moments reflection I realized that this must necessarily be either Banks' pit or my own, since (to the best of my knowledge) there was no other similar construction in the orchard. It was the work of seconds to determine that if it were indeed Banks' the bear was no longer present.

We started on the bear's trail a few hours after dawn the next morning. Though I had been unable to mark the bear properly (my aerosol marking can, which had been in my hip pocket, had unfortunately discharged while I was evading him) Banks had succeeded (as he himself said) in "giving it to him right in the face" when he encountered the creature in the orchard while coming back to resume his post after a brief sojourn at the main farm building. Anticipating the return of Commissioner Cowly in the morning he had, a few seconds before, prudently "misplaced" his assult rifle in the mud; and since he had left the Kap-Tscher gun in his "blind" he had possessed nothing except the marking spray ("and his legs" as he humorously remarked) with which to defend himself from the bear. Luckily these had proved sufficient.

Wet weather, as Commissioner Cowly explained to me before we set out, holds scent and is thus ideal for displaying the talents of trailing dogs. This day was ideal, the rain of the night preceeding having continued almost until our "jump off" time, when it gave way to sleet. The dogs were whimpering with excitement as they were led out, and had several times to be restrained from returning to the truck. "Wanderer" as "Commissioner Cowly" explained to me, would be put on the scent first. "The best method," he told me (to quote him directly), "of working with a bloodhound is to allow him to smell some possession or article of clothing of the prey he is to seek; a handkerchief, underwear, or a dirty sock is ideal." I was about to ask if it would be necessary to "start" the dogs with a tuft of hair torn from the bear's pelt (since it would be manifestly impossible to use an article of clothing—properly so called—except, possibly, in the case of a fugitive circus bear) when I noticed Banks carrying a soiled handkerchief. For a moment, I confess, I felt incredulity; but it soon developed that the handkerchief was Banks' own, and contained one of the bear's droppings (technically called a "spore"), a number of which had been discovered near the spot where I had inadvertantly touched his nose. "Wanderer" took one long sniff and howeled mournfully —the overture of the hunting song of the pack!

It was good to be alive that morning in the rain-grey woods, where the icicles shaped themselves at the tip of every leaf. The dogs were soon out of sight, and we—Commissioner Cowly, Mr. Swint, Banks, and I—followed them by sound alone, Banks interpreting every note of the canine chorus for us: "Hear that," he (Alexander "Sandy" Banks, the Preditor Control Agent employed by the Wildlife Management Commission) would say, "that's Nip!" Or, "That's Tuck!"

We had traversed nearly three miles of rough, wooded country (bears are extraordinary travelers despite their normally relaxed and even indolent dispositions, and when pursued by half a dozen or so large dogs followed by men with guns will often keep up the chase hour after hour until they are ready to drop, although on other occasions they may seek to escape by climbing trees, hitching rides on trains, or other such slights) when the hounds met their first check. We found them milling about in an open lumbering "cut" (informally used, after the lumbering operations were complete, for solid wastes disposal) through which a small stream ran. "They've lost the scent," Commissioner Cowly explained, "and are casting for it." At that moment Sweet Sue "got the part", and raising her head she voiced a series of yelps more highly pitched and feminine than those of the larger dogs and, having thus announced her discovery, disappeared into the trees. "Gawdam dog's on a rabbit track," "Sandy" Banks commented.

"I don't believe it," I replied. "I think she has found the bear."

I should have known better than to pit my slender skills against those of such an experienced woodsman as (Sandy) Banks. "Bear went down that creek," he explained to me, "t' throw off the dogs. The scent," (spore) "won't last on running water."

It seemed obvious that the ice was too thin to have supported the weight of the bear, and I pointed this out to Banks, but he directed my attention to a series of holes, each about a foot long and six inches in width, in which the ice was just beginning to re-form. "Them's his steps," he said. "You notice how they're only about as far apart as a bear would walk? And if you'll look real close at the back edges of them you'll see blood where he cut hisself."

Traces of this sort (technically known as "spore") are most important, and I was stepping out onto the ice to examine them for myself when, quite unexpectedly, the trecherous surface gave way beneath one of my boots, which was plunged to the calf into the icy water. Fortunately the tough leather saved my Achilles' tendon from injury, but before I could draw it out the boot was filled to the top. This occasioned a good laugh all around, but it was one in which, since I was already feeling somewhat ill (I believe as a result of the apples I had eaten the preceeding night), I was unable to join as heartily as I would have wished. "Got a boot full of water, don't you," Mr. Swint remarked when the laughter had subsided. "You better take it off."

I was already attempting to do this, and eventually, with the help of a knife I borrowed from Banks, I succeeded, dumped out the freezing water, and squeezed out my sock. My foot, I noticed, had become an interesting blue color.

At that moment a small gray rabbit came dashing out of the woods, dodging backward and forward in that erratic way rabbits have, and throwing up sprays of icy water as it passed. Mr. Swint threw my boot at him, and Commissioner Cowly a stick, the latter so well aimed that it broke the animal's back. We were just going over to look at him (before he dragged himself to safety, for he was still able to make fairly good time by pulling himself along with his front paws, and the dogs did not seem to have noticed him) when "Sweet Sue" emerged from the woods with remarkable speed, followed by what I at first took to be a much larger dog. Before Banks could bring the Kap-Tscher gun into play both animals had disappeared into the trees again. It was (or had been) the bear.

All was not lost, however. Old "Wanderer" picked up the trail as soon as it was pointed out to him by Banks, and in a trice he—with Nip and "Tuck" not far behind, and trailed by Lancelot (the bull terrier) who up until then had appeared somewhat disenchanted with the entire proceeding—was running on a headhigh scent. In a few minutes their baying was transformed into shrill yelping. "They've got him!" Commissioner Cowly exclaimed, crouching to halt Wanderer who, having apparently been savagely used by the bear, was just then running past us in the opposite direction. Maddened by excitement the dog fastened to his hand, and it was necessary for Mr. Swint to kick him ("Wanderer") several times before he would let go.

A few steps further and we were at the spot where "Bruin" had taken his stand. Salt water from an oil drilling operation had killed fifty or a hundred acres of timber here, and his back was protected by a huge, dead oak. Here he stood ready to maul with utmost vicuiousness any of the dogs who ventured to attack him. I raised my camera for a picture, and as I did so I could see from the expression of dispair that crossed that coal black face that he believed it to be a gun. His look of relief when the camera made only a harmless click was quite comic. It was at this moment, however, that "Sweet Sue" who, more than any of the other dogs had been holding him at bay, standing (brave dog!) squarely before him and keeping up a constant high-pitched yipping, was seized by the hindquarters by "Launcelot" the bull terrier, who perhaps feared that she was getting too close to the bear. Unfortunately, with that "dead game" instinct of his race the white dog did not release her even when he had succeeded in dragging her backward several yards into a clump of withered bushes, and for a few seconds it appeared that the bear might attack us. Banks saved the day, putting four Kap-Tscher darts into the brute in rapid succession, after which Mr. Swint and I took turns until the supply of darts was exhausted. Even so, Commissioner Cowly, always solicitous for the welfare of anyone even remotely connected to his department, insisted on Banks striking the head of the now unconscious bear with a large stone before he would declare it officially "safe". Then—too soon it seemed!—the hunt was over. The quarry lay still, and the thought came to me, as it always does at the end of such adventures, When and Where shall I ever again find such friends or such sport? And will anybody buy this? There was no sound in all the woods save the thrashing and panting of the five dogs in the dead bushes and the soft hiss of "Banks' " spray can as he "marked" the bear.

Dennis O'Neil writes comic strip continuity for a living. He does this with good conscience and with all the art he can bring to bear. He has recently begun to branch out into fiction without pictures other than those evoked by the words alone. He has here written a story of extreme situations.

> *—I don't think I'll die a "natural" death because I'm not sure there are any left.*

> —Seymour Krim

Dennis O'Neil
NOONDAY DEVIL

—And in the roaring of the filthy storm, he thought he heard the voice of his Master, and in the dark, churling clouds he thought he glimpsed his Maker's face.

But was it the countenance of the Lord? Or were those the features of his mortal father? Or did he see the scowl of a monsignor he had once served? The priest could not be certain.

A flash of lightning gleamed on the oily rain that streamed from his hair; a peal of thunder numbed his ears. He listened to the sudden, echoing silence that followed, listened to silence shape words:

. . . cast you out, unclean spirit . . .

A gust of wind from the north momentarily deafened him. Then:

. . . snatch from ruination and from the clutches of the noonday devil . . .

Again, the thunder. And finally, the whisper of an old man, an infinitely weary and suffering old man, a plea:

. . . help Me . . .

The priest lurched forward, arms outstretched, groping at the blackness, crying, "How, O Lord? Tell me how."

But he sensed he was alone.

Awoke: the patch of brown grass beneath his head was already dry, last night's mud reverted to fine gray dust. Sunlight hurt his eyes through closed lids. He raised his upper body, rested on an elbow and looked. Nothing had changed. The buildings—barn, chicken coop, farmhouse—were as they had been these past few mornings, stark planes of glaring white, the sheen of sun almost tangibly heavy upon their surfaces; the distant hills shimmered in the heat, colorless apparitions dotted with tiny dark cylinders, the remains of the forest; and the sky was the color of sour milk, as usual. A new chapter of Genesis: "And on the eighth day, the Lord created bleach, and did spill the bleach over the firmament. Lo and behold."

He tried, briefly, to recall the dream, or hallucination, he had experienced during the storm. He couldn't. Nor could he remember why he had gone out in such foul weather. No matter. He stood, ignoring the throbbing in his skull and joints, and the sharper stab of pain on his skin, and walked to the well. He cranked up the bucket, put in a cupped hand, slopped water into his mouth. He grimaced, spat: the water was oily-bitter, the taste of brake fluid. "So it's reached my well now," he said aloud.

He turned, and started toward the barn. As he drew near, he could hear the clink of metal striking metal, and guessed what he would find Clarissa doing. He was right. Pushing past the sagging door, he saw her bent awkwardly over the engine of the Ford, wrench in hand. Odd bits of machinery were scattered around her bare feet.

"Morning," he said.

"Just a second, Ben." She twisted a bolt, set her tool down carefully on the fender, pivoted, and kissed him on the lips. "You didn't come to bed," she said accusingly. "Have you found another virgin to seduce?"

"Hardly. I'm a man of the cloth, remember? I have my priestly duties."

"You haven't said a Mass since way before we left the city."

"The old bread and wine trick isn't *all* a priest has to do."

"You sure as hell weren't running a bingo game."

"Maybe I was hearing a confession."

"Whose? Has the Tin Hitler been converted?"

"To the best of my knowledge, Oscar is still the complete agnostic."

"If not the Tin Hitler, who?"

"You'll never know."

Clarissa stepped back, and lifted the wrench. "God, you can be exasperating. Guessing games. Tin Jesus *games.*"

"Easy, Clar," he said, touching her shoulder. "I was joking."

"Just like the old days in the parish hall, huh? Jolly Father Ben, the regular fella. A hearty goddam for the men, a wink for the women, a tickle for the young girls. *More* than a tickle for one young girl. At *least* one."

"Not fair, Clar. I never . . . made love to anyone else, ever."

"You say."

"I say. Hey, let's stop fighting, okay? Peace."

"I'm sorry, Ben. I'm sort of twisted out of shape today."

"Understandable. I should make allowances for your delicate condition." He patted her swollen belly. "How's the Little Padre?"

"Alive and kicking—*boy,* does he kick."

"Good. Sign of a healthy baby."

"How do *you* know?"

"I have lots of brothers and sisters. Mama was a righteous Catholic lady."

"I'll bet."

"Apart from that, how are you feeling? Better?"

"About the same. The sores are bothering me."

"Let's check them," he said, grasping her elbow, leading her from the humid shadows to the glare outside.

"They're no worse than yours," she protested.

He peered at her closely, beginning with the ridge of scab at her hairline, then dropping his gaze to the mottled cheeks and nose—dark crimson bruises crisscrossed with glistening red lines; to her hard, shrunken nipples, brown and faintly moist; to the protruding stomach, blotched with tiny, pus-filled craters; and to the feet, the shocking feet, blue veins bulging and shiny with oozing blood. He controlled a shudder, squeezed his eyes shut and, for an instant, saw her as she had been the first time he dared embrace her—a lithe creature of seventeen, mischievous, inviting, desirable. Afterward, lying on his cot, he had stroked her, slid his palms down her soft flesh, marveling at the flawlessness of her complexion. That had been— what? A year? Less—eleven months. Had she changed so much in eleven months? Had the world?

He felt her fingers tousling his hair. "I'm no beauty queen, huh?"

"They're improving, the sores," he lied. "And sure, you're a beauty queen. I'll thank you not to speak ill of the woman I love."

"Do you still? Love me?"

"Both of you. Can you doubt it?"

"You have the damnedest habit of answering a question with a question. But you're nice, anyway."

"I'm exasperating."

"Exasperating and nice."

They went into the barn. Clarissa returned to the Ford. Ben leaned against a wall, watching her.

"Why the urge to play with the heap?" he asked.

She glanced at him over her shoulder. "Ben, we'll *need* the car. Little Padre is due in a week or two. We'll need a way to get to a hospital, or at least a doctor. I won't be able to *walk*."

"We agreed to have the baby here."

"Oh, yeah. *No,* I mean. Ben, you're not *trained.* Neither is the Tin Hitler—not that I'd let him come near me. Suppose something went wrong? A breech birth, or something. You'd want a doctor close by, wouldn't you?"

"Sure. Only . . . things may not be normal in the city."

"It's a chance we'll have to take."

Ben began a reply, checked himself, sighed and said, "Think you can get her operating?"

"She *is* operating. I've made certain of that. Now I'm tuning her."

"Your daddy was quite a teacher."

"Of automobiles, he was." She grinned: for a second, she was again young, and unblemished. "Of lecherous priests, no."

At the door, Ben said, "I'll see how Oscar is doing."

"Give him a goose-step for me."

Ben crossed the yard and halted by the well; observing Clarissa's sores had reminded him of his own. He considered bathing them, decided against it. The liquid—to call it water would be profane—couldn't possibly help. Probably the stuff would cause further infection. Or maybe not. He shrugged and continued on, across a square, barren patch of ground behind the house. When they had arrived, this acre had been a garden; soon, it became a graveyard. The first to die was Sally, Clarissa's kid sister. Next, Bobby and Billy, twin orphans, Ben's favorite altar boys. Finally, last week, Mrs. Satterwaithe, a fortyish widow, the St. Bernard's rectory housekeeper. Cause of deaths, unknown. The four had simply slowed, and stopped, like ill-used wind-up toys. The condition, the undoctorable malaise, was common in the city; apparently, the casualties brought it with them. *Rest in peace and—amen, brethren.* They were dead, period. Out of sight, out of mind. Actually, they weren't out of sight—the squat crosses and the mounds of dusty soil were blatantly visible. To plant them here, between the house and the road—this was Oscar's idea, Oscar's notion of psychological scarecrows. Visitors were *not* welcome.

Oscar was squatting on his sleeping bag, mopping his brow with his empty left sleeve. The barrel of his carbine rested on the middle strand of the barbed wire fence; the butt was clutched under the stump of his missing limb. He nodded curtly as Ben approached.

"Morning, Major," Ben said pleasantly. "Hot one today."

"Always is," Oscar answered. "Getting hotter. Greenhouse effect."

"Yes, the smog, and so forth."

"Father, there is no 'so forth.' There is the greenhouse effect."

"Of course." Ben hunkered down and contemplated his companion. Major Oscar Robbins, U. S. Army, retired, was lean and tan, extremely fit except for a slight paunch and the missing arm. Incredibly trim, was the major: Ben wondered how he maintained the crew cut of his thick gray hair, how he kept his uniform relatively free of wrinkles. Ben and the rest, even Mrs. Satterwaithe, had discarded clothing early in their stay; the major insisted on wearing his.

"Seen anyone today?"

"Someone's coming now," said the major. He pointed in the direction the carbine was aimed.

Ben squinted, saw what appeared to be a formless dot against the milky sky, wavering, dissolving, reforming in the heat-shimmer.

"You plan to chase him?"

The major said, "I do, unless he has supplies. He has food, medicine, I'll greet him." The major shifted position, sitting on his heels and steadying his weapon. "I seem pretty—*crass*—to you, Father? Lacking in Christian virtue?"

"You don't claim to be a Christian."

"Correct. I profess survival. The soldier that survives, wins, by definition. Frankly, I don't believe we're going to win, but I am habituated to the effort. 'Do not go gentle into that good night. Rage, rage, against the dying of the light!' "

Ben chuckled. "You amaze me, Major. I hadn't expected Housman from a—"

"—from a mere military man, Father? I enjoy poetry—as an ornament. As substance, it's useless. By the way, I quoted Dylan Thomas, not Housman."

Oscar's mood changed, as it often did. He abandoned drill-field terseness, and became a classroom dogmatist. He said, "The problem with modern civilization is, it mistook amusement for importance. Now it's too late to rectify the mistake."

"You're that pessimistic?"

"I'm that realistic. The trouble with your kind is, you don't *like* harsh facts. Ignore them and they'll go away, you say. This farm, for example. Your basic tenet was good—the city was unlivable, so retreat to the country, establish a self-sustaining community. But you brought no knowledge of farming, and practically no tools. If I hadn't happened along, you would have starved, or gone slinking back."

"I think we did fairly well, for city folk."

"Sure you did," the major snorted, "after I organized you, rationed the food, formulated a program. If men like myself had seized the governments twenty years ago, there might have been a chance to stop the so-called 'ecological crisis.' We didn't. The civil libertarians outshouted us."

"You're against individual freedom?"

"I'm *for* survival, at any cost."

"I don't doubt your intentions, Major. Your wisdom, though . . ."

"Been to the pantry lately?" Without warning, the major switched to his drill-field personality. "Empty. Tasted the water? Foul. Water table's polluted. We grab anything that guy has."

Following the major's gaze along the carbine barrel, Ben saw that the dot had changed color, to a motley of pastels, and resolved itself into human shape. The chorus of a half-forgotten song tinkled in Ben's mind: *O have you brought me hope, and have you paid my fee, or have you come to see me hanging . . .*

"Far enough," the major barked, centering his sights on the man's chest. The newcomer halted ten feet from the fence. He reminded Ben of a misplaced mannequin, strayed from the boys' department into the jumbo men's department during a fire sale. His sport shirt hung in folds; the bottoms of his orange jeans trailed in the dust; and, most absurd of all, a cheap camera dangled from a frayed strap around his neck. He was holding a bundle of soiled blue blanket.

"Hello," he shouted, too loudly. "Had a speck of trouble a while ago, on Highway 70. Our station wagon threw a rod."

Highway 70, Ben remembered, was twenty-five miles east. The ludicrous man had trekked a considerable distance.

"I was hoping to find a garage and a mechanic—and a restaurant," he said. "I can pay for our meals. Every store we passed was closed. Is it a holiday?"

"What's in the blanket?" the major demanded.

"My son, Jimmy. He's an infant, two months old. I couldn't leave him with the wagon. He's feeling a shade under the weather. Hot weather's hard on the youngsters. They get colicky. I forgot to introduce myself. I'm Perce Macdonald. I'm a foreman at the aircraft plant. Mister"—this directly to the major—"is that gun loaded?"

"It is."

"I have plenty of money," Macdonald said hastily. "I'm flush. All we'd like is a hamburger or two. I'll chop one into tiny pieces for Jimmy. He ought to be able to digest a little meat. I'll give him part of mine. A root beer would go good. I'll pay plenty. You name the price."

"This station wagon of yours," the major said. "What'd you bring along?"

"Extra gasoline and stuff. Jimmy's toys. We're bound for Colorado. The wide open spaces, for me and Jimmy."

"Extra gasoline?"

"Three five-gallon drums. I'll trade you a drum for a hamburger."

The major stood, hefted the carbine. "I might trade. Lead me to the gas, show it to me."

"Wait." Ben stepped forward, unlatching the gate, placing himself between the major and Macdonald. "I may go with you, to the highway. I can give you a lift. I have a . . . chore in the city."

"Be glad of your company, sir," Macdonald said. "But I wouldn't head for town if I was you."

"Is it bad?"

"Depends on your preference. For me and Jimmy, it was uncomfortable."

"Riots? Looting?"

"No sir, none of that. People just kind of sitting around. Your listlessness, it is. An engineer at the plant blames it on the radiation."

"Radiation? Did someone explode a bomb?"

"No sir. It's from the sun."

"As I figured," Oscar Robbins muttered. "Nitrogen wastes pushed upward on heat currents. Combine with the ozone, transform it to nitrous oxide. No ozone, no protection from ultraviolet. Whence come the sores."

"I don't care to hurry you people," Macdonald said apologetically, "but Jimmy will be getting hungry, and we'll be sorry. He has a cry loud as a police siren, I swear."

"Can I see him?" Ben asked.

Macdonald hugged the blanket tight, and a tear leaked down his scabbed cheek, and he moaned. Then he smiled wide, and thrust the blanket into Ben's grasp, and babbled cheerfully, "Surely, sir. He's my boy, he'll be a basketball player, mark my words, I was short, Jimmy will be tall, tallness is on his mother's side, 'course he won't neglect his studies—"

A stink of decay rose to Ben's nostrils. Trembling, overwhelmed with anticipation of the unspeakable, he pinched the blanket to him, hesitated, in quick blinks looked at the sterile hills, the dry pastures, the garden that was a graveyard, the weeping, babbling Macdonald—the whole desolate vista—and then delicately raised the cloth. He gagged. The thing was not, had never been, a child. A horror, a travesty, an outrage; the issue of human loins, nonetheless.

. . . *And the word was made flesh, and dwelt among us.*

Ben licked his thumb, rubbed saliva on the thing's head, and whispered, "I baptize thee in the name of the Father, the Son and the Holy Ghost."

"*Amen,*" said the Lord. Yes, the Lord God Himself. Not Ben's mortal parent, nor a monsignor—*He Is Who Is* spoke.

Sudden, splendid happening, a true conversion, Saul on the road to Damascus. Ben was a priest, ministering to his flock. Fully a priest. More a priest than ever, alive with the joy of his vocation. His priesthood had lain dormant, waiting to blossom; at last it had, and he was very, very happy.

He gave Jimmy, newly blessed, to Macdonald. "He'll be the terror of the basketball court, no doubting it."

"May I see him?" Clarissa said from behind Ben.

The priest whirled, startled. Clarissa was at the gate; her hands were clasped on her belly, her brow furrowed.

"Get the fuck away," the major commanded. An act of kindness, the priest realized; Oscar, too, had glimpsed Jimmy.

"It's best to let the tyke sleep," the priest said.

"Ben," Clarissa said, "they've begun. The contractions. Little Padre is early."

"That settles it. We're going to the city."

The major waved his gun at the sky. "You won't have to, Father. The city is coming to you."

And it was true. On the horizon, there was a gritty gray line, like charcoal smudged on oilcloth. As they watched, the gray congealed, proceeding steadily, rapidly, blotting the milky whiteness.

"What is it?" Clarissa whimpered.

"Meteorological disturbance," the major said. "Smog's concentrated, riding the wind." The drill instructor peeled back to reveal the tart lecturer. "When I was in a jungle, once, my arm pinned in the wreckage of a jeep, hostiles firing mortars, my outfit decimated—I gave myself a fifty–fifty chance. I wasn't worrying about death. I knew safety existed. My problem was reaching it. Now—water septic, air poisoned, hell, the sunlight itself a killer—I'd be a goddam fool to give myself a chance. No way to outrun everything."

"Despair is a grievous sin," the priest said.

"By your reasoning, the truth is a sin. I'll be leaving you. I don't wish to die in your company. No offense."

Shouldering his gun, tucking his dangling sleeve into his belt, Oscar Robbins marched up the road. The priest made a sign of the cross after him.

"Ben—*please!*" Clarissa was bent double, hugging her midsection.

"Mr. Macdonald, will you and Jimmy kindly accompany Clarissa to the house?"

"Surely."

"I want *you,* Ben," the girl pleaded.

"I'll join you shortly. I have a chore. I must be about my Father's business."

Buffeted by wind, the priest walked to the graveyard and asked, "What *is* your business, Lord?"

"A noonday devil is abroad. Exorcise him."

The priest ran to the barn, to the car, and found his copy of the Latin Rite where he had left it, in the glove compartment.

And in the filthy storm, he opened the book and read aloud: "I cast you out, unclean spirit, along with every Satanic power of the enemy! every specter from hell! every savage companion!"

The part of him that was fleeting heard the echo of the major's shot, and something of the screams of the woman his wife on first sight of the creature their son, but he did not heed these distractions, for the part of him that was eternal was absorbed in the holiest of tasks.

"And therefore tremble in fear, now, Satan, you corrupter of justice! you begetter of death! you betrayer of nations! you robber of life! you prince of murderers! you inventor of every obscenity! you enemy of the human race!"

The darkness did not conceal the sacred words, for the grace of God shone upon them: ". . . snatch from ruination and from the clutches of the noonday devil this being made in Your image—"

Thus did Benjamin and his Maker together struggle with the Prince of Evil, and neither could foresee the victor—

Has no one a good word for pollution? If anyone
has, it will be Lafferty. And sure enough, he does.

So, as a matter of fact, has the tireless *Freep*
columnist:

*. . . Find a spot on the recycling chain that
(a) takes minimal effort and (b) is profitable
enough to make it worth your while, or to support
good works . . .*

*There is a commune in the Hollywood Hills
which has turned a twelve-year-old Volkie bug and
a home-built trailer into seven hundred dollars a
month, collecting re-cyclable paper, glass and
metal. There are four people involved in the work,
and they work a day and a half a week. They
do it this way: they mimeo some flyers, which they
stick on or under doors, stating that they would
call once a month to collect—free! free!—any of
the below-mentioned materials (glass, etc.), if the
recipient of the flyer would only put the stuff
where it could be hauled, etc.*

*Then our stalwarts follow the flyers a week later
and knock on the doors, reminding the occupant
of the flyer and sticking it in his mind, thus committing him, Then, of course, they come around
and collect. And they even sweep-up behind themselves. (Takes five minutes and impresses . . . the
neighbors.) At home, they sort, crush and bundle,
and once a month they deliver. And pick up their
checks!*

*Six days a month. Seven hundred dollars. That's
not a bad living.*

Here's a better one.

*I found three people (well, two people and a
commune) who do nothing but haul junk cars
away (Free! Free!) and sell them at a scrap-metal
compressor in West L.A. The commune puts ads
around and gets most of their response from them.
The two individuals just cruise the alleys. The
commune has a tow-truck, but both the individuals
use funky old pick-ups with home-built trailers—*

one with a power winch, one with a hand cranked affair.

And all three enterprises average a thousand dollars a month! After expenses! The commune has reaped the additional benefit of three or four extra vehicles, built out of salvaged parts.

The compressor people pay forty dollars a ton for hulks, and take them with seats, plastic, teeth, hair and eyeballs, so no stripping is necessary. And the average American . . . wagon weighs about two tons. On a good day, so one hulk-picker told me, you can score three bodies. Let's see, at eighty bucks a heap, that's . . .

So the main thing is to perform the necessary service which our hypocritical, token-solution society isn't providing. We must bring the mountain to San Fernando Valley, since Mahomet is too tired from designing new improved detergents to go to the re-cycling center.

We must do this in joy and sympathy, and in the knowledge that we are all what we must be, and we must be what mother earth needs.

—Ecommando Tactics (L.A. *Free Press*)

> Garbage-pickers of the world, unite! You have nothing to lose . . . You have nothing . . . You have nothing . . . You have . . .

R. A. Lafferty
SCORNER'S SEAT

1

Kyklopolis is one of those communities that originated in the Panic Past; yet there is very little of panic in its makeup. It is one of those settlements of "Wheelies" and "Boaters," who are em-

ployed (we do not know whether intentionally so employed) at
the cleansing of certain river junctions; and cleansing them nearly
as well as (and much cheaper than) can be done with Purification
Locks. There is a feeling that such communities should be permitted to continue in their somewhat obsolete function.

Kyklopolis is, even more than most such settlements, a closed
religious enclave. It has withdrawn from the world and it stead-
fastly refuses to learn anything from the rest of the world. It does
send out one pilgrim yearly to teach the rest of the world. This
leaves one small question: does the rest of the world have anything to learn from Kyklopolis?

Oddly there *is* one small thing that some of us in the rest of the
world would like to learn from Kyklopolis. How do the sewer
workers of that settlement get the local form of euglena algae or
cloaca algae (the scum-wort) to mutate? How do they induce the
anaerobic reversal in it, changing it from an oxygen robber to an
oxygen producer? How do they make it act like a plant instead of
an animal? We have only most inefficient methods of reversing
these rare euglenas. The Kyklopolitans have, apparently, an easy
and efficient way of bringing this reversal about as an annual
change. The yearly pilgrims out of Kyklopolis do not seem to understand the method of the reversal, do not seem in fact to com-
prehend our questions about it. We believe that their trigger to
the change is a compounded wave (probably within the auditory
range). But just what is it? And why are we unable to duplicate it?

HARVESTER REPORT

I hold this Seat till with transmuting howl
I fair the scum-wort that before was foul,
And close the circles of our cyclic day:
The Eco-log and eke the sarco-phay.

—SCORNER NUMBER 33

"What is a girl like you doing in a nice place like this?" he asked
her. "Let me take you out of this and back where you belong."

"Back to Sewer Nine?" she mocked (these were old jibes or jokes). "But I really come from Sewer Nine," she said. "I was raised there."

Her name was Circle Shannon and she was a nice roundish young woman. That was the impression she always gave Roger Meta, nice, roundish and twinkling. And perhaps the impression he gave her was of unhurried strength, easy bulk and ghost-shine.

They had never seen each other by sunlight. They had never touched each other except by accident. They both worked in the covered sewers, traveling those underground pools and streams and sometimes floods in their flat-bottomed boats that could go nearly anywhere. What light got into that under-city world was accidental; and yet there was light. It was at least as strong as good starlight. They were workers in Sewer Seven. The boats of both of them had a phosphorescent shine on them, dim, green, underground and underwater fire.

Roger Meta was scooping muck from the bottom of the sewer with a muck-scoop or muck-dredge. It was skilled labor. One broke up the new-formed muck-ridges that were not of a pattern, and sometimes one deposited muck on the old-pattern ridges that had been breached. The deep ridges were intended to give a rippling baffle effect to the waters, to turn the waters over.

The muck-scoop had a hinged handle, for the waters of the sewer were twice as deep as the roof was high. Roger piled the muck in the fore-end of his muck-barge; and Circle Shannon came and picked stars out of it as they talked sparingly. Circle was a snail-picker and slug-picker, and these slimy creatures shined like faint stars where they were imbedded in the surface of the resurrected muck.

Circle also plucked snails and slugs from the walls and ceilings of Sewer Seven, from the floating scum islands of the sewer flow; from the deeper water of it also, for she could sense the location of the small creatures variously. And while she took certain large snails and slugs (knowing exactly which were ready to take) she left other smaller seedling snails (from Sewer Five); and here in Sewer Seven they would always grow and scavenge well. She had now perhaps five hundredweight of snails and slugs gathered, half the safe lading of the boat.

"Grendel is in Sewer Seven this night, Roger," she said. "Beware of him."

"You do not know where Grendel is," Roger Meta answered softly. "Nobody ever knows where he is. If one knew, that one might avoid him a little."

"All girls and women know when he is near," Circle insisted. "We have the scent and the sense of him always. I tell you that he is in this very sewer now, and quite near."

"Grendel has nothing to do with girls and women," Roger stated. "He is male forever, and he combats and devours only males. You have enmity against another creature. We have enmity against Grendel."

"Be you warned, man," Circle said again, "he is quite near. But I do not know whether he devours tonight."

So they worked away in their boats quite near to each other, Circle Shannon who was a nice roundish young woman, and Roger Meta who was a young man of easy bulk and ghost-shine. This was at night in one of the closed sewers under the town of Kyklopolis.

This Grendel of whom they had spoken with a trace of fear was a sewer monster. He was a water-monster beyond description, and he may have been the last of his race. He had the jaws of a giant Crocodile (this is all hearsay; nobody has seen him clearly and lived to tell about it). He had the gullet of Behemoth himself so that he could swallow a man whole. He had a human head and face and eyes, except for the great jaws below and the horrible mark above. His great arms were longer than a barge-boat, more powerful than a power-dredge, sometimes jointed like those of a man, sometimes writhing like the tentacles of an octopus or a kraken. There is a story that in another country and another time (the low middle ages) a hero tore one of the arms off Grendel. Do not believe it. The hero tore one joint of one finger off, no more.

Grendel loved foul water: it was his grazing and his home. For this reason he resented having the water cleansed. For this and other reasons he devoured male humans, especially those of the sewer families. Or a young boy in his bed above might hear a call in his sleep and come and tumble down one of the access holes and into the calling jaws. A youth might go beyond where he was supposed to go and lean too far out of his barge and be taken. A full man in his strength might be gulped alive and whole even when most warned and wary. The Scorner himself, when his year was finished, when he had ruled with reason and with intuitive unreason, when he had broken at last and set up his howling clamor, would most often rush and cast himself into the sewer at its foulest place. And there Grendel would have him and eat him alive. Grendel particularly loved the yearly Scorner.

Well, why did not the men of Kyklopolis get together in great numbers with many boats and torches and weapons and hunt out and kill this Grendel? Should such a peril be allowed to live? But this is to ignore who Grendel really was, to forget of what race he was the last surviving member. For Grendel, who had once been completely human, was of the race of Cain. Moreover, Grendel was not only the descendant but also the murderer of the murderous Cain. He had disregarded the Mark of Cain and had killed its bearer. Then the Mark of Cain was transferred to Grendel himself. It was prohibited to kill him; it was prohibited by God to kill him.

The sewers of Kyklopolis were full of ghosts and ghost stories, and perhaps the starkest of them was Grendel. There is no denying that Grendel had his ghostly elements, just as he had his human and monstrous and fishy and devilish elements.

"It is told to me, Roger Meta, that you are nephew or stepson or somehow heir of John Legacy, he who is next person to die in our town," Circle Shannon was saying as she brought her boat nearer to that of Roger. "This is told to me but you did not tell it to me. Who did you tell it to?"

"I have told it to nobody at all," Roger said. "I haven't enough expectation to tell it to anyone, to presume on anyone with such slim hopes."

"Tell it to me, Roger Meta," Circle said, "and I may be able to supply such additional expectation and hope as is needed. He had the name of John Laketurner. His name has been changed legally to John Legacy, which means that he is the next to die. And you are somehow his heir. I supply the hope. Should I be a hopeless and empty woman forever?"

And Circle touched this Roger gently on the arm; gently but meaningfully. It was the first time they had ever touched except by accident.

"There are four of us who are equally heirs," Roger explained. "These four are myself, Charley Goodfish, Harker Skybroom and Jaspers Rerun. The predictions, the rimes, the cryptic remarks of Scorner himself do not indicate which of us has the advantage. After all, my foster uncle John Laketurner received the name of John Legacy only two days ago. Even after that it is not sure that he is the next to die. Often fate falls one way when it has been notched and chopped to fall another. It is said that one of us four will indeed receive the belly or birth blessing for his companion from the dying uncle, that another of us four will be the next Scorner, that still another of us (in addition to Scorner) will be killed by Grendel, and that the fourth one of us will go as yearly pilgrim to countryside and world. I will not be as I am when another season has gone, but I haven't high hope of legacy."

"Carol Bluesnail is declared companion of Charley Goodfish already," Circle said. "Twicechild Newleaf is declared companion of Harker Skybroom. Velma Green is declared companion of Jaspers Rerun. Now I, Circle Shannon, become declared companion of you, Roger Meta. I repeat: I do not wish to remain a hopeless and empty woman forever. Do you understand me?"

"I understand you," Roger Meta said, and he rubbed the palm of his hand on her cheek. It was the first time he had ever touched her.

That is the way it was in Kyklopolis. The count was kept constant. This was rigidly enforced by the Scorner, who had to be such a hard man that in one year he would break to pieces, being unable to bend. But if the count should drop by one or more then things could be put in motion to restore it to where it had been. If John Legacy should die soon (how could he not die soon since he had been named for it?) then it could be arranged for someone to take his place.

The selection of the man to be Scorner was a curious business. Following the yearly break-up and death of the old Scorner, all the people of the town would consider who the next Scorner should be. They would look; and after a bit they would all be looking at the same man. He might protest, he might try to refuse, but he would know himself to be the man. And always he would serve his term.

The Scorner was the autocrat, the absolute ruler of the town for his life in office. No other town had quite the same arrangement. To keep the town constant and continuing it was necessary that the Scorner be very stern, that he scorn all normal human sentiment. To keep the count constant required that the Scorner have rights of life and death over the inhabitants. It required also that he have rights over the air and the water, over the muck-spreading, over the land crops and the grazing, over the euglena and other algae, over all land and water plants and animals and fish, over the river and its divergencies.

As to the river and its related waters, there were two theories. One was that it was the purpose of the town of Kyklopolis to purify the river, to pass it on clearer and more fishful than it found it; that it was for this reason that Kyklopolis existed at that river junction.

The other theory was that the river, even in its putridity, was meant to serve the town and its people, that all rivers were meant to serve towns and peoples. The same for the air: it was meant to nourish even by its noxiousness.

Only the Scorner in office held instinctively the position that these two purposes were the same, that Kyklopolis was rightly named (the Circle City, the Cycle City, the Wheel City); and that if there were enough such towns and cities in the world, the world would be redressed.

The redressing of the world had to be very slow, however: too much haste could tip it even further out of balance. It was for this reason that the aid given by Kyklopolis to the rest of the world was not massive. It consisted, in fact, of one pilgrim a year sent out into the world to carry the message of balance and purification. How effective was the work of the pilgrims wasn't known. No one of the yearly pilgrims had ever been heard from again after his departure.

"How many are the ghosts tonight!" Circle Shannon cried out, "and how glowing and lowering! I believe that they will have a party."

"I believe that we will have a party also," Roger Meta called, and he poled his boat nearer to that of Circle. "A snail told me so, a fish told me so," he said. "I believe that the other three heirs of John Legacy will come down to have party with us just when it begins to dawn above and their night's work is over with. And I believe that they will bring with them their three declared companions."

"Why then we will have our party along with that of the ghosts," Circle said, accepting it easily and completely that the six visitors really would come down. "And *there* is a great fish to serve for our party. It's unusual that there be any fish so large as he before the time of transmutation."

She speared the big fish with a fish spear. She loaded it, flopping and hopping, into her snail-boat. And they brought their two boats to the shelf of rock and muck where the ghosts were gathering.

The sewer ghosts were made mostly of methane gas. So then there was nothing to them but glowing swamp gas? Hold there, hold! There was much more to them. Of what are you mostly made yourself? And is there no more to you than that?

Each of the dimly glowing hovering gas ghosts had his own person and personality. They could not communicate directly with human persons in words. The only sound they made was like the gurgling of water. It may indeed have been the near gurgling of water; it may have been that the ghosts were really soundless. We don't think so. The gurgling was always to be heard in the presence of the ghosts; it was often but not always to be heard in their absence.

There was real acquaintance and friendship between the sewer ghosts and the sewer workers. They knew each others' names, they were good company. Often it would have been lonesome, for ghost or for person, had it not been for the company of the other.

A hatch cover was raised in the ceiling of Sewer Seven. It showed a pale circle of pre-morning light and one last fading star. Then persons came through the hatch hole and down the old iron ladder to the shelf of rock and muck. Six persons: Roger Meta had not met all of them before; Circle Shannon had not met any of them: but both knew the names and persons of all six, just as they knew the names and persons of the sewer ghosts.

There were three unhurried strong young men from above with the day-shine on them: Charley Goodfish, Harker Skybroom, Jaspers Rerun. There were three sparkling and roundish young women: Carol Bluesnail, Twicechild Newleaf, Velma Green.

"I am blind, I am blind," Twicechild cried. "One does not see by the light here; it is less than starlight. Here we must sense each other by other senses than sight. Harker, my declared companion and man, I have never sensed you so before."

"Circle Shannon and myself have never seen each other by sunlight," Roger Meta was saying. "We have been declared companions for less than one hour: we touched each other for the first time less than an hour ago. It may be that we will see each other by sunlight during the coming day."

"Yes, you will go up when we go up, as soon as the party is over," Charley Goodfish told them. "There *will* be a party, will there not? Carol Bluesnail had the intuition that there would be a party and she told the other five of us that we were called to come with her to it. It would be embarrassing if she were mistaken and there was no party intended."

"There *will* be a party," Circle said pleasantly. "A providential fish appeared and I captured it for the party. And these globs of almost-light that you see here are our friends the sewer ghosts. They eat nothing at all, but they are good company."

"I thought that you were only sewer legends," Twicechild Newleaf said to the tallest and most garish of the ghosts. "I had no idea that you were real, but I have not been in the sewers before, or not since I was a child."

The tallest and most garish of the methane ghosts bowed in courtly fashion and gurgled like water. He did not use words, but he did communicate to Twicechild that he and the other ghosts were indeed real, that they were friendly, that they regarded themselves as mentors and guardians of the humans who labored in the sewers.

Carol Bluesnail had brought several large onions. Really, there is no having a party without onions, and the sewer workers in particular appreciate onions. Twicechild Newleaf had brought several small dressed birds (she was a fowler by profession). Velma Green had goat cheese. Charley Goodfish had a crock of honey wine. Harker had brought cloud-clover, those small edible seedlike particles that are precipitated out by the sky-sweeps and must be gathered from balloon, they being too light ever to fall to earth in quantity. Jaspers Rerun had brought euglena bread: this is made from that peculiar algae where it is taken from the river below the sewers and after the yearly mutation. And Roger Meta had a clay jug of turtle meat that had been preserved in its own fat since last year's burgeoning period.

Charley Goodfish, the beekeeper, the honey and wax man, produced and lit and set a wax candle. Above this he put a cupped pan on a little support; and into the cupped pan he placed pieces of the providential fish that Circle Shannon had taken and was now cutting up.

"Is there any further fuel?" Charley Goodfish asked. "What do the people in sewers do about fuel and burning? Above land these are very touchy subjects."

"Our friends, the sewer ghosts," Circle said, introducing them in one of their functions. The methane-gas ghosts came one after another and passed through the candle flame, turning it into a small but roaring fire. The providential fish was quickly cook-fried in the cupped pan, and no one of the sewer ghosts was greatly diminished by his contribution. There was plenty of methane gas in the sewers at all times and the ghosts could always assimilate it to themselves in whatever quantity was needed.

It was good party then with eating and drinking and some singing. The song had the curious quality of echoing and re-echoing through that whole watery underground. It was absorbed by every surface and depth there, and it would be given back gradually. Weeks later, little wisps of that song would be given back by the slimy walls and overheads, by the thickish waters, by the scum-wort or euglena algae (especially in its mutation time), even by the sewer ghosts, who retained scraps of old song to mix later with their water-gurgling sound.

The eight young human persons became very close in their emotions. They promised and pledged various things, in particular that no one of them would take unfair advantage in obtaining the belly blessing or birth blessing from that dying man named John Legacy. They agreed that the eight of them would go together that very day (it was daytime now in the world above) to John Legacy and see if the business of the blessing could be settled quickly. Then they touched and kissed each other, and made an eight-way friendship forever.

The six of them went up the iron ladder and through the hatchway to morning light. And Circle Shannon and Roger Meta poled and floated their boats to that place where Sewer Seven reached the loading banks. There they could discharge the snails and slugs and muck to the morning workers who distributed such. They had never gone together before. They were right on the edge of daylight now, and they had never seen each other by daylight.

Two great hands, one on each side, came up out of the black-green water and seized the muck-boat of Roger Meta by the very gunwales. Each of the hands was as wide as the boat was long, twice as wide as a man's height. One joint of one finger of one hand was missing, had been missing for fifteen hundred years. There were no other hands anywhere like these. They were the hands of the monster Grendel.

2

The means of enforcing a constant population in Kyklopolis is unknown. The people of the town simply accept it that there may not be a birth till there has been a corresponding death to make room for it. The moral power of the ruling Scorner seems to have much to do with this inhibition: a tradition beyond understanding reinforces it. The people believe so strongly that they will be sterile until they have received the belly blessing or birth blessing that they are indeed sterile.

HARVESTER REPORT

To wash the water and to scrub the air
This be our part and everlasting share:

But never quite to kill our filthy friend
Or, purpose gone, we come to empty end.

—SCORNER NUMBER 33

Great jaws gaping in the murky water below, and black water pouring over the wales of Roger Meta's muck-boat.

"I cannot reach you, Circle," Roger called, "but I give you the blessing from here. My life goes now. Replace it."

"No," she said stoutly. "I go with you if you go." And she was into the water with a fish spear and after Grendel. A spear like that wouldn't even scratch the hide of Grendel.

But it didn't happen then. It wasn't meant to happen. There was a giggling of devils (it was sometimes said that Grendel was composed of a whole nation of them inside his curious form). Grendel released the boat and slid down into deepest water. There were water spouts then with brimstone in them, hideous sounds that set one to retching, stench that roared, and guffaw that rotted the marrow. It was the monster Grendel laughing underwater.

"Mine is another of the four fates then," Roger spoke, shaking. "He doesn't take me today."

Then it was suddenly a very joyful day, after Circle and Roger had turned their boats over to the unloaders and processors where Sewer Seven comes into daylight and mingles with the other waters. The two young sewer workers climbed up the banks to the ragged outskirts of Kyklopolis. They blinked like dirty moles at the morning light, but that light is a healing thing even for sewer people. They saw each other by daylight for the first time. They were pleased about it, and a little shy.

They were just within that wall of Circle Stones that bounds the Circle City and separates it from the Countryside and the rest of the World. These circle stones are stone wheels standing up, about a meter in diameter, with holes in the middle of them, just touching each other, ten thousand of them if one counts the similarly shaped and sized buoys that complete the circle out in the river just beyond the purifying sewers. It would seem that this little stone wall, free-standing and unmortared, could not keep anything out, but it could keep the world out.

Could not one easily leap over it? No. To do so would be to be vaporized by lightning bolt. Try it and see! Only once a year might an assigned Pilgrim leap over it without self-destruction.

Circle Shannon and Roger Meta left the dangerous bounding fence and started into deeper and more vital Kyklopolis itself. How beautiful, how idyllic was the cyclic city as it stirred itself into morning light. Little children bringing Night Charleys and Honey Buckets out of their houses and bringing them to the men who pushed the night soil barrows. Spriggers (they were the so-called "Green Children" who could make things grow) bringing out the little pots of green sprigs that had sprouted the day before and now raised their heads to the morning light. The spriggers brought their plants to the sprig masters, who would set them in the new muck being spread that morning. Constant renewal in even the very small things. No path used more than three days. Then it was abandoned (lest it should become dusty), mucked, and sprigged and sodded.

"The Scorner has reigned a year and a day," Circle Shannon said. Sheep were grazing the clover growing of the rooftops of the buildings, and chickens were clucking and pecking up there between and among the sheep. The bees also grazed the clover of its nectar, and the edible locusts grazed it of its black-leaf. All things fit together.

"The Scorner will probably break up today or tomorrow," Roger said, "though there is a case of a Scorner reigning as long as a year and four days. Some men do not break as quickly as others."

People going by on one-, two-, four- and eight-man bicycles, going always roughly and joyously for mostly they went on first-day or second-day paths through the blue-stem grass and the rice-grass, scattering the seeds like small clouds in the air, bringing the birds in cloud-sized flights, bringing the fowlers who took the birds. Only in the more dense center of the city were there rocked and covered bicycle roads, with the sodding and growing on the roofs of them. But it was good to stir the grass and constantly renew the paths in the other areas. The bicycles were the only wheeled vehicles in Kyklopolis the Wheel City. Certainly no motor vehicle could go there.

They saw Scorner now, up in his own Scorner's Seat, the highest
point in the city: and the balloons and the sky-brooms were all located in that region today. The curiosity about the Scorner was a
natural thing. His breaking up marked the turning and renewal of
the year.

One hundred, two hundred, three hundred windmills turning.
Windmills also were made in the Bicycle Factory, which was the
only industry in Kyklopolis. More than half of the one thousand
water fountains of the town were already spouting, and the others
were being put into operation as the workers arrived. The smaller
fountains were operated by workers who pedaled in a sort of stirrup
and saddle arrangement very like cycles. They raised the putrid
and polluted water into the sun and air, raised it again and again,
turned it over and over. Muck-men worked in the fountains, just as
Roger Meta worked in the sewers, and filled carts with the fertile
but pungent precipitate. Air and sun and motion, and a bit of additive
that the additive men dripped into the one thousand fountains every
day, and wonders were done. Black water, brown water, green water,
golden water, even silver and white and clear water sometimes. The
fountains were a crowning beauty of the town.

The Scorner's Seat was a sort of pagoda. It was set up on poles
with ladders for visitors going up to it. It had a deep pitched roof
with turned-up edges. It had to be resodded and resprigged often,
and it was now grazed by only three mountain goats.

Leading men of the various trades and divisions went up the ladders and reported to Scorner every day: and received their stern instructions from him. That is the way that Kyklopolis was governed.

Scorner was stern in everything and was absolutely sound in his
judgments, though it is said that he had been a gentle and rather
slow-witted man until his office possessed him. Now the potato and
turnip men, the cereal men, oats, barley, wheat, rice men came to him
for their quotas and instructions. And the grass men—the grass men
were in trouble. There was discussion that grass might have to go,
being a plant that requires an intermediary animal to turn it into human food. The clovers (including the peanuts especially) had already
cut deeply into the province of grass, enjoying certain advantages

(the edible root-nodules) as well as greater productivity per square meter even for grazing, and they were nitrogen fixers as well as superior oxygen producers.

"When the last grass is gone, Kyklopolis will have lost something," a grass man moaned, but the Scorner sternly reduced the grass space in favor of cereal and clover. "Even clover will have to go sooner or later," the Scorner said. It was possibly the last thing he would say, for he made a sign that he would confer no more that day: and the leading men all left him.

Circle Shannon and Roger Meta had been eavesdropping or balloon-dropping on Scorner out of curiosity. It was this way: they had met one of the other heirs, Harker Skybroom, who was a balloon man. He was off duty but he had joined the loungers around the Scorner's Seat. Now a balloon was going up, and he invited himself and Circle and Roger to go along with the balloon operator, who was his friend. And when they had reached a certain height they had signaled the winch-operator to hold it there so that they might hear something of the Scorner's business. After all, the Scorner was public property and was almost always in view.

Now they signaled the winch-operator again, and they went up and again up, very high. The hydrogen-filled balloons (hydrogen by electrolysis was another thing produced at the Bicycle Factory, Kyklopolis' only industry) were captive on strong cable and were wound into the high air by hand winch. The winch on its heavy base was wheeled, so that the balloons might be sent up over a different part of the town every day, wherever the air was heaviest. The balloons served as rough air purifiers. The operators sprayed certain things into the smog, animate as well as inanimate things. The smog was transmuted in that vicinity. After all, smog is only polluted air, and pollution is only an extreme form of fertility.

Vertical thermal drafts were created by the balloons. This meant further aeration of the air. Cloud-clover was created out of some of the smogs; this was the sky-manna too light to fall to earth; it was a cloud of small edible seedlike particles too light to fall. But it could be gathered by the sky-sweeps of the balloons. And it could be grazed by those smog-eating miniature "cattle," certain midges and insects that were seeded by balloon. And these "sky-cattle" were taken by birds, which in turn were taken by fowlers. And also there was a mysterious Fortean dribble, sweet and fragrant from the transmuted fog. The actual food taken out of the smogs was of some consequence, the fertility rained down was considerable, and the sky-pollution was absorbed or scattered. It was clear air mostly over Kyklopolis, and wherever the air was befouled it could be cleared in a few hours with the balloons and their various sky-sweeps.

One could, perhaps, see to a considerable distance from the high balloons. But what one saw from them was unregistered or quickly forgotten. It was only the Countryside and the World, things that could hardly be of interest to citizens of Kyklopolis.

They came down again, the operator, Circle Shannon, Roger Meta and that remarkably gentle big man Harker Skybroom. Circle and Roger and Harker found that bee-man Charley Goodfish. He was the man who talked to bees, who got all sorts of information from them, who brought some of this information to Scorner, who even brought special bees to Scorner when that stern man wished to question them more closely. Charley was the master of all honey products, and he and his co-workers maintained ten thousand hives or nations of bees. Many of these were set just inside the circle stones that were the walls of the city. Clearly many of the nations of the bees did traffic with the nectars of the Countryside and the World, but this is a thing we will be silent on.

The growing party found Jaspers Rerun, who made euglena bread and other things from what might be considered waste material. Jaspers was fascinated with the euglena algae. He was fascinated with all the waters, though he was neither a sewer man nor a river man. He was even fascinated with the water-monster Grendel, much too fascinated with him. But Jaspers did not seem to have the staying qualities, not as Charley Goodfish, for instance, had them.

They found Carol Bluesnail. They found Twicechild Newleaf. They found Velma Green. Their party was now to the full count of eight. Theirs had become, in the late of the night before, an eight-way friendship forever.

"We will go now to John Legacy," Twicechild said. "We are all pledged that no one of us will take unfair advantage in obtaining the birth blessing from him. And we are also pledged to see whether the matter of the blessing cannot be settled very quickly."

"Does any of us know where John Legacy may be found?" Roger asked.

"No one of us knows," said Harker Skybroom. "When a man has assumed the name of Legacy he leaves his proper home to die elsewhere. It is always to a secret place that he goes. It is always a secret how he summons his heir, for it is not with words or sign. If it were, then someone besides the heir might intercept and go also. And it is a most deep secret how he gives the birth blessing, how he is able to confer fertility to one who was not fertile before."

"Well then, we all walk in a secret," Circle Shannon said in a jolly mystic way. "Come, come, walk, walk! I believe that we will hardly take one step out of the way. What can be kept secret from such fine folks as we are? Were we not the ones we would not walk the way. But we are the ones. Come, come all."

They walked through the poke patches and the onion patches. They walked wetly through the rice patches. Circle plucked a snail from the water-land edge here and set it in her hair by her ear. Three bees came and settled on Charley Goodfish and perhaps they talked to him. Two birds came down onto Twicechild Newleaf, who was a fowler by profession. All of these unhuman informants seemed to agree on the direction of the walk.

The party came to a very small house with a lone kid grazing the grass of its roof. They all knew that John Legacy was inside, waiting happily to give the birth blessing, waiting less happily to die.

3

The solitary and impassioned ruler of Kyklopolis is afraid to break the cycle on which that settlement is based. The fact is that the small region has now become a religious fossil of the old Pollution-Purification rite. It becomes an enacted struggle in every detail of the life there: the elements are not real, they are surreal.

The fact is that there is no regional pollution at all except that created on this special spot. After all, the Pottawattamie Purification Locks are only sixty kilometers upstream from Kyklopolis. The river runs clear from the locks and it runs clear to the very borders of Kyklopolis. And the air of the region has been clear for thirty years, excepting deliberate pollution in this one small area. The pollution in Kyklopolis is actually created and maintained by the massive toxic waste from (of all things) a bicycle factory which has a metallurgic operation so inefficient and of such poisonous throw-off (solid, liquid and vapor) as to stagger the imagination and to preclude any doubt that it is accidental. It isn't.

The second item in the pollution there traces to the incredible mutational development of what we first believed was the simple euglena algae; whatever it is, it isn't simple. This rogue euglena, *in one of its seasonable forms,* chokes the waters completely, befouls the entire sewer and river system, crowds out almost all fish life with its robbing of the water of its oxygen. It even engenders belief in a local Devil or Water Monster, the counterpart of the town-ruling Scorner, but also the destroyer and absorber of the Scorner. This whole euglena blockage could, of course, be flushed out at any time, but the cyclic religious beliefs of the town would have to be flushed out also.

Then, once a year, the Scorner dies violently, the maleficent euglena becomes a beneficent euglena providing water, oxygen and food for a great burgeoning of fish, and the blockage cleanses itself. We have here acted out the relics of grotesque pollution and grotesque purification, both out of that queer (now even nostalgic) period known as the Panic Past.

We cannot say that the pollution in Kyklopolis is deliberately maintained, for there is no element of deliberation possible here. But it is stubbornly and insanely maintained.

We still wonder, though, by what trick (we are almost certain that it is an audio trick) the yearly change in the uncommon euglena algae is brought about.

SECOND HARVESTER REPORT

Round and round, be we lord or lout?
How'd we get in it? How to get out?
Who be the Circle's nearest kin?
Where oh where does the wheel begin?

—SCORNER NUMBER 34

The eight of them moved into the little house in one silent tight bunch. Had they been called indeed? Were they heirs in reality, and how had it come about?

Inside, the bed had been overturned and broken. John Legacy was on the floor, but he was neither prone nor supine. He had gathered himself into a bundle like a belligerent buffoon. He'd not die willingly, but he'd not die fearfully either. And he'd said once that he wouldn't die in bed.

"I might not die at all," he bawled at them now out of the middle of a great grin. "I may transmute instead. Today is the day of the great transmuting. What shall I transmute into, a great frog?"

"I'd respect you none the less if you did." Circle Shannon spoke with absolute seriousness. "Would you be happy so?"

"Nay, I'd still be on the recurring wheel, and I want off it," the old man said. "Ah, it is my four heirs with their pledged companions. You have chosen them well, my boys, or perhaps it is that you have been well chosen. You are my heirs, and yet no one of you has seen me before and no one of you has a drop of my blood. How did the knowing that you were my heirs come into your heads and into the heads of this town? I put that knowing into the heads, that's how it happened. You have not seen me, but I have often seen you. I've long been habited to watch young men at work, and I have seen that you four are less entrapped than others. What? Did a ninth visitor just enter this terminal house?"

"No, good John Legacy, only we eight have entered," Twicechild Newleaf told him gently.

"Wrong, fine girl," the old man said. "A ninth visitor *has* just entered and his name is death. Ah, but I'll die in my tongue last place of all. I have things to say yet. Do you know where this town went wrong all those years ago? Do you know where the whole world almost went wrong? Pollution, you see, is an overabundance of death: it cannot be cured by commanding an underabundance of life. We commit that error in Circle City."

"Good John Legacy, will you give one of us the birth blessing now?" Carol Bluesnail begged. "I'd not mention it, but you begin to turn blue and you'll die before you realize it."

"Oh, I give the birth blessing to all of you then," John Legacy gasped out of his blue-faced pain. "You all be fertile now. Go and hold union and conceive. You are quickened."

"But there are four couples of us," Harker Skybroom protested gently, "and your going will leave room for only one new birth."

"There are four different fates for the four couples of you, and I tell you it will work out even. Before the day is over some of you will yourselves give the birth blessing, but more than four is not mine to give. Go and conceive."

"But, good John Legacy," Roger Meta began to speak. And then he finished it lamely. "He's beyond words." John Legacy was dead, and it is fruitless to argue with a dead man.

The four couples went out. They felt themselves quickened. They felt themselves fertile. They went off, couple by couple, to their own places. They gave the mutual blessing. They held union. And it is believed that they conceived.

The birth blessing from one surnamed Legacy—it always works.

It was afternoon of the day. The howl began (there is no other word for it); it was the witless, soulless, hopeless howl. A man was breaking up in body and brain and spirit: a solitary and impassioned man, too stern to bend, he had to break. A year and a day's frustrations and entrapments erupted into the horrifying transmuting howl.

Were there any mercy in that town the very arteries of grief would burst at that awful wailing woe that shook the whole region.

Who talks of grief? Who calls for mercy? No, no, it is joy everywhere in a town awakened to afternoon gladness. It is glee. It is gaiety unconfined. The whole town rushed to the river and sewers to watch the great transmutation. The Scorner was dying in loud râle and wail in his high seat, and the universality of the town rejoiced.

Not quite all, perhaps. There is some question of the disposition of four couples who were united in an eight-person friendship. One couple (Roger Meta and Circle Shannon) was already at home in the sewer and had seen the transmutation many times. "But I'll see it no more," Roger said mysteriously. "I'll be out of it now and away."

Harker Skybroom and Twicechild Newleaf did not join in the rejoicing. They were frozen in a white-faced fear and horror which neither could understand. They did not go to watch the transmutation. There would be transmutation enough in themselves.

But Charley Goodfish and Carol Bluesnail went gladly to the viewing, as good citizens should. And Jaspers Rerun with Velma Green went at a run in feverish eagerness. People were singing as they went on foot and bicycle to watch the changing of the waters. Some of them even sang the new "Four Fates" song, which prophesied what would happen to four new heirs:

> One be the Constant Townsman deft,
> The Pilgrim one, and one the Scorner,
> And one a dazzled man who left
> His wife a Grendel-widow mourner.

The sewers were fragrant as new-mown hay now, and all the waterways were teeming with life and food. Minnows were seeded by minnow-men, minnows came from nowhere and everywhere and feasted on the wonderful transmuted euglena algae. One could actually watch them grow to bigger and bigger fish. From the navigation channel, which had always run clear and pure parallel to the contrived Kyklopolis waters, fish leaped the barrier to feast on this new pasture and to grow to even bigger fish. Turtles came and frogs, crabs and river lobsters, slack-water shrimp, all fine water things; they came or they were brought, and they would grow and grow. For six months, all through the winter, the waters would be burgeoning with life. They then would choke and die again.

On one point, speculation of outsiders had been correct. The trigger for the transmution of the euglena algae was an audio one, a high complex sound that nobody had been able to duplicate. It was the death howl, the death wail of the Scorner, and nobody could duplicate it who had not suffered in strictness as the Scorner had suffered for one year.

Perhaps the happiest of the happy people was Jaspers Rerun. He had always been delighted by the yearly purification and now he felt that he had a special part to play in it. He did. He plunged into the renewed waters. He was taken in one gulp by the monster Grendel. Grendel was happy now with his holiday prey, the people were happy that Grendel was happy, even the widow Velma Green was almost happy and very proud.

The people were singing their national hymn that referred to those critical times of more than thirty years ago:

> The World a dark smoker, nor Nero to fiddle;
> We drew us a Circle and lived in the middle.

Such solidarity as the people of Kyklopolis showed was rarely to be found.

Meanwhile, back in the center of town, the body of the Scorner had been tumbled out of its high chair onto the turf, and hackers were hacking away at it. They drew it, and the rich entrails were divided among the men of the leading crops. They quartered it, and the quarters were given to the four quarters of the town; there is incomparable fertility in the body of a dead Scorner, and none of it must be wasted. (Grendel had already dined: he'd not get this Scorner.)

Then men went ritually with lighted lanterns (though it was still clear day) to look for the new Scorner. They looked here and there. Then more and more men were looking in the same place and at the same man. They were looking at the white-faced terrified Harker Skybroom. They seized that gentle big man and dragged him out. They dragged him up to the Scorner's Seat and made him Scorner.

Now he would be (for the good of the community) stern and inhuman and relentless for his one year, and then he would die with the terrible transmuting howl. It was the long line of dedicated Scorners who had made the close-built town of Kyklopolis able to feed and support itself though completely cut off from countryside and world.

Roger Meta was pilgrim. All had looked at him as pilgrim, as all had looked at Harker as Scorner. And Roger, fleet-footed now, lost no time leaving the town. What message he carried is not known (the town would never hear of any of the pilgrims again), but he leapt over the barrier of circle stones (the lightning holding its bolt for this once-a-year passage) and was gone from there. His going left room for all of John Legacy's birth blessings.

But what is this? There cannot be a second pilgrim in one year. That is illicit. Nevertheless, Circle Shannon was coming after Roger her man at a pretty good rate of speed.

"Hey, sis, want a birth blessing? I'm leaving. So's he within me. Have two."

"Oh yes, oh yes," two young women said, and Circle gave them birth blessings.

Then it was over the circle-stone fence with her. And lightning death?

Circle stood (outside the town now, in the World) with head tilted back and arms akimbo. The lightning hurled itself at her and she flinched not at all. It froze, it almost grinned, it parted, it struck and split three circle stones; but it left Circle Shannon unscathed.

> Who be the Circle's nearest kin?
> Where oh where does the wheel begin?

"Wherever it begins, it ends right here," Circle expounded. "My nearest kin is already quickening within me, and my other nearest kin is half a kilometer ahead. I run into countryside and world. I run after him."

Circle Shannon ran after her man Roger Meta in the deepening darkness.

It is not only fashionable, it is also correct, to consider the relationship of an organism to its environment as a "transaction." Living creatures on Earth exist and can go on existing only in a balanced relationship, one with another, peoples with place. There is only one place: Earth.

Barry Malzberg has always written about bizarre transactions, with consummate artistry. For me, especially, since (as worrywarting editor) I threw him a title that had been haunting me, and asked him to see what he could do with it, "The Battered-Earth Syndrome" is the living end.

Barry N. Malzberg

THE BATTERED-EARTH SYNDROME

I

SIXTY-SEVENTH DREAM FESTIVAL: Down old 46, the engine on high, cylinders lurching power, beer cans trailing from the windows and what in hell is that son of a bitch in the old Cad ahead trying to do to us? With a roar Nick cuts him off, pulling into lane then to move to the top of the tach and in the rear-view we see the Cad wobble, shriek, leave the road in plumes and dust. "Fuck him," Nick says, tossing a beer can to the sky, we see it twinkle and then fall against a motel sign. "Fuck you *all*."

Speed increases, we roll. Laughing, tumbling, moving against one another in the back. Margo and Junior; Mickey and me. (I will never see Margo, Junior or Mickey again.) Nick alone in the front as befits the driver. *Hamburger Hurrah, Jack's Very Top Best Buys,* the *Hostess Motel,* the empty field in the distance on which the cars are stacked, stacked and stacked, burning in their haze . . . and I feel Mickey's breast under my palm, lean down to knife her with a kiss while Margo and Junior struggle, are they really struggling, what is going on here? and Nick rocks the car, back and forth we scoot on the lanes of 46, tremors shooting up through my ass, which increases the need, I reach for Mickey, clamber against her and at just that moment the old Cad reappears or I think it is the old Cad, swinging out to overtake and then cutting in front and Nick, cursing, has no choice except to brake; the car screams, we all scream and go piling off the road with a jounce and clank, rolling free then across the fields and smashing with a whine into the office of the Hostess Motel, cheap rooms at bargain rates, transients always welcome and everything becomes bloody and confused; I fall to the seat of the car, fall past the office of the Hostess Motel Mickey wheezing all the way, hostess herself greeting us from under an impacted bumper and oh—

II

SIXTY-SEVENTH DREAM FESTIVAL: Coming against the wind we see the deer for the first time, poised on a ridge, blinking. Nick pokes me, hoists his rifle. "Let's get the son of a bitch right now," he says and lifts the rifle, I lift my rifle, center in on the animal. "No," Nick says, "this is mine, first kill," and I lower my rifle, Nick always has first shot: Nick always drives the car, Nick always gets first crack at the ass and none of this is fair but on the other hand this is the way it was assigned. "Watch this," Nick says giggling and pulls the trigger, the deer falls, the deer opens like a bloody sack in the distance, rivers of its thin blood pouring down the ridge and the ridge becomes 46 and 46 is filled with traffic, here we are standing on the highway cars tearing past us, the blood still coating stone, Nick giggling with panic. "They had no right, no right to do this," he says, "it isn't fair, they can't switch on us like this all the time," but too late for this non-sense; here comes a diesel and the diesel is bearing down on us, beer cans pouring from the windows, and I try to brace myself for the impact but *before* the impact—

III

INTERIM: "How long have you felt this way?" the short thing asks me. I would gesture to answer but being bound as usual find it almost impossible to reply. "Tell me," the short thing says. "Tell me everything from the beginning. You are being unresponsive, you know. You are being highly unresponsive."

"Go to hell," I say which is the only reasonable statement under the circumstances, blast them, "leave me alone." Nick is also in the room although I cannot see him from my particular angle of vision. He is however moaning and cursing throughout his own interrogation. I cannot hear the questions but I can hear his answers. Nick has not yet learned, may never learn, how to deal with them.

"You must understand," the short thing says, "that you have suffered a terrible injury, something in your own background which causes you to strike out—"

"Go to hell," I say. "Drop dead. Leave me alone," and so on and so forth, struggling all the way but keeping my cool because unlike Nick I have learned that the situation can be managed if you *do not show temper*.

"To strike out repeatedly," the interrogator says, "and you have not yet learned; you understand that until you learn we must repeat and repeat the process—"

"Eat it," I say and thrash around a bit, Nick screams in the background, the short thing leans toward me simpering, fitting down the lenses again and before I have a chance to set myself it all begins again but nevertheless—

IV

SIXTY-EIGHTH DREAM FESTIVAL: In the city I take the short route to center, me driving this time, Nick in the back grinning. Gun in my back pocket, ready for use. Never come into the city without a gun. "Take 'em over," Nick says, "we're going to take them over."

Cut right at the river. Now I can see the water itself; brown it lies before us, small objects dipping and cresting in the oily filth: cigarette cartons, prophylactics, the scent of dead animals, a drowned car whose hood peeps up shyly, its chrome ornamentation covered with insects. Something floundering in the water but I will not investigate.

"Used to be pure," Nick says, "at least that's what I hear," and laughs, Nick is always laughing: through fair and foul, in whatever circumstances that laugh carries us through (we do everything together). Kill the engine. To our left, way down on the docks, we hear screams as bodies are unloaded into the water. "Two hundred years ago it was clean," Nick says. "Wonder what happened to it?"

"Who knows?"

"Going to take over the city," Nick murmurs. "Going to take over this thing. Let me out." He leans against his door, it heaves open, he staggers to the ground and wanders toward the river. I get out and follow him at a distance, touching my gun. This is Nick's idea; I would not interfere. Dream festivals alternate or in any event this is the rumor. Nick looks over the river, small shapes bobbling in there as we come closer, swaddled in murk. "Look at it," he says, "look at this." He unzips his fly and pisses in the river.

"Good," I say, "good, good," and try to do the same but when I make the attempt something has happened to my urethra or perhaps it is only tension I am talking about; I am unable to release water and stand there pinned against the river, foul wind rising and against my eyes, the wind bringing tears as I lock there unable to finish, Nick smirking at me and this one goes on for a long time, too long by far and how much of this can I take and oh—

V

SIXTY-EIGHTH DREAM FESTIVAL: Later we prowl the city looking for a Kill but there is no one at large in the city; they have heard the reports and are locked in. Up and down the blocks we drive the motor whimpering, the car squeaking, and finally pull to the side against a gutted building in which mad dogs, held by chains, bark.

There is a CONDEMNED sign on the building and underneath it writing saying that the area will be renewed but I am more interested by the dogs who scream in human voices. "Big buggers," Nick says, chewing gum now, and, taking out his guns, shoots the dogs. One, two, three, flopping in the stillness. "They're going to renew this," Nick says, moving from the car to ease a foot between railings and kick at the carcasses. "Wonder what it's going to be like?"

"Beautiful. It will be beautiful."

"Renewal," Nick says, "renew everything," and puts a few more bullets into the corpses, they shake, the CONDEMNED sign falls to the walk with a clang and as Nick and I turn toward one another to face this new situation I see something in his eyes and he sees something in mine and it must be the same thing because I realize that we have nothing left in the world to do and where the hell is the car and how did we get here and what are they doing to us and what is this supposed to prove and anyway—

VI

PAUSE: "Measures," the short thing says, "we must take measures. You are not responding. You fail to show insight. We are becoming impatient."

"What do you want?" I say, "what do you want of us?"

"We want you to understand. We want you to realize the source of your acts. We want to change lives, incorporate understanding, help you know—"

"I don't need any of it Jack," I say and close my eyes. "Get lost with your insights and understanding because this is our life and we are the future and that is exactly the way that everything is supposed to be."

"You don't realize," the short thing says. It is gibbering. Although I find it impossible to deduce expressions from the alienness I can sense that it has lost control of the situation or so fears. "You are not even trying. We've never had anything like this. Your responses are totally blocked, you will not even accept the reality of what you have created. We want to help you but—"

"But what?" I ask. I turn for the first time to look for Nick but he is not there which is unusual; this is my first solitary situation. "Don't do me no favors."

"But you won't be helped. You won't even accept empirical verification. Never before have we had—"

"Where is he? Where is Nick?"

"Your friend," the short thing says, "your friend is not here anymore. He was unable to make adjustments."

"You mean you cracked him."

"We will not talk about your friend. We will talk about you only. Your situation—"

"You broke his mind," I say bitterly. "You broke Nick. You and your damned dream festivals. Those aren't dream festivals—"

"We will not discuss this. We will fixate upon your own situation. Your need to strike out, your need to abuse. Don't you realize? The environment is not discrete; it is bound to you. You are your world. And furthermore—"

It is babbling. The short thing is babbling. I stand, I throw off the shackles (they were only a state of mind) and confront it whole.

"I'm not afraid anymore," I say, "there's nothing you can do with my mind."

"You don't understand. It is only your mind that exists; only your mind that—"

"You can't touch me. I can do everything I want to do. You broke Nick but I'm stronger than him and you'll never break me."

"Punish," the short thing says, "the urge to brutalize. The uncontrollable urge, why my God, you people are—" It stops, seems to gain some control. "Stop this," it says in a harsher tone. "This will get you nowhere."

"Yes it will."

"You will simply re-enact over and again impulses which you can never purge. You will destroy—"

"Free," I say. "I'm free." I back away from the thing and will myself from the room. This is the way that it is done. There are no doors in their rooms. Ever. Nor rooms in their dream festivals. The room flickers, I depart.

"You fool," the thing says behind me, "you brutal *fool,*" but too late for any of that. Now I am gone and like Nick I will learn to piss in the river.

VII

SIXTY-NINTH DREAM FESTIVAL: I lie in emptiness, the sands absorb me. In the dream I have then *Hamburger Hurrah, Jack's Best Buys* and the *Hostess Motel* are burning but I do not feel the flame; I am encased in ice and everything moves away slowly and then more quickly and I wait to come out of this dream festival as I have come out of all the others and I wait and I wait and I wait and oh what can I say, I was just trying to shape the thing up and I wait and I wait

There are *alternatives. Research is under way on a number of weird and logical power sources. The movement of the tides . . . is under serious consideration as a power-generation force. Solar energy has yet to be studied thoroughly, let alone tapped. Methane shit-converters are in steady use in a number of rural communities. (Talk about killing two birds with one stone! A unit that eats garbage and produces electricity!) Steam is again being dragged out of the closet. Even yeast is being made to produce power.*

So there are *other means to run our world. There are ways to power things without polluting. There are sources as yet untapped, free for the taking. Ionization; colloidal suspension generators; stasis plants; magnetic and polarity converters. There are even men who are seriously looking for ways to use the very motion of the universe to generate power! It's far too early to laugh any of these things off. We can never say for certain that any one or all of them won't work. The only thing we* can *say and be sure of being right is that if we continue using our current power-generation methods, we will all die.*

—*Ecommando Tactics* (L.A. *Free Press*)

If some of the younger writers here represented might be considered to be on the dean's list, Poul Anderson must certainly be considered one of the deans. As a writer, he has always taken a proper interest in problems; but he is a positive force; he takes his joy in thinking up workable solutions.

Poul Anderson

WINDMILL

—and though it was night, when land would surely be colder than sea, we had not looked for such a wind as sought to thrust us away from

Calforni. Our craft shuddered and lurched. Wickerwork creaked in the gondola, rigging thrummed, the gasbag boomed, propeller noise mounted to a buzz saw whine. From my seat I glimpsed, by panel lights whose dimness was soon lost in shadows, how taut were the faces of Taupo and Wairoa where they battled to keep control, how sweat ran down their necks and bare chests and must be drenching their sarongs even in this chill.

Yet we moved on. Through the port beside me I saw ocean glimmer yield to gray and black, beneath high stars. A deeper dark, blotted far inland, must be the ruins of Losanglis. The few fires which twinkled there gave no comfort, for the squatters are known to be robbers and said to be cannibals. No Merican lord has ever tried to pacify that concrete wilderness; all who have claimed the territory have been content to cordon its dwellers off in their misery. I wonder if we Sea People should—

But I drift, do I not, Elena Kalakaua? Perhaps I write that which you have long been aware of. Forgive me. The world is so big and mysterious, civilization so thin a web across it, bound together by a few radio links and otherwise travel which is so slow, it's hard to be sure what any one person knows of it, even a best-beloved girl whose father is in Parliament. Let me drift, then. You have never been outside the happy islands of the Maurai Federation. I want to give you something of the feel, the reality, of this my last mission.

I was glad when meganecropolis fell aft out of sight and we neared the clean Muahvay. But then Captain Bowenu came to me. His hair glowed white in the gloom, yet he balanced himself with an ease learned during a youth spent in the topmasts of ships. "I'm afraid we must let you off sooner than planned," he told me. "This head wind's making the motors gulp power, and the closest recharging station is in S'Anton."

Actually it was northward, at Sannacruce. But we couldn't risk letting the Overboss there know of our presence—when that which I sought lay in country he said was his. The Meycan realm was safely distant and its Dons friendly.

One dare not let the accumulators of an aircraft get too low. For a mutinous moment I wished we could have come in a jet. But no, I understand well, such machines are too few, too precious, above all too prodigal of metal and energy; they must be reserved for the Air Force. I only tell you this passing mood of mine because it may help give you sympathy for my victims. Yes, my victims.

"Indeed, Rewi Bowenu," I said. "May I see the map?"

"Of course, Toma Nakamuha." Sitting down beside me, he spread a chart across our laps and pinpointed our location. "If you bear east-northeast, you should reach Hope before noon. Of course, your navigation can't be too accurate, with neither compass nor timepiece. But the terrain shouldn't throw you so far off course that you can't spy the windmills when they come over your horizon."

He left unspoken what would follow if he was wrong or I blundered. Buzzards, not gulls, would clean my bones, and they would whiten very far from our sea.

But the thought of those windmills and what they could mean nerved me with anger. Also, you know how Wiliamu Hamilitonu was my comrade from boyhood. Together we climbed after coconuts, prowled gillmasked among soft-colored corals and fanciful fish, scrambled up Mauna Loa to peer down its throat, shipped on a trimaran trader whose sails bore us around this whole glorious globe till we came back to Awaii and drank rum and made love to you and Lili beneath an Island moon. Wiliamu had gone before me, seeking to learn on behalf of us all what laired in the settlement that called itself Hope. He had not returned, and now I did not think he ever would.

That is why I volunteered, yes, pulled ropes for the task. The Service had other men available, some better qualified, maybe. But we are always so short of hands that I did not need to wrangle long. When will they see in Wellantoa how undermanned we are, in this work which matters more than any other?

I unbuckled, collected my gear, and went to hang on a strap by an exit hatch. The craft slanted sharply downward. Cross-currents tore at us like an orca pack at a right whale. I hardly noticed, being busy in a last-minute review of myself.

Imagine me: tall for the Meycan I would claim to be, but not impossibly so, and you yourself have remarked on the accidents of genetics which have blent parts of my ancestry in a jutting Inio-like nose and coppery skin. Language and manners: In sailor days I was often in Meycan ports, and since joining the Service have had occasion to visit the hinterlands in company with natives. Besides, the deserts are a barrier between them and Calforni which is seldom crossed. My Spanyol and behavior ought to pass. Dress: shirt, trousers, uniform jacket, serape, sombrero, boots, all worn and dirty. Equipment: bedroll, canteen, thin pack of dried-out rations, knife, *spada* slung across back for possible machete work or self-defense. I hoped greatly I would not need it for that last. We learn the use of weapons, as well as advanced judo and karate arts, in training; nonetheless, the thought of opening up human flesh made a knot in my guts.

But what had been done to Wiliamu?

Maybe nothing. Maybe Hope was altogether innocent. We could not call in the armed forces unless we were certain. Even under the Law of Life, even under our covenant with the Overboss of Sannacruce, not even the mighty Maurai Federation can invade foreign territory like that without provoking a crisis. Not to speak of the hurt and slain, the resources and energy. We *must* be sure it was worth the cost— Now I do go astray, telling this to a politician's daughter who's spent as much time in N'Zealann as Awaii. I am too deeply back in my thoughts, as I clung there waiting.

"Level off!" Taupo sang from his seat forward. The ship struggled to a somewhat even keel. Evidently the altimeter said we were in rope's length of the ground.

Rewi, who had been beside me, squeezed my shoulder. "Tanaroa be with you, Toma," he murmured underneath the racket. He traced a cross. "Lesu Haristi deliver you from evil."

Wairoa laughed and called: "No need for deliverance from shark-toothed Nan! You'd never catch him in those dunes!" He must always have his joke. Yet his look at me was like a handclasp.

We opened the hatch and cast out a weighted line. When its windlass had stopped spinning, I threw a final glance around the cabin. I wouldn't see this gaiety of tapa and batik soon again, if ever. Supposing Hope proved harmless, I'd still have to make my own way, with mule train after mule train from trading post to trading post, to Sandago and our agents there. It would not do to reveal myself as a

Maurai spy and ask to use Hope's transmitter to call for an airlift. That could make other people, elsewhere around the world, too suspicious of later strangers in their midst. (You realize, Elena, this letter is for none save you.)

"Farewell, shipmate," the men said together; and as I went out and down the rope, I heard them begin the Luck-Wishing Song.

The wind tore it from me. That was a tricky passage down, when the cord threshed like an eel and I didn't want to burn the hide off my palms. But at last I felt earth underfoot. I shook a signal wave up the rope, stepped back and watched.

For a minute the long shape hung over me, a storm cloud full of propeller thunder. Then the line was gathered in and the craft rose. It vanished astonishingly fast.

I looked around. Deserts had never much appealed to me. But this one was different: natural, not man-made. Life had not died because water was gone, topsoil exhausted, poisons soaked into the ground. Here it had had all the geological time it needed to grow into a spare environment.

The night was as clear as I've ever seen, fantastic with stars, more stars than there was crystal blackness in between them, and the Milky Way a torrent. The land reached pale under heaven-glow, speckled by silver-gray of scattered sagebrush and black weird outlines of joshua trees; I could see across its rises and arroyos to hills on the horizon, which stood blue. The wind was cold, flowing under my thin fluttering garments and around my flesh, but down here it did not shout, it murmured, and pungencies were borne upon it. From afar I heard coyotes yip. When I moved, the sandy soil crunched and gave a little beneath my feet, as alive in its own way as water.

I picked my guiding constellations out of the swarm overhead and started to walk.

Dawn was infinitely shadowed, in that vast wrinkled land. I saw a herd of wild sheep and rejoiced in the grandeur of their horns. The buzzard which took station high up in sapphire was no more terrible than my gulls, and no less beautiful. An intense green darkness against rockslopes red and tawny meant stands of piñon or juniper.

And it was April. My travels around western Meyco had taught me to know some of the wildflowers I came upon wherever shade and moisture were: bold ocotillo, honey-hued nolina plume, orchids clustered around a tiny spring. Most, shy beneath the sage and greasewood and creosote bush, I did not recognize by name. I've heard them called bellyflowers, because you have to get down on your belly to really see and love them. It amazed me how many they were, and how many kinds.

Lesser animals scuttered from me, lizards, snakes, mantises; dragonflies hovered over that mini-oasis on wings more splendid than an eagle's; I surprised a jackrabbit, which went lolloping off with a special sort of gracefulness. But a couple of antelope surprised me in turn, because I was watching a dogfight between a hawk and a raven while I strode. Suddenly I rounded a clump of chaparral and we found each other. The first antelope I'd ever met, they were delightful as dolphins and almost as fearless: because I was not wolf or grizzly or cougar; their kind had forgotten mine, which had not come slaughtering since the War of Judgment. At least, not until lately—

I discovered that I cared for the desert, not as a thing which the books said was integral to the whole regional ecology, but as a miracle.

Oh, it isn't our territory, Elena. We'll never want to live there. Risen, the sun hammered on my temples and speared my eyeballs, the air seethed me till my mouth was gummed, sand crept into my boots to chew my feet and the jumping cholla lived up to its name, fang-sharp burrs coming at me from nowhere. Give me Mother Ocean and her islands. But I think one day I'll return for a long visit. And . . . if Wiliamu had lost his way or perished in a sandstorm or otherwise come to natural grief in these reaches, as the Hope folk said he must have done . . . was that a worse death than on the reefs or down into the deeps?

—Rewi Bowenu had been optimistic. The time was midafternoon and the land become a furnace before I glimpsed the windmills. Their tall iron skeletons wavered through heat-shimmer. Nonetheless I felt a chill. Seven of them were much too many.

Hope was a thousand or so adults and their children. It was white-washed, red-tiled adobes centered on a flagged plaza where a fountain played: no extravagance in this dominion of dryness, for vision has its own thirst, which that bright leaping slaked. (Flower beds as well as vegetable gardens surrounded most houses, too.) It was irrigation ditches fanning outward to turn several square kilometers vivid with crops and orchards.

And it was the windmills.

They stood on a long hill behind the town, to catch every shift of air. Huge they were. I could but guess at the man-years of toil which had gone into shaping them, probably from ancient railway tracks or bridge girders hauled across burning emptiness, reforged by the muscles of men who themselves could not be bent. Ugly they were, and in full swing they filled my ears with harsh creakings and groanings. But beauty and quietness would come, I was told. This community had been founded a decade and a half ago. The first several years had gone for barebones survival. Only of late could people begin to take a little ease, think beyond time's immediate horizon.

Behind the hill, invisible from the town, stood a large shedlike building. From it, handmade ceramic pipes, obviously joined to the mill system, led over the ridge to a great brick tank, just below the top on this side. From that tank in turn, sluices fed the canals, the dwellings and workshops, and—via a penstock—a small structure at the foot of the hill which Danil Smit said contained a hydroelectric generator. (Some days afterward, I was shown that machine. It was pre-Judgment. The labor of dragging it here from its ancient site and reconstructing it must have broken hearts.)

He simply explained at our first encounter: "The mills raise water from the spring, you see, it bein' too low for proper irrigation. On the way down again, the flow powers that dynamo, which charges portable accumulators people bring there. This way we get a steady supply of electricity, not big, but enough for lights an' such." (Those modern Everlast fluorescents were almost shockingly conspicuous in homes where almost everything else was as primitive as any woods-runner's property.)

"Why do you not use solar screens?" I asked. "Your power supply would be limited only by the number of square meters you could cover with them."

My pronunciation of their dialect of Ingliss passed quite easily for a Spanyol accent. As for vocabulary, well, from the start I hadn't pretended to be an ordinary wandering worker. I was Miwel Arruba y Gonsals, of a *rico* family in Tamico, fallen on ill days when our estates were plundered during the Watemalan War. Trying to mend my fortunes, I enlisted with a mercenary company. We soldiered back and forth across the troubled lands, Tekkas, Zona, Vada, Ba-Calforni, till the disaster at Montrey, of which the *señores* had doubtless heard, from which I counted myself lucky to escape alive. . . .

Teeth gleamed in Smit's beard. "Ha! Usin' what for money to buy 'em? Remember, we had to start here with no more'n we could bring in oxcarts. Everything you see around you was dug, forged, sawed an' dovetailed together, fire-baked, planted, plowed, cultivated, harvested, threshed, with these."

He held out his hands, and they were like the piñon boles, strong, hard, but unmercifully gnarled. I watched his eyes more, though. In that shaggy, craggy face they smoldered with a prophet's vision.

Yet the mayor of Hope was no backwoods fanatic. Indeed, he professed indifference to rite and creed. "Oktai an' his fellow gods are a bunch of Asians, an' Calforni threw out the Mong long ago," he remarked once to me. "As for Tanaroa, Lesu Haristi, an' that lot, well, the sophisticated thing nowadays in Sannacruce is to go to their church, seein' as how the Sea People do. No disrespect to anybody's faith, understand. I know you Meycans also worship—uh—Esu Carito, is that what you call him? But me, my trust is in physics, chemistry, genetics, an' a well-trained militia." For he had been a prosperous engineer in the capital, before he led the migration hither.

I would have liked to discuss philosophy with him and, still more, applied science. It's so hard to learn how much knowledge of what kind has survived, even in the upper classes of a realm with which we have as regular intercourse as we do with Sannacruce.

Do you fully realize that? Many don't. I didn't, till the Service academy and Service experience had educated me. You can't help my sorrow unless you know its source. Let me therefore spell out what we both were taught as children, in order then to point out how over-simplified it is.

The War of Judgment wiped out a number of cities, true; but most simply died on the vine, in the famines, plagues and worldwide political collapse which followed; and the reason for the chaos was less direct destruction than it was the inability of a resources-impoverished planet to support a gross overpopulation when the industrial machinery faltered for just a few years. (The more I see and ponder, the more I believe those thinkers are right who say that crowding, sensory deprivation, loss of all touch with a living world in which mankind evolved as one animal among millions—that that very unnaturalness brought on the mass lunacy which led to thermonuclear war. If this be true, my work is sacred. Help me never to believe, Elena, that any of the holiness has entered my own self.)

Well, most of the books, records, even technical apparatus remained, being too abundant for utter destruction. Thus, during the dark centuries, barbarians might burn whole libraries to keep alive through a winter; but elsewhere, men preserved copies of the same works, and the knowledge of how to read them. When a measure of stability returned, in a few of the least hard-hit regions, it was not ignorance which kept people from rebuilding the old high-energy culture.

It was lack of resources. The ancestors used up the rich deposits of fuel and minerals. Then they had the means to go on to exploit leaner substances. But once their industrial plant had stopped long enough to fall into decay, it was impossible to reconstruct. This was the more true because nearly all human effort must go into merely keeping half-alive, in a world whose soil, water, forests and wildlife had been squandered.

If anything, we are more scientific nowadays, we are more ingenious engineers, than ever men were before—we islands of civilization in the barbarian swamp which slowly, slowly we try to reclaim—but we must make do with what we have, which is mostly what the sun and living things can give us. The amount of that is measured by the degree to which we have nursed Earth's entire biosphere back toward health.

Thus the text we offer children. And it is true, of course. It's just not the whole truth.

You see—this is the point I strive to make, Elena, this is why I started by repeating the tricky obvious—our machinations are only one small force in a typhoon of forces. Traveling, formerly as a sailor, now as an agent of the Ecological Service, I have had borne in upon me how immense the world is, how various and mysterious. We look through Maurai eyes. How well do those see into the soul of the Calfornian, Meycan, Orgonian, Stralian . . . of folk they often meet . . . and what have they glimpsed of the depths of Sudamerca, Africa, Eurasia? We may be the only great power; but we are, perhaps, ten million among, perhaps, twenty times our number; and the rest are strangers to us, they were blown on different winds during the dark centuries, today they begin to set their own courses and these are not ours.

Maurai crewmen may carouse along the waterfront of Sannacruce. Maurai captains may be invited to dine at the homes of merchants, Maurai admirals with the Overboss himself. But what do we know of what goes on behind the inner walls, or behind the faces we confront?

Why, a bare three years ago we heard a rumor that an emigrant colony was flourishing in the Muahvay fringe. Only one year ago did we get around to verifying this from the air, and seeing too many windmills, and sending Wiliamu Hamilitonu to investigate and die.

Well. I would, as I said, have liked to talk at length with this intelligent and enigmatic man, Mayor Danil Smit. But my role as a *cab'llero* forbade. Let my tale go on.

They had received me with kindness in the settlement. Eager curiosity was there too, of course. Their communal radio could pick up broadcasts from Sannacruce city; but they had turned their backs on Sannacruce, and anyhow, it's not what we would call a thriving cultural center. Periodic trips to trading posts maintained by the Sandagoan Mercanteers, albeit the caravans brought books and journals back among the supplies, gave no real satisfaction to their news-hunger. Besides, having little to barter with and many shortages of necessities, they could not afford much printed matter.

Yet they seemed, on the whole, a happy folk.

Briun Smit, son of Danil, and his wife Jeana gave me lodging. I shared the room of their five living children, but that was all right, those were good, bright youngsters; it was only that I was hard put to invent enough adventures of Lieutenant Arruba for them, when we lay together on rustling cornshuck pallets and they whispered and giggled in the dark before sleep or the dawn before work.

Briun was taller, leaner and blonder than his father, and seemingly less fervent. He cultivated hardly any land, preferring to serve the community as a ranger. This was many things: to ride patrol across the desert against possible bandits, to guard the caravans likewise when they traveled, to prospect for minerals, to hunt bighorn, antelope and mustang for meat. Besides crossbow and blowgun, he was deadly expert with ax, recurved hornbow, sling, lasso and bolas. The sun had leathered him still more deeply than his neighbors and carved crow's-feet around his eyes. His clothes were the general dull color—scant dyestuff was being made thus far—but flamboyant in cut and drape and in the cockade he bore on his curve-brimmed hat.

"Sure, Don Miwel, you just stay with me long's you've a mind to," he said out of the crowd which gathered when I made my dusty way into town.

"I fear I lack the skill to help you at farming, sir," I answered quite truthfully. "But perhaps I have some at carpentry, ropework and the like," which every sailor must and a landed aristocrat might.

Jeana was soon as delighted by what I could do as by what I could tell. It pleased me to please her—for instance, by making a bamboo-tube sprinkler grid for her garden, or a Hilsch arrangement out of sheet metal not immediately needed elsewhere, that really cooled the house whenever the frequent winds blew, or by telling her that Maurai scientists had developed insects and germs to prey on specific plant pests and how to order these through the Mercanteers. She was a small woman, but beautifully shaped beneath the drab gown, of elfin features and vivid manner and a fair complexion not yet bleached by the badlands.

"You have a lovely wife, *señor,* if I may so," I remarked to Briun, the second evening at his home. We sat on the verandah, taking our ease after the day's jobs. Our feet were on the rail, we had pipes in our right hands and mugs of cider in our left, which she had fetched us. Before us stood only a couple of other houses, this one being on the edge of town; beyond gleamed the canals, palm trees swaying along their banks, the first shoots of grain an infinitely delicate green, until far, far out, on the edge of sight, began the umber of untouched desert. Long light-beams cast shadows from the west and turned purple the eastern hills. It was blowing, coolness borne out of lands already nighted, and I heard the iron song of the unseen windmills.

"Thanks," the ranger said to me. He grinned. "I think the same." He took a drink and a puff before adding, slowly now and soberly: "She's a reason we're here."

"Really?" I leaned forward.

"You'd learn the story regardless. Might as well tell you right off, myself." Briun scowled. "Her father was a forester o' rank in Sannacruce. But that didn't help much when the Overboss' eye lit on her, an' she fourteen. He liked—likes 'em young, the swine. When she refused presents, he started pressurin' her parents. They held out, but everybody knew it couldn't be for long. If nothin' else, some night a gang o' bully boys would break in an' carry her off. Next mornin', done bein' done, her parents might as well accept his bribes, hopin' when he was tired of her he'd find a poor man who'd take another gift to marry her. We'd seen cases."

"Terrible," I said. And it is. Among them, it's more than an angering, perhaps frightening episode of coercion; they set such store by virginity that the victim is apt to be soul-scarred for life. My question which followed was less honest, since I already knew the answer: "Why do the citizens tolerate that kind of ruler?"

"He has the men-at-arms," Briun sighed. "An', o' course, he don't directly offend a very big percentage. Most people like bein' secure from pirates or invaders, which the bastard does give 'em. Finally, he's hand in glove with the Sea People. Long's they support him, or at least don't oppose an' boycott him, he's got the metal to hire those soldiers." He shook his head. "I can't see why they do. I really can't. The Maurai claim to be decent folk."

"I have heard," I said cautiously, "he follows their advice about things like reforestation, soil care, bio-control, wildlife management, fisheries."

"But not about human bein's!"

"Perhaps not, Mister Briun. I do not know. I do know this, however. The ancestors stripped the planet nearly to its bones. Unless and until we put flesh back, no human beings anywhere will be safe from ruin. In truth, my friend, we cannot maintain what technology we have except on a biological basis. For example, when almost everything has to be made from wood, we must keep the forests in equilibrium with the lumberers. Or, since the oil is gone, or nearly gone, we depend greatly on microbial fuel cells . . . and the fuels they consume are by-products of life, so we require abundant life. If the oil did come back—if we made some huge strike again, by some miracle—we would still not dare burn much. The ancestors found what happens when you poison the environment."

He gave me a sharp look. I realized I had stepped out of character. In haste, I laughed and said: "I have had more than one Maurai agent lecture me, in old days on our estate, you see. Now tell me, what happened in Sannacruce?"

"Well—" He relaxed, I hoped. "The discontent had been growin' for quite a while anyway, you understand. Not just Overboss Charl; the whole basic policy, which won't change while the Sea People keep their influence. We're becomin' too many to live well, when not enough fallow land or fishin' ground is bein' opened for use."

I refrained from remarks about birth control, having learned that what seems only natural to a folk who spend their lives on shipboard and on islands, comes slowly indeed to those who imagine they have a continent at their free disposal. Until they learn, they will die back again and again; we can but try to keep them from ravaging too much nature in the meantime. Thus the doctrine. But, Elena, can you picture how hard it is to apply that doctrine to living individuals, to Briun and Jeana, eager hobbledehoy Rodj and little, trusting Dorthy?

"There'd been some explorin'," he continued after another sip and another pungent blue smoke-plume trailed forth into the evening. "The good country's all taken where it isn't reserved. But old books told how desert had been made to bloom, in places like Zona. Maybe a possibility closer to home? Well, turned out true. Here, in the Muahvay, a natural wellspring, ample water if it was channeled. Dunno how the ancestors missed it. My father thinks it didn't exist back then; an earthquake split the strata, sometime durin' the dark centuries, an' opened a passage to a bigger water table than had been suspected before.

"Anyhow, Jeana's case was sort of a last straw. Her dad an' mine led a few pioneers off, on a pretext. They did the basic work of enclosin' the spring, diggin' the first short canal, erectin' the first windmill an' makin' an' layin' the first pipelines. They hired nomad Inios to help, but nevertheless I don't see how they did it, an' in fact several died o' strain.

"When the rest came back, families quietly sold out, swappin' for wagons, tools, gene-tailored seed an' such. The Overboss was took by surprise. If he'd tried to forbid the migration, he'd've had a civil war on his hands. He still claims us, but we don't pay him any tax or any mind. If ever we link up to anybody else, I reckon it'll be Sandago. But we'd rather stay independent, an' I think we can. This territory will support a big population once it's developed."

"A heroic undertaking," I said low.

"Well, a lot died in the second group, too, and a lot are half crippled from overwork in those early days, but we made it." His knuckles stood forth around the handle of his mug, as if it were a weapon. "We're self-supportin' now, an' our surplus to trade grows larger every year. We're free!"

"I admire what you have done, also as a piece of engineering," I said. "Perhaps you have ideas here we could use when at last I go home again. Or perhaps I could suggest something to you?"

"Um." He sucked on his pipe and frowned, abruptly uncomfortable.

"I would like to see your whole hydraulic system," I said; and my heart knocked within me. "Tomorrow can you introduce me to the man in charge, and I go look at the water source and the windmills?"

"*No!*" He sprang from his chair. For a moment he loomed over me, and I wondered if he'd drop his pipe and snatch the knife at his belt. Shadows were thickening and I couldn't make out his face too well, but eyes and teeth stood aglisten.

After a long few seconds he eased. His laugh was shaky as he sat down. "Sorry, Don Miwel." He was not a skilled liar. "But we've had that kind o' trouble before, which is why I, uh, overreacted." He sought solace in tobacco. "I'm afraid Windmill Ridge is off limits to everybody except the staff an' the mayor; likewise the springhouse. You see, uh, we've got just the one source, big though it is, an' we're afraid o' pollution or damage or— All right, in these lands water's worth more than blood. We can't risk any spy for a possible invader seein' how our defenses are arranged. No insult meant. You understand, don't you, guest-friend?"

Sick with sorrow, I did.

Still, the Service would require absolute proof. It seemed wise to bide my time, quietly study the layout for a few weeks, observe routines, gather bits and pieces of information, while the dwellers in Hope came fully to accept Miwel Arruba.

The trouble was, I in my turn came to accept them.

When Briun's boy Rodj told me about their winter visitor, his excitement glowed. "Clear from Awaii, he was, Miwel! A geologist, studyin' this country; an' the stories he could tell!" Quickly: "Not full of action like yours. But he's been clear around the world."

Wiliamu hadn't expected he would need a very thick cover.

Not wanting to prompt Briun's suspicion, I asked further of Jeana, one day when he was out and the children napping or at school. It bespoke a certain innocence that, despite the restrictive sexual customs, none looked askance at my hostess and me for the many hours we spent alone together. I confess it was hard for me to keep restraint— not only this long celibacy, but herself, sweet, spirited and bright, as kindled by my newness as her own children.

I'd finished the sprinkler layout and hooked it to the cistern on the flat roof. "See," I said proudly, and turned the wooden spigot. Water danced over the furrows she hoed alone. "No more lugging a heavy can around."

"Oh, Miwel!" She clapped small work-bitten hands. "I don't know how to— This calls for a celebration. We'll throw a party come Saddiday. But right now—" She caught my arm. "Come inside. I'm bakin'." The rich odors had already told me that. "You get the heels off the first loaf out o' the oven."

There was tea as well, rare and costly when it must be hauled from Sina, or around the Horn from Florda. We sat on opposite sides of a plank table, in the kitchen dimness and warmth, and smiled at each other. Sweat made tiny beads on her brow; the thin dress clung. "I wish I could offer you lemonade," she said. "This is lemonade weather. My mother used to make it, back home. She died in Sandstorm Year an' never— Well." A forlorn cheerfulness: "Lemonade demands ice, which we haven't yet."

"You will?"

"Father Danil says prob'ly nex' year we—Hope'll have means to buy a couple o' fridges, an' the power plant'll be expanded enough so we can afford to run them."

"Will you build more windmills for that?" A tingle went through me. I struggled to be casual. "Seems you already have plenty for more than your fluorolights."

Her glance was wholly frank and calm. "We have to pump a lot o' water. It don't gush from a mountainside, remember, it bubbles from low ground."

I hated to risk spoiling her happiness, but duty made me press in: "A Maurai geologist visited here not long before, I have heard. Could he not have given you good advice?"

"I . . . I don't know. That's man talk. Anyway, you heard how we can't let most of ourselves in there—I've never been—let alone strangers, even nice ones like you."

"He would have been curious, though. Where did he go on to? Maybe I can find him later."

"I don't know. He left sudden-like, him an' his two Inio guides. One mornin' they were gone, nary a word o' good-by except, naturally, to the mayor. I reckon he got impatient."

Half of me wanted to shout at her: *When our "Geological Institute" radioed inquiries about its man, your precious village elders gave us the same answer, that he'd departed, that if he failed to arrive elsewhere he must have met with some misfortune on the way. But that wouldn't happen! Would it? An experienced traveler, two good natives at his side, well supplied, no rumor of bandits in this region for years past. . . . Have you thought about that, Jeana? Have you dared think about it?*

But the rest of me held my body still. "More tea?" she asked.

I am not a detective. Folk less guileless would have frozen at my questions. I did avoid putting them in the presence of fierce old Danil Smit, and others who had spent adult years in the competition and intrigues of Sannacruce city. As for the rest, however . . . they invited me to dinner, we drank and yarned, we shared songs beneath that unutterably starry sky, several times we rode forth to see a spectacular canyon or simply for the joy of riding. . . . It was no trick to niggle information out of them.

For example, I wondered aloud if they might be over-hunting the range. Under the Law of Life, it could be required that a qualified game warden be established among them, directly responsible to the International Conservation Tribunal. Briun bristled a moment, then pointed out correctly that man always upsets nature's balance when he enters a land, and that what counts is to strike a new balance. Hope was willing to keep a trained wildlife manager around; but let him be a local person, albeit educated abroad, somebody who knew local conditions. (And would keep local secrets.)

In like manner, affable men assigned to duty on Windmill Ridge told me their schedules, one by one, as I inquired when they would be free for sociability. My work for the younger Smit household had excited a great deal of enthusiasm; in explaining it, I could slip in questions about their own admirable hydraulic system. Mere details about rate of flow, equipment ordered or built, equipment hoped for—mere jigsaw fragments.

Presently I had all but the final confirmation. My eyewitness account would be needed to call in the troops. What I had gained hitherto justified the hazard in entering the forbidden place.

A caravan was being organized for Barstu trading post. I could accompany it, and thence make my way to Sandago. And that, I trusted, I feared, would be my last sight of these unbreakable people whom I had come to love.

The important thing was that no sentry was posted after dark. The likelihood of trouble was small, the need of sleep and of strength for next day's labor was large.

I slipped from among the children. Once I stepped on a pallet in the dark, the coarseness crackled beneath my bare foot, Dorthy whimpered in her blindness and I stiffened. But she quieted. The night was altogether deserted as I padded through the memorized house, out beneath stars and a bitter-bright gibbous moon. It was cold and breezy; I heard the windmills. Afar yelped coyotes. (There were no dogs. They hadn't yet any real need for them. But soon would come the cattle and sheep, not just a few kept at home but entire herds. Then farewell, proud bighorn and soaring antelope.) The streets were gritty. I kept out of the gray-white light, stayed in the shadows of gray-white houses. Beyond the village, rocks barked my toes, sagebrush snatched at my ankles, while I trotted around to the other side of the Ridge.

There stood the low, wide adobe structure which, I was told, covered the upwelling water, to minimize loss by evaporation and downfall of alkaline dust into it. From there, I was told, it was lifted by the mills into the brick basin, from which it went to its work. Beyond the springhouse the land rolled upward, dim and empty of man. But I could make out much else, sage, joshua trees, an owl ghosting by.

My knife had electromagnetic devices built into its handle. I scarcely needed it to get in, save for not wanting to leave signs of breakage. The padlock on the door was as flimsy as the walls proved to be thin. Pioneers in a stern domain had had nothing to spare for more than the most pathetic of frauds.

I entered, closed the door behind me, flashed light from that gem-pommel on my knife, which was actually a lens. The air was cold in here, too. I saw moisture condensed on pipes which plunged into the clay floor and up through the roof, and somehow smelled it. Other-wise, in an enormous gloom, I barely glimpsed workbenches, tool-racks, primitive machinery. I could not now hear the turning sails of the windmills which drove the pumps; but the noise of pistons in crudely fashioned tallow-lubricated cylinders was like bones sliding across each other.

There was no spring. I hadn't expected any.

A beam stabbed at me. I doused my own, reversed it to make a weapon, recoiled into murk. From behind the glare which sought about, a deep remembered voice said, more weary than victorious: "Never mind, Miwel or whoever you are. I know you haven't got a gun. I do. The town's firearm. Buckshot loaded."

Crouched among bulky things and my pulsebeats, I called back: "It will do you less than good to kill me, Danil Smit"—and shifted my position fast. The knife was keen in my hand, my thumb braced eas-ily against the guard. I was young, in top shape, trained; I could prob-ably take him in the dark. I didn't want to. Lesu Haristi knows how I didn't want to, and knows it was not merely for fear of having to flee ill prepared into the desert.

He sighed, like the night wind beyond these walls. "You're a Maurai spy, aren't you?"

"An agent of the Ecological Service," I answered, keeping moving. "We've treaty arrangements with the Overboss. I agree he's a rat in some ways, but he co-operates in saving his land for his great-grandchildren . . . and yours."

"We weren't sure, me an' my partners," Danil Smit said. "We fig-ured we'd take turns watchin' here till you left. You might've been honest."

"Unlike you—you murderers." But somehow I could not put anger into that word, not even for Wiliamu my shipmate and his two name-less guides.

"I s'pose you've got backup?" he called.

"Yes, of course," I said. "Losing our first man was plenty to make us suspicious. Losing the second . . . imagine." Leap, leap went my crouch-bent legs. I prayed the noise of the pumping masked my foot-thuds from him. "It's clear what your aim is, to grow in obscurity till you're so large and strong you can defy everybody—the Federation itself—from behind your barrier of desert distances. But don't you see," I panted, "my superiors have already guessed this? And they don't propose to let the menace get that big!"

You know I exaggerated. Manpower and equipment is spread so thin, close to the breaking point. It might well be decided that there are more urgent matters than one rebellious little community. Wiliamu and I might be written off. Sweat stood chill upon me. So many seas unsailed, lands unwalked, girls unloved, risings of Orion and the Cross unseen!

"You haven't realized how determined we are," I told him. "The Law of Life isn't rhetoric, Danil Smit. It's survival."

"What about our survival?" he groaned.

"Listen," I said, "if I come out into view, can we talk before Tanaroa?"

"Huh? . . . Oh." He stood a while, and in that moment I knew what it is to be of a race who were once great and are no longer. Well, in their day *they* were the everywhere-thrusting aliens; and if they devoured the resources which were the very basis of their power, what could they expect but that Earth's new masters would come from the poor and forgotten who had had less chance to do likewise? Nevertheless, that was long ago, it was dead. Reality was Danil Smit, humbled into saying, "Yes," there in the dark of the shed, he who had seen no other way than murder to preserve his people's freedom.

I switched my own flash back on and set it down by his on a bench, to let light reflect off half-seen shapes and pick his beard and hands and pleading eyes out of the rattling, gurgling murk. I said to him, fast, because I did not like saying it:

"We suspected you weren't using a natural outflow. After centuries, the overnight discovery of such a thing would have been strange. No, what you found was a water table, and you're pumping it dry, in this land of little rain, and that breaks the Law of Life."

He stood before me, in the last rags of his patriarchy, and cried: "But why? All right, all right, eventually we'll've exhausted it. But that could be two-three hundred years from now! Don't you see, we could use that time for livin'?"

"And afterward?" I challenged, since I must keep reminding myself that my cause is right, and must make him believe that my government is truly fanatical on this subject. (He would not have met enough of our easy-going islanders to realize crusades are impossible to us— that, at most, a tiny minority of devotees strive to head off disaster at the outset, before the momentum of it has become too huge.) My life might hang upon it. The shotgun dangled yet in his grasp. He had a good chance of blasting me before I could do more than wound him.

I went on: "Afterward! Think. Instead of what life we have today, to enlarge human knowledge and, yes, the human spirit . . . instead of that, first a sameness of crops and cattle, then a swarm of two-legged ants, than barrenness. We must resist this wherever it appears. Otherwise, in the end—if we can't, as a whole species, redeem ourselves—will be an Earth given back to the algae, or an Earth as bare as the moon."

"Meanwhile, though," he said desperately, "we'd build aqueducts . . . desalinization plants . . . fusion power—"

I did not speak of rumors I have heard that controlled fusion has in fact been achieved, and been suppressed. Besides its being an Admiralty secret, if true, I had no heart to explain to the crumbling old man that Earth cannot live through a second age of energy outpouring and waste. One remote day, folk may come to know in their blood that the universe was not made for them alone; then they can safely be given the power to go to the stars. But not in our lifetimes.

Not in the lifetime that Wiliamu my comrade might have had.

I closed my teeth on the words: "The fact is, Danil Smit, this community was founded on the exhaustion of ground water vital to an entire ecology. That was a flat violation of the Law and of international covenants. To maintain it, you and your co-conspirators resorted to murder. I'll presume most of the dwellers in Hope are innocent—most believe there is a natural spring here—but where are the bodies of our men? Did you at least have the decency to give them back to the earth?"

The soul went out of him. Hope's founding father crept into my arms and wept.

I stroked his hair and whispered, "It could be worse, it could be worse, I'll work for you, don't give up," while my tears and his ran together.

After all, I will remind my admirals, we have islands to reclaim, stoninesses in the middle of a living ocean.

Give the pioneers topsoil and seeds, give them rainwater cisterns and solar stills, teach them palm and breadfruit culture and the proper ranching of the sea. Man does not have to be always the deathmaker. I know my proposal is a radical break with tradition. But it would be well—it would be a most hopeful precedent—if these, who are not of our kind, could be made into some of our strongest lifebringers. Remember, we have an entire worldful of people, unimaginably diverse, to educate thus, if we can. We must begin somewhere.

I swore I would strive to the utmost to have this accepted. I actually dared say I thought our government could be persuaded to pardon Danil Smit and his few associates in the plot. But if an example must be made, they are ready to hang, begging only that those they have loved be granted exile instead of a return to the tyrant.

Elena, speak to your father. Speak to your friends in Parliament. Get them to help us.

But do not tell them this one last thing that happened. Only think upon it at night, as I do, until I come home again.

We trod forth when dawn was whitening the east, Danil Smit and I. Stars held out in a westward darkness, above the dunes and eldritch trees. But those were remote, driven away by fields and canals carved from the tender desert. And a mordant wind made the mills on the ridge overhead creak and clang and roar as they sucked at the planet.

He raised a hand toward them. His smile was weary and terrible. "You've won this round, Nakamuha, you an' your damned nature worshipers," he said. "My children an' children's children 'ull fit into your schemes, because you're powerful. But you won't be forever. What then, Nakamuha? What then?"

I looked up to the whirling skeletons, and suddenly the cold struck deep into me.

Ted Thomas says that there has been horse racing for two thousand years and (regardless of what other species may die out) there will continue to be horse racing for a predictable two thousand years in the future, at least. Ted Cogswell extrapolates (leaving horses out of it for the moment) that there may come a time when, because of the exhaustion of natural resources, man will not be able to pollute enough, and the environment will begin to shift back to its primitive form . . . That might be disastrous because (I say) we have already adapted. *Do you think your many-times great-great-grandparents could survive on the L.A. freeway? Do you think they could breathe what passes for air in New York City without strangling on every breath? As the balance of nature shifts, so do we.*

Ted Thomas is a lawyer, and very persuasive. Ted Cogswell is a professor, and very instructive. The two of them together have evolved a Cogswell Thomas; the creature is an author, and very inventive.

Cogswell Thomas
PARADISE REGAINED

When Petro Anthos stepped out of the matter transmitter on the planet Hel, the guards promptly surrounded him and searched him for weapons. It was the one thing they did well. As long as the condemned man reached Hel free of weapons, there was little to worry about from him. So they searched him, found nothing, and turned him over to a resident work group. Jennings took him in charge, snarled at him in front of the guards, and then put his arm around his shoulders when they had him in the barracks dome.

Jennings said, "You're in luck."

Anthos looked at him; this was a thing he had not known, that Hel was peopled with lunatics. Fifty light-years from Earth; a vicious penal colony where one breath of the atmosphere brought choking, gagging, painful death; hard labor seven days a week; a trickle of survival food supplements from Earth in exchange for a daily quota of coal; a place so deadly that its mere existence all but eliminated crime from the populations of Earth. Here he was in the first five minutes of a twenty-year sentence, and a work gang chieftain put an arm around his shoulders and told him he was in luck. Anthos looked at him.

Jennings was a short stocky man with a potbelly that did not jiggle the slightest bit when he walked. He was dirty and grimy and his clothes were in tatters, but he had a calm air of authority about him that could be felt. Now that he thought about it, Petro Anthos realized that having the arm around his shoulders had probably kept him from screaming. Jennings said, "You're a gas chromatographer, aren't you?"

Anthos nodded numbly.

"Okay. Now, we don't have enough time for you to think much about this, but we have to include you in on an escape plan we've worked out."

Anthos' heart lurched. He choked and stammered, "Escape? I thought . . . Through the matter transmitter? I saw the other end just now. You can't possibly . . ."

Jennings impatiently waved him quiet. "Not through the matter transmitter. That's impossible. We've found a place on this planet where we can live outside. I know, I know"—he waved again as Anthos started to talk—"you've heard that no human being can live outside the domes or outsuits on this planet. Well, you're almost right. But we've found a place, a small valley, that's barely livable. Once we get to it, we can make it more livable in time. We need a good group to do it, though, and we need a gas chromatographer. We had one, Al Chertsey, but he got a little careless last week and inhaled one good breath of white damp. Burned out his lungs. God, he died hard. You know what it's like?"

Anthos nodded. They had made it all too clear to him before they had sentenced him to Hel. The atmosphere would not support life, nor did it screen out the harmful solar radiations. Men had to wear outsuits equipped with back tanks to hold air, special breathing apparatus, protective helmets to keep out radiation and cold. Even the flora and fauna of Hel wouldn't support human life; they did not contain the vital trace compounds. The local foodstuffs were one of the secrets of Earth's hold on Hel. Supplemental nutrients were passed in through the matter transmitter only in response to the quotas of coal that were passed out to Earth. And the ultimate irony was that Earth did not even need the coal, although it had none of its own. Coal was a status symbol, something to be burned in little pots in the living rooms of the very wealthy. Anthos nodded. He knew what it was like.

Jennings said, looking around at several other men and women gathered near, "It won't be easy, in the valley, not for a while. But if we're going to work twelve hours a day, seven days a week, we might as well be doing it for ourselves, not a bunch of sybarites back on Earth." He looked at Anthos. "You with us?"

Anthos hesitated. He was thin and frail, and the thought of hard physical work appalled him. But he was a tough-minded chemist, a good gas chromatographer who called the shots as he saw them, which was why he was here in the first place. In the year A.D. 2688 on Earth, one simply does not, as Anthos had done, give analytical results flatly opposed to the analytical results of the Federal Horse Racing Board of Analytical Examiners concerning a urine analysis of a certain Derby winner. Despite all the changes of men and animals on Earth, it was still possible to spike a horse and chemically induce an extraordinary burst of speed.

Jennings noted the hesitation and said, "Let me introduce you to our people. Ed Jackson, mechanical engineer. So is Frank Stand over there." Anthos nodded to two grimy people. "Milly Franks and Lenore Meyers are chemists." Anthos would not have known they were women. "Sy Smith, electrician; Willy George, nothing much but a hard worker; Ernie Hilgard, biologist; Pete Standage, historian; Lex Parker, teacher." Jennings named a few more, and Anthos had the definite feeling that this was the cream of the penal colony.

Anthos said, "I'm in."

"Great," said Jennings. "Now, here's the plan. We go back into our tunnel in half an hour. The coal is almost exhausted, and the tunnel is due to be sealed off in another month. We've found that five kilometers down the tunnel it reaches almost to a bend in a sealed tunnel from the old workings, and we've cut a small tunnel to it and stored explosives and food and equipment and some air tanks and even an air compressor. The tunnel has a lot of white damp in it, but we think we can get all of us through it okay. And at the other end we got a small tunnel to the surface."

Anthos looked at him and said, "So you go up to the surface and die."

"No. It opens into the damnedest valley you ever saw, kind of sealed off from the rest of the planet's surface. We can live there. It won't be easy, but we can stay alive and work to make the valley more livable. We figure in five years we can convert the valley to a place even better than Earth. That's why we need all the skills of all these people." Jennings waved at the group around him. "See what we do? We blow up the tunnel we're working in, right to the surface so it fills with white damp. But we're in the abandoned tunnel, which we've blown shut. The guards will just take a look in the working tunnel, and when they find it filled with white damp they'll figure we're all dead and just seal it off and forget about us. Life's cheap here. What do the guards care for a few dozen prisoners? So we go on to our valley and make it livable."

Anthos' hand shook as he smoothed his mustache, but he nodded and said, "You need me to monitor the atmosphere, and things like that, I suppose. You have the makings for a gas chromatograph?"

Jennings, noting the shaking hand, put his own hand on Anthos' shoulder and said, "We've got a good supply of equipment. We'll make out." He looked around and said, "In fifteen minutes we move out. Take everything you can stuff in your clothes."

The group scattered, leaving Anthos standing alone. He felt very much alone as he looked for the first time at the dome that served as living quarters for the prisoners. It was dark and smelly, and quiet, with a tang in the air that he knew was a trace of the white damp, seeping into the dome from outside. Bunks with webbing for mattresses formed a circle around the outer perimeter of the dome, sticking straight out from the walls. Everything was smudged gray to black from the ubiquitous coal dust. He put his hands in his pockets, and as he felt how empty they were and realized he had absolutely nothing in the world except the dirty clothes he stood in, depression welled up inside him so strong he began to gasp. In an instant Jennings was at his side, arm around him again, saying nothing. Anthos forced himself to breathe normally. He said to Jennings, "How do you stand the noise level in here?"

"You get used to it. Okay. Time to go." The group went out the lock to the sealed vehicle which took them to the lock at the mouth of the workings. They entered and rode for an hour to the end of the tunnel and got to work with pick and shovel. The guards got back on the tram and left. What happened then was a nightmare of unreality for Anthos.

With practiced speed the group moved a mile back down the tunnel and planted a series of explosives. They littered the floor with unusable junk from the mining gear, even including a blown air tank. They opened the small side tunnel and planted a charge in it. Climbing over the charge, they all crawled into the side tunnel, panting from the exertion, choking on the foul air, taking turns breathing from the tanks. Dimly, Anthos heard the roar of the explosion and cowered from the wave of coal particles and rock dust that engulfed them and threatened to suffocate them all. In the sealed tunnel the dust was better but the white damp was worse. The group shouldered all the equipment they could carry, and took turns pulling and dragging the air compressor. Every hour they stopped, fueled the compressor with powdered coal, recharged the air tanks, and went on. The buzzing in Anthos' ears grew louder until he could no longer hear the harsh panting from his companions. Everything grew blurred and his muscles began to twitch and refuse to obey his will. He reached the point where he could barely stand. He put a hand on the cold wall to steady himself. He felt someone ease him to the floor of the tunnel and hold the facepiece of an air tank to his nose. Slowly his twitching muscles stilled and his breathing became normal. In five minutes he was able to sit up and look around. Jennings said to him, "The others are opening the tunnel to the valley."

Anthos found his voice and said, "At least we're out of prison."

"We'll miss it, but we'll manage. We'll miss it. But we'll get back there a few years from now."

Anthos had started to turn away, but then Jennings' words sank in. He turned back. "What?"

"Oh, yeah. I didn't mention it before. Once we get the valley in shape, we'll take over the whole planet. Not many guards. With the matter transmitter out of commission it will take Earth fifty years to get a ship here. We'll be ready for them by then."

Anthos heaved himself to his feet, indignant protests forming in his mind, but a call from the darkness said, "Tunnel's through. Let's go."

Jennings patted Anthos on the shoulder, saw that he was able to walk, and went into the small mouth of the tunnel and worked his way up. Anthos had to follow, and then he stepped out onto the surface and looked around.

He was standing near one edge of a giant, natural saucer measuring some six kilometers in diameter. A ring of mountains enclosed the saucer, and the shaft through which he had just emerged lay near the base of the south rim. Scattered around the rim of mountains were spots of orange light, marking the raw throats of active volcanoes. Plumes of steam and smoke poured out of fissures all over the floor of the valley. The entire valley was filled with a light haze that almost obscured the sun overhead. Yet Anthos knew that without the haze the valley would be unlivable under the unfiltered, harsh radiation of the sun. And he could breathe. He could stand on the surface of Hel and breathe. When he inhaled deeply, he coughed, for there was the barest trace of white damp in the air. But he could breathe. He looked at the floor of the valley more carefully. A great, clear lake lay in the center, measuring perhaps three kilometers in diameter. It was fed by a wide, rushing stream that sprang from the rocks halfway up the east rim. And bordering both the stream and the lake was a broad belt of greenery. Anthos was too far away to see the nature of the green things growing, but some of it stood higher than the rest and looked very much like trees.

Jennings said to all of them, "Well, there it is. May not be much but at least it's livable. And we'll make it much better. We've got almost all the raw materials we will ever need, right here. So let's not waste time. We'll break up into groups. One group will find us temporary places to live. Another will go back and finish bringing all the stuff we hid in the tunnel. Another'll start looking for anything here we can eat. Another . . ." Jennings went on, and then picked people for the groups. Ten minutes after they arrived in the valley they scattered to start their work. They worked until they could no longer stand, and then they rested. They worked harder than they had ever worked as prisoners mining coal.

The days blended into weeks and months, and in four years they accomplished what they had thought would take them five.

Jennings called them together in their outdoors meeting place and said, "Well, I think we are ready to move on to the next step. The valley is in good, livable shape now, and except for one critical trace compound, we are more than self-sufficient. And we can get new supplies of that compound when we take over the main camp. We're ready to move."

Anthos said, "I'll take the group that handles the demolitions. I want to make certain that no one gets hurt. That all right with you, Colonel?"

"Wouldn't want it any other way." Jennings smiled at Anthos, smiled at the changes four years had made in him. Anthos was lean as a slat, broad as a board, all sinew and whipcord. His mustache had grown greater and rattier than ever, and his large, liquid brown eyes missed nothing as they snapped over the landscape. Anthos, the gas chromatographer, had evolved into Jennings' second-in-command. Jennings continued, "Set it up, Petro. Do it tomorrow."

The operation went smoothly. The guards were not very alert and were easily enticed out of the transmitter building. After the explosion, Anthos' men quickly went in and carefully fused all remaining components. Then, from a safe distance, Anthos explained that all of them, guards and prisoners alike, were totally marooned, and that the only salvation for any of them was to join Jennings' group in the valley. Wisely, Anthos told them not to make up their minds now, but that he would be back the next day for their answer; Anthos wanted it to sink in that there would be no more supplies coming from Earth, that the only Earth-type atmosphere existed in the valley, that even the air in the domes would slowly go bad.

When Anthos returned the next day, everybody was ready to join him in the trip to the valley. The guards were huddled with their weapons in one group, and the prisoners were in a separate group. Anthos collected the weapons and made it clear that they were all in this together, guards and prisoners alike. It took three days to get all the people from the site of the prison domes to the valley. The guards were moved last, and Anthos stayed with them. He watched their faces as they came up out of the tunnel into the valley and looked around. Then he took them to the meeting place where Jennings was waiting to talk to them. They sat down, hundreds of them. From where they sat, they had a fine view of the valley.

Jennings waved out over the valley and said, so all of them could hear, "There it is. Almost perfect Earthside conditions." The haze and smoke in the valley were so thick the rays of the sun could no longer penetrate. Long streaks of yellow flames licked along the surfaces of exposed coal veins, burning, pouring dense clouds of smoke into the air. Jennings said, "Just inhale. Good sulfur dioxide and nitrous oxides, plenty of carbon dioxide and carbon monoxide. When we first got here, the sky was blue—think of that!—you could hardly breathe for the oxygen in the air. Why, that white damp was like the Earth's atmosphere seven hundred years ago, before our forefathers changed it. The sun shone right through here most of the time. Can you imagine what it was like? Look at the lake down there—it was as blue as the sky! Fortunately we found some phosphate deposits, so we loaded the lake with them. Just look at it now—rich, green, nutritious water." The lake was jelly-thick with algae, and bubbles of marsh gas could be seen breaking the surface here and there. Jennings said, "We even have fish in there, but we only began to extract mercury two months ago, and we haven't yet been able to bring the mercury content of the carp up to the point where they are edible. Another few months. Feel the temperature? We're up to one hundred degrees F. now and going up all the time. It'll soon be normal; there's plenty of carbon dioxide in the air now, and we have a greenhouse effect. We've only got one immediate problem. We can't yet make a critical dietary compound, dichlorodiphenyltrichloroethane. But it is non-biodegradable, and there is an enormous amount in the sewage deposits of the prison camp, so we'll go back and extract the DDT and use it as a food supplement until we can make it. Like it so far?"

Guards and prisoners alike nodded and clapped. Jennings held up his hand for silence. "The best is yet to come. What we've done here we can do to the rest of the planet. We've done some exploring, and there are extensive oil pools available. We can flood the streams, rivers, lakes and oceans with oil to kill off most of the harmful oxygen-producing organisms. We'll burn open coal veins to cut off the harmful sun rays and give us carbon dioxide, carbon monoxide and the sulfur compounds we need in the air. By eliminating the native flora and fauna we ought to be able to reclaim huge portions of the planet, or maybe even the whole thing. We'll spray with DDT so the plants and animals will take it up and become nutritious. It won't take too long to get a proper greenhouse effect working for the whole planet. We'll make a second Earth here. Are you with us?"

A roar of approval went up, cheers, whistles, shouting. On and on it went. A guard leaped from his seat in the front row, went up to Jennings and shook his hand and turned to the assembled crowd. They slowly quieted as they saw he wanted to say something. He shouted, "Four months ago, just four months ago, I came to Hel from Earth. And I want to tell you now that this place," he waved his hand out toward the valley, "makes me feel more at home than any place I've been since I left New York City. I say we make the whole planet livable."

The cheers were deafening.

Gene Wolfe, without seeking the honor, muscled
his way into this collection a second time by sheer
merit.

Gene Wolfe

BEAUTYLAND

The first time I saw Dives he was down on the sidewalk coughing
his lungs out; an old lady had his mask up on the tip of her umbrella,
and a kid, a tall, pimply kid with bushy hair and thick glasses, had
been tripping him every time he tried to grab it from her. I went over
to them and said, "You better give that back or he'll die," and the old
woman was going to, but the kid grabbed it from her and threw it
down in the gutter; I couldn't give it to him to put back on with that
stuff on it, but I kicked the kid and managed to flag a T-E-E aircab,
and once I had him in there he was all right. I took off my own mask
and told the driver to cruise; like all of them the windows showed the
city the way it's supposed to look after it's rebuilt, so that if you believed it you'd give your ass to be born a hundred years from now.

Dives (I'm going to call him that because his mother didn't)
thanked me and tried to give me some money. I didn't take it—there
was quite a bit of it, and I figured if he let go of that much that easy
the thing to do was get close to him, not piss it away for a few
lousy Cs.

The first thing I noticed about him was that his nose had been
broken a lot, like an old fighter's; and there were a bunch of little
scars on his face. I found out afterward that they were from surgery
to erase bigger scars, and one of his eyes was solid state. After a while
he said, "Where are we going?" and I said anywhere he wanted to,
that I figured he might be a little shaky yet and I'd drop him off.
Naturally I was figuring he'd want to go home, and then since I'd
pulled him out of trouble and turned down his money he'd have to
have me in for a drink and we'd be buddies.

He said, "Why don't we go to my apartment for a drink?" and gave his address to the autodriver (a Park Avenue address that sounded like a million) and the funny thing was that I could see him seeing through me and not caring. He was thinking: This guy sees I've got money; so he figures he's going to be my friend—okay, that's the only kind I'm ever going to have, and maybe he plays pinochle. I didn't like it but I figured I'd better go along.

He bought a new mask from the driver, but it turned out he didn't really need it, because it *was* a million-dollar address like I thought, and we could jump right out of the totally enclosed environment of the aircab into the big one of his building without even putting anything on. "Neat," I said, looking around his private lobby, and it really was neat, all hologram walls, real as hell, a big valley way up in the mountains somewhere, where you couldn't see a road or a house or anything at all, and the trees and bushes and weeds and everything were all green, like nothing was killing them.

"A piece of property I used to own," he said.

I said, "I bet it don't look like that now."

Then he said, "No, it doesn't . . . when I was trying to promote it I called it Beautyland—ever hear of it?" and when I shook my head one of the biggest damn androids I ever saw came out of the wallpaper—that was what it seemed like—and shook me down. He was brand new and his platinum trim said he had all the gadgets and he moved in that easy, gentle way they do when all their skin's two-centimeter armor plate.

I stayed mighty still, believe me, until he was finished; then I said, "That was some kind of password, huh? I should of said I heard of it."

Dives said, "Have you?"

"Like I said, no. But if you want me to lie a little that's okay." Then I thought it might be a good move to remind him of what I did for him, so I said, "Listen, why don't you take the big guy here with you when you go out, then you wouldn't need me," and the android nodded and said, *He is right they have hurt you again, Master.* He had the kind of deep voice they always give them.

The rich guy (that was a two-grand suit, by the way, if I ever saw one) just shrugged and said, "I think I owe them a chance at me from time to time. Come on in and we'll have that drink."

It was real class. The android took our verbal orders and relayed them to the Barmaster, then served them on a tray. Dives had brandy and I had vodka on the rocks, and when I picked it up he said, "You've been in prison, haven't you?" I nodded and told him they were called Social Reorientation Farms now and asked him how he knew, and he said he had spent some time on one himself. Naturally I asked him where, and when he had got out.

"Over a year ago. I was only there for six weeks—I had tried to kill myself, but it passed pretty quickly."

I told him that was lucky—I'd tried to make a killing and spent over eight years.

He wasn't paying much attention. He said, "I saw people drinking like that there. They fermented mash in the back of the laundry, but ice was nearly impossible to get, and when they had it they drank the way you do—holding the biggest piece in their mouths and drawing the liquor past it. That was why you didn't know about Beautyland; you were in prison."

I said I'd never try to defraud anyone else again; they'd gotten all that out of me.

"And I'll never try to take my own life again, either. At least, not directly." He pulled out a remote control for the android and hit the OFF button. I could see the thing turn off all right, and after a minute he threw the control into a far corner of the room. "That wasn't my only defense," he said, "but it was my principal one, and I won't use the others."

I said that was okay by me, but if someone came busting in I was going to make a dive for the control and turn it right back on again. I would have done it too—I've never had that much muscle on my side and I would like just once to see how it feels.

He said, "I don't think you'll want to turn him back on after you've heard me; I want to tell you about my valley."

I said, "Suppose after I've heard you I *don't* want to break your neck."

"Then we'll play chess. Or whatever you want. That valley belonged to me, and I loved it. You saw it."

I said, "Sure."

"But I couldn't live in it—to live in it would be to spoil it, to ruin it. You saw that. I thought of selling it to the government, but you know what has become of the national parks; developers offered me a lot of money for it—at least, what I thought was a lot of money then —but I knew what they were going to do if I sold my land to them. Meanwhile I had to take a job in a factory to live."

I was looking around at his apartment. I said, "Then you got a real bright idea."

"I thought I did. I thought I had figured out a way to make money out of the valley without destroying it. Using the land as collateral I got a loan, and with the money I had a biological survey made. Let me show you one of my ads."

He had it all set up and ready to roll. The TV wall went on and showed the same kind of picture that had been out in the lobby—I guess the same place—and one of those plastic voices said, "They call it BEAUTYLAND, and only you can save it." Then the picture turned to fire.

Dives said, "We had every tree, every damn plant, numbered. The idea was that we were going to sell them, item by item. There were eighteen rabbits in the valley and we named them all and got a picture of every one of them. There were six deer—I guess they may have been about the only wild deer left in the United States—and we named them too. I wanted three hundred thousand each for those deer; the highest-priced tree was a hundred and fifty thousand—it was an oak that must have been a couple of meters thick. See, the idea was that we were going to destroy anything that wasn't bought."

I said, "Give me that again."

"Anything the world didn't pay for—or somebody in it—I was going to burn. It all belonged to me, and they couldn't stop me. I had a flame projector made; you saw it a minute ago, because we used it in shooting that spot." He turned off the TV with a wave of his hand. "What they did pay for would be saved forever. None of this Mickey Mouse stuff the government does—we were going to build a wall around the place and keep everybody out. It could be photographed if you wanted from towers on the outside, but that was as close as anyone would be allowed to get. But first anything that wasn't paid for by somebody burned. You see, I thought someone would pay for all of it, or nearly all."

I asked, "How did you do?"

"We didn't," he said. "A few old ladies bought wild flowers and that was the end of it."

I waited for him to go on, and after a long time he said, "We called the best rabbit Benny Bunny, and a big part of the campaign was geared around the slogan Save Benny Bunny for Beautyland. Benny Bunny was supposed to cost fifty-five thousand. I got five hundred *toward* saving him from some elementary school in New Jersey; I sent it back and they wrote me later they used the money to buy some sparrow tapes."

"So you burned the stuff?"

"We burned it," he said, "yes."

I waited for him to tell me how he had swung it.

"I went back to the office I had rented," he said, "one morning after it had become apparent that the whole thing wasn't going to work. Our deadline was past, and our deadline extension was past, and the bank was closing in on me, though they must have known I didn't have any way to pay them off. I had talked to the media the night before and told them I didn't have the heart to burn the things myself—I was going to hire somebody to do it."

I kept on waiting.

"There was a line there, waiting for me to come. It went around the block twice—all kinds of people."

"Looking for jobs?"

"That's what they said, but that wasn't really it—I talked to some of them and they just wanted to do it. One of them—about the fifth or sixth one I talked to, I think—tried to bribe me. You can probably guess what came next."

"You put on a new campaign," I said.

"I didn't have to—I just announced it. I doubled and tripled the price of everything, but I was a sucker there—I could have gotten more for the deer and the rabbits. And the birds. They fought each other to pay my price for those."

I said, "You should have auctioned them."

"Yes, I should have, but it's too late now. We did it at night so the flames would show up on camera better—I got three million for the TV rights—and Benny Bunny got clear down onto one of the inter-states before the man who had paid out a hundred and sixty-five thou-sand for the privilege nailed him. As it was he nearly lost him to a station wagon; he was the president of a big oil company, so I thought that was kind of ironic."

I said that I imagined there had been a lot of little quirky things like that.

He nodded and said, "I thought you might like to know how I made my money," and I told him I didn't give a damn as long as it was there.

Colin Saxton is primarily a painter; his wife does most of the writing in the family. (Both construct a mean mandala.) Colin is a gentle man; paints; wins prizes; teaches; cultivates his roses; meditates. . . .

By now it is clear that more than half of the creative people here examining science fiction's first paradigm: world-saving, *offer pretty gloomy prognoses. Approximately 50 per cent see us irretrievably on the butter-slide. Several more see us saved—but only in spite of ourselves: by the inscrutable workings of bureaucracy, or by virtue of evolutionary pressures producing survivor-types with the morals of weasels, lynx-eyed scoundrels. Some postulate that we may be saved by engineering methods or by application of conservation principles. Very few look to the counterculture for solutions.*

Dr. René Dubos elsewhere takes respectful account of the mystical leanings of the young people of the Aquarian Age. In a fine and hopeful book (published during the summer of 1972 by Scribner) he suggests a scientific theology, and argues that there is en theos, A God Within.

Transcendentalist Jack Grant, yet another of the pilgrims to California, has set up the Lamplighters Roadway Press in Los Gatos (44 Fairview) to publish and distribute a subjective "whole-person catalogue," what he refers to as a "catalogue of energy systems," The Geocentric Experience. *This book (alternatively referred to by virtue of the transposition sign in its very title as* The Egocentric Experience) *is a three-dollar mind-trip.*

Both Dubos and the varied and wonderful authorities cited by Grant allow for—nay, insist upon —the validity of some kind of inner divinity (personal, worldwide, universal, any/all of those) and the possibility of some kind of genius loci. *Shades of Teilhard de Chardin! Shades of shades! Personal salvation may be the only workable route.*

Colin Saxton

THE DAY

Ben slowly uncrossed his legs, rocked forward onto his knees and stood up. He looked carefully around his room, allowing the familiar objects to reaffirm their existence; to communicate their essential identity. Mind quiet, he absorbed the flow of impressions, feeling himself become in turn each shape, nuance of color, density of shadow, quality of hardness or softness and spatial parameter. He listened to the first stirrings of activity within the village. Somewhere a dog barked and was quickly called to silence.

The feeling of oneness with the rest of the tribe, renewed each morning in the hour of silence, receded as he ate a simple breakfast of rye bread and fruit followed by a drink of goat's milk.

The sun was just rising over the distant horizon as he stepped out onto the patterned stones of the street. For a moment he looked directly into the bright orange disc and experienced subtle sensations moving within him, the response of life to life.

In the early morning sun the white houses of the village were a luminous pink patchwork of coral and blue-violet shadow. Their simple cubic shapes radiated outwards from the Central Hall. The Hall itself dominated the scene, a tall octagonal building with a shallow domed roof of clear glass. Its walls were inlaid with blue, green and orange tiles, forming a different complex design on each of its eight sides. For a few seconds the rays of the rising sun striking the glass roof at a certain angle produced another sun in the heart of the village.

Ben followed the street that pointed directly north. He walked between the small gardens that changed into larger orchards as the spaces between the radial arms of the village grew wider. Thoughts about the coming events of the day began to build up in his mind. This was the most important day in the life of the tribe. The ceremony had no name; if it had to be referred to it was simply called "The

Day," although there were those who in the circle of their intimate friends referred to it as "The Going Over." "The Day" recurred every ten years and coincided with the vernal equinox.

After a few hundred yards the street ended, its carefully shaped and patterned stones terminating in a simple but ingenious knot design. The ground now began to rise steeply, a well-trodden path spiraling to the top of the conical hill that overlooked the village.

Ben looked towards the crest of the Hill; two of the eight massive stones that crowned the apex could be clearly seen silhouetted against the blue-green sky. From this distance they were not very impressive, two short black sticks with a splinter of light between. Tough thorn bushes scattered the slope and an occasional pine speared upward, its branches touched by a new fresh green. Below in the shallow valleys, oak, beech, larch and horse chestnut clustered close by the many small streams. The Hill was strewn with numerous large stones, some seemingly precariously balanced on the steeper slopes, others apparently thrusting out jagged tips from deep underground. On a rough circle bounding the Hill about halfway up, the streams had their source, springing out of the ground from some vast reservoir.

A few early spring flowers spotted the grass on either side of the path and brought to Ben's mind an image of the great Mandala of rose petals that lay under the glass dome of the Hall. By nightfall another ring of petals would be added to the design and the tribe would file past in silent thanksgiving.

Ben was now more than halfway to the top of the Hill. He stopped and sat down on a weather-rounded rock; translucent beads of dew sprinkled the grass at his feet and a nearby bush sparkled in the now clear bright sunshine. Ben's eye was attracted by one particular dewdrop. It was about a yard away and clung to the very tip of a spiked blade of grass. It shone with a brilliant ruby light. By moving his head very slowly Ben could see all the colors of the spectrum appear in sequence focused into a pinpoint of intensity by the tiny drops of dew. Once again he felt the stirring of subtle but powerful forces within him, and glanced briefly at the bright sun. He felt vividly alive, more so than he could ever remember, and this was as it should be, for today he played his most important role yet for the well-being of the tribe. Today he was one of the four "Callers of the Ways."

He stood up and looked around; he should be able to see at least one of his fellow Callers. Yes, about half a mile away to his right and a little lower down, a tiny figure in a pale blue garment moved along the hillside. That was Glyn, the Caller to the West. Jan was Caller to the North; he would be on the opposite side of the Hill; and Sam was somewhere to his left just out of sight. Sam was Caller to the East.

Each Caller started the ascent of the Hill from the appropriate cardinal point. Four paths spiraled up the Hill from each of these points; they never touched or crossed and the paths ended under the twin towering stones that marked each cardinal point on the crest of the Hill.

Ben walked on, the air was scented with new grass, and damp earth. Here and there he moved through pockets of rich-smelling pine. Not the slightest breeze disturbed the absolute stillness. The sky was now an unbroken blue, pale and shimmering at the horizon, deepening to an intense ultramarine at the zenith.

As the Callers neared the top of the Hill they naturally came closer to each other and for the first time Ben saw Sam rounding the slopes two hundred yards ahead. Looking back, Glyn came into view round the opposite shoulder of the crest. Jan would not be seen until he stood by the northern stones on the very top of the Hill. No more than four hundred feet above him the great stone columns of the eastern gate reared majestically against the deep blue sky. Roughly carved from graygreen granite, the stones were over forty feet tall, their surfaces even from this distance sparkling and flashing as the sun struck the myriad facets of quartz and mica. Eventually the Callers reached their allotted positions. Ben stood between the massive stones of the southern gate and looked across the shallow bowl-like depression that was the actual top of the Hill. Jan was standing in the northern gate, the green of his robe blending harmoniously with the color of the stones. He raised his hand in salute, then turned to his left and repeated the gesture to Sam, and then again to Glyn in the western gate. The other three Callers followed in turn the same ritual greeting.

Sitting on the short springy grass with his back against the sun-warmed stone, Ben looked down in the direction of the village. About three miles beyond the termination of its radial arms the green of the landscape ended. From there on out to the horizon in every direction a sulfurous ocher lay over the land. Perhaps thirty miles away a range of hills hazy and blue with distance showed faintly against the brilliant sky, their feeble color the only relief in the unremitting drab yellowness. From his vantage point Ben could see where the running streams disappeared again underground. Their points of exit formed a rough circle half a mile short of the perimeter of the fertile land. A number of irrigation ditches had been dug which carried the priceless water to the very edge of the desolate plain. Here the water seeped into the lifeless dust, making irregular dark patches like bruises on a corpse.

It will not always be like this, thought Ben. Tomorrow will see a gain of a few yards, seeds will be sown, crops will be harvested in the autumn, all from ground that has resisted every attempt at cultivation over the last ten years. And that was why "The Day"—this day—was so important in the life of the tribe. There were other reasons. The great enigma of the ceremony was the very center of the spiritual life of the community, linking them directly to the unknowable, making them beneficiaries of powers beyond their comprehension.

Looking towards the base of the Hill, nearly a thousand feet below him, Ben could just make out the movement of tiny figures, two to each path. The Elders and their Helpers were beginning the ascent. In about an hour he would start preparing himself for his function as a Caller of the Way.

Meanwhile he let his memories of earlier training rise into his thoughts. For five years, since he turned twenty, he had attended weekly meetings with the head man and the four senior Elders. He and the other three Callers had listened repeatedly to the myths of the tribe. They had practiced meditation, occasionally fasted, done exercises of breathing and posture. They had run to the top of the

Hill and down again five times in a day, pushing their bodies beyond exhaustion.

Once a year they kept a three-day vigil at their gates, awake and listening. A protracted exercise in listening, until every nerve became sensitized to the slightest sound, inner or outer . . . until blades of grass crashed and ground together . . . and a wild symphony screamed through the veins.

From time to time they had asked: "What is expected of us on "The Day," what must we do?" And they were told: "At dawn you will climb the Hill and take up your positions at the gates. When the Elders and their Helpers arrive at the summit you will practice silence and wait. When the time arrives you will call the ways."

"But how *do* we call the ways, what must we do, what must we say? How do we know when the time has arrived?"

The head man, and the Elders had replied: "You will know when it is time, and you will know what to do." Further questions were ignored and the attention of the four young men redirected to the myths of the tribe or the practice of exercises. Today was the day and Ben was no wiser as to his specific function, but he was calm and waited with confidence.

He stood up, positioned himself between the huge stones, and looked directly south. One hundred yards below him two dead tree trunks formed a second gate. Seen between them, halfway down the hill, a tall white stone shone in the sun. Above the top of the stone but half a mile further out, a small lake reflected the deep blue sky. Further out still, appearing to be directly above the lakes, was a small circular copse of trees. And in line with all these, on the very edge of the desolate world beyond, a tall wooden tower. From this distance it looked like a tiny dark twig pushed into the yellow plain. These features marked out with precision the south way.

Ben sat down again, crossed his legs and tucked his feet under him. He closed his eyes, made no attempt to concentrate on anything and sank into a semi-conscious reverie. Images floated in his mind, memories of childhood, fragments of myth. He heard again, dreamlike and in random order, the voices of his parents, the Elders and the head man. Strange forms and colors, fragments of music, pictures of houses, stones, trees, water rose sharp and clear into his mind, and as quickly faded. One image repeated itself over and over again: The large circular design of rose petals in the Central Hall. Its white center shone like a bright star and the concentric rings of pink, yellow, orange and red glowed with an unnatural intensity. Whenever this image appeared Ben would hold on to it for a short while, absorbing its power and beauty.

He was drawn out of his reverie by the sound of footsteps close by. Opening his eyes, he found it difficult to focus in the brilliant sunshine; slowly color came back to his surroundings and the clarity of his perceptions returned.

The Elder of the South was approaching the gate. A Helper followed close behind, a large wicker basket on her shoulders. Ben stood up and moved aside. The Elder passed between the massive stone columns. His gaze never wavered to right or left and his features were totally impassive. Ben watched them move towards the center. The other three Elders and their Helpers were already waiting.

The eight figures sat in a circle, facing inwards: the four Elders at the cardinal points, the Helpers between them. The Elder for the North wore a vivid green robe, the one for the west blue, east yellow and south red. The Helpers, all women, were dressed in white.

The Callers now sat crosslegged, each between the huge stones of the gates, facing away from the central group.

Ben closed his eyes and sought deep within himself for silence. Soon he was held in some timeless state, a strangely dynamic stillness, in which, paradoxically, as the stillness deepened—energy increased. In the world outside the sun neared its apogee. A slim patch of shadow, cast by the inside face of the eastern stone of the southern gate, steadily diminished. Within moments both inner faces of the gate were in sunlight.

Ben felt a sudden rise in the subtle energies; an intolerable sense of pressure built up within him. Then a great voice exploded in his chest:

"CALL THE WAYS."

Beyond all sense of himself, like a puppet jerked to its feet, he lurched upwards, pointed due south and shouted in a loud clear voice that was not his own:

"MAKE CLEAR THE WAY!"

The utter calm that followed was a profound shock and dragged him back to his senses. He continued to look out to the distant horizon, tense, waiting.

Very far away, bridging sky and land, a vertical knife edge of pale blue light trembled and wavered. As Ben stared at the phenomenon it grew in height and intensity. The space around it seemed to heave and buckle, distorting the contours of the distant hills.

With a sudden flash of understanding Ben knew that the vibrant thread of light was hurtling towards him at tremendous speed. Starting from somewhere beyond the horizon its apparent increase in size was a visual effect of its rapid advance. Already the dazzling, vibrating knife edge reached almost to the zenith. A terrifying crack in space, burning with a wild cosmic energy, warping the air around it, hurtling along the Way, straight as an arrow towards the southern gate.

Ben had just time to realize that the same thing was happening along the other ways before the uncanny force swept over and through him. A fierce white energy surged up his spine and exploded in his head. Powerful currents streamed through his limbs. Every hair on his body was erect and quivering. There was a wild buzzing like a million angry bees, a crackling and humming and an intense smell of ozone.

Ben felt his life energy drawn from him in one convulsive wave before he collapsed unconscious.

The dour Elders were struck simultaneously by the wild force. Their bodies were vaporized on the instant and a column of blinding white light speared upwards from the top of the Hill. In seconds it faded. Total stillness and silence returned.

The four Callers were lying on their backs between the stones of the gates, their heads turned towards the center of the Hill. The four Helpers lay feet towards the center, their heads pointing southeast, southwest, northwest and northeast. All eight bodies were stiff and terribly pale. The air above the shallow bowl of the hilltop was filled with gently falling rose petals. Soon the ground and the eight prone figures were covered with a crimson scented carpet. Not a breath of wind disturbed the delicate forms.

Down in the village in the lower room of the Central Hall the rest of the tribe raised their heads from their chests, opened their eyes, uncrossed their legs and slowly stood up. In silence the head man served them each a drink from a massive silver chalice and then passed round some small oat cakes. They drank and ate in silence.

After about an hour the figures on the hilltop opened their eyes. A few crimson petals slid from the motionless faces. With great care the Callers and the four Helpers rose to their feet. The women began to fill their baskets with rose petals, clearing a path towards each Caller. The Callers then helped to fill the baskets. All worked in complete silence until every single petal had been collected.

The air was still heavy with perfume as the eight people started down the Hill towards the village. When they arrived at the Central Hall the sun was very low in the west. They entered the Hall and climbed the stairs to the upper room. The great circular image glowed in the fading light. The rose petals from which it was made never faded. There were already eighteen concentric rings, the petals that formed the center were at least one hundred and eighty years old. The Callers stood at the cardinal points of the circle and the Helpers spread the freshly gathered crimson petals to form a new outer ring.

When they had finished, the rest of the tribe came and stood in silent communion gazing at the miraculous Mandala. A new moon cast its pale radiance through the clear glass roof.

Next day, at dawn, the whole tribe walked out to the edge of their land. Where previously the sulfurous waste had touched the edge of grass, a twelve-yard strip of rich dark soil encircled the whole territory. The tribe unloaded their bags of seed and joyfully sowed the whole of the new ground.

For the next three days they celebrated with complete abandon.

Mike Price is a young Canadian poet who looks
more like Geo. Alec Effinger than Geo. Alec Effinger does, except on his best days. His work has
appeared both in magazines and books inside Canada, but this may be his first appearance in the
United States.

Coupling the ideas of the regenerative ability
and the end result of overcrowding is a fortuitous
grisliness. The poems are independent entities
about *very* independent entities.

D. M. Price

TWO POEMS

starfish

one.

five-legged dancer
come to earth and left
above tide's line—
unless I step in,
you're sure food
for these gulls
chuckling down the beach.

but the old fisher
man (where'd he come
from?) says
some mumbling about
throwing just one leg
of a star back in
to the sea
and the whole thing
grows back, a perfect

reflection of itself.
in fact, he goes on,
if you really like stars,
and gulls as well,
you could cut 'im in half,
feed half to the gulls (the
flock edged closer, gibbering),
cut what you got left
in half again, keep one piece
if you have a tank of your own,
and chuck the rest
back in the water.
you'd still come out ahead
and so would the star(s) and
so would the gulls.
that's ecology, son.

old man, that's a tall one
you've just slipped me,
thinks I, turning back
from the star to ask
him whether (hey! where'd
he go?)—

an academic question: old one-eye,
gull grandaddy,
used my turned back
as a safe-conduct,
chopped off all of the star
he could safely carry (-half-)
and escaped, jeering
the halfwit he'd left
holding the halfstar.
well, that's it,
little sea beast; i can feel
how eager you are,
in your squirming, to have done

in the proper place,
rather than this slum
of highest tide. thus,
i cock my arm,
and spin you out,

like SOOOooooo . . . !

and where do you think
that damned old beachrat
went (where do you think)?
think no more on it.
think no more on the star, either.
that's ecology, son.

two.

late in the evening,
i brought the lady back
for a walk on the beach that
the gulls had deserted
in favour of their own little Rite
of Spring (from which,
coincidentally, we'd just returned)
down near the river's black mouth.
the lady tried to walk
out to the line
where the sea bisects Antares
from his double on the calm water;
cried out, hopped out, ran (pleasantly)
to me. starfish are adaptable:
she'd been knee-deep in them!

later, we counted stars mirrored
on the ocean. where's Cepheus?
she asked. out in the sea,
i swear someone snickered.

BILLENNIUM: A NOTE TO DEADCAT

the manual says one cat to a room
 in the interests of crowd control.

the manual should know; it represents
consensus of the best opinions
on how best to become angels. all agree
the best start is to learn to live together,
in which cause, a scientist
in an amsterdam technohive developed
the optimum manner of fitting two million people
to a room not much larger than a closet
and, what's more, to keep them quiet!
if it sounds as if there are merely two or three
of us in here, the noise is too great; that
is unavoidable: the vertices
of otherwise smooth walls make our backs itch
infernally. at any rate,
the cat keeps us quieter than any threat.

on the cold sand
the great wings closed around the sybil and i;
we passed the glass places beneath the enormous eyes
where the angels refined their brilliant ores.

however, i have seen a cat
touch the angels' magic
and die instantly.
passive though we are, we resent power
that great and,
hell, he was a good cat. . . .

the manual says one day we will be angels,
that we must learn to live together.

oh, that we are, that we are.

the official manual will be very surprised
the day we are given our wings (so to speak)
and we return the earth to ape and whale.
we'll enjoy ourselves.
we may have to hit every hick planet
between here and the Rim, but by the time
we're finished there
won't be a corner in the universe

left alive, mate.

A. E. van Vogt needs no introduction. This is, after all, the man who wrote *Slan;* who created (and created, and created, and created) Gilbert Gosseyn. Every so often he comes up with some- one so endearing or so strange or something- unusual that you can't forget the character. The protagonist of "Don't Hold Your Breath" fits un- der one of those headings.

Just the same, as someone has remarked: "It's getting a little thick out there, friends. Pretty soon it's going to be 'in goes the bad air, out goes the bad air; in goes the bad air . . .'

"But don't let it worry you. The oceans will keep us going after the trees are all dead and we've concreted Amerika over. Why, even with the pres- ent rate of pollution the oceans should be able to regenerate the atmosphere in less than ten thou- sand years.

"All we have to do is hold our breath until then."

A. E. van Vogt

DON'T HOLD YOUR BREATH

As old earth's last hour approached, the conspirators grew desperate. They had located among the remnants of mankind an odd survival type. Unknown to him—it was always a male—they placed one of their members (always a woman) near him, as their final hope. The crisis would be when the woman left suddenly.

Though the crazy talk had been going on for years, I had got to age thirty-two when it started in earnest. About the change that was coming. No oxygen in the atmosphere after May 11. Thirty-two days from now. Who do they think they're scaring? Not me, Art Atkins.

"Make up your mind!" That was mostly what you heard when you tuned in on any of the media. "Sign into your nearest tent, and do it now before the last-minute rush."

I had my girls, and my game, and my superswank apartment and the whole luxury bit; and that nonsense was really beginning to be a nuisance. Most of my time with a girl was usually taken up these nights with arguing her out of making a run for the nearest tent.

—For Pete's sake, I pointed out in my most patient manner, there's nothing in a tent but a little more oxygen. It's only a stopgap. I ought to know. I'm one of the contractors that helped build the local one.

After you'd said that a few hundred times to a sobbing armful of gleaming feminine flesh, it got to be pretty boring; and what followed was no longer that great, either.

This morning, the phone rang shortly after ten. When I picked up the receiver, the picture that flashed on the screen was of Mona. Mona was my latest addition—added her to my select collection only six months ago. Right now, she was all dressed up.

"I'm dropping out, Art," she said.

"Look," I said, not exactly amused, but playing it straight, "how can a drop-out, drop out?"

"Oh, you will have your joke," she said in a miffed tone. On the telescreen, she made that movement of hers. Tossed her golden hair. The first time I saw her do that, it just about drove me out of my mind with erotic excitement; and I wasn't entirely immune to it this minute either. I grew aware that she was speaking again. "I mean," she went on, "I'm going to move into the tent. This air is too much for me."

"You've been listening to those crazy people," I accused. "I told you not to."

"Well, maybe you'd better listen to them, too," she flashed. It was a moment of uncontrol, and I could see her make an effort to get back into calmness. She managed it, and said, "Next month is the big day, and that's close enough to midnight for me."

"*What* big day?" I asked, pretending not to know.

I was talking to a blank screen.

I didn't get around to calling her back until afternoon; in case she expected a quick reaction, and a begging Art Atkins, thank you, no. When I phoned, the ringing signal came back many times, but nobody answered. It penetrated finally that maybe she really meant it.

Okay, okay. Grudgingly, I looked up the tent number, and dialed it. A computer voice said, "Sorry to inform you, sir, no personal calls are accepted for tent inhabitants from the outside except from authorized phones."

I replaced the receiver sort of gently, but grinding my teeth. Finally, I just sat there, shaking my head. It was amazing. Those people out there never failed to do their madness. Always big and *first* with bastards like that was putting up barriers. Doing something to be difficult. So be it . . . I was finally resigned—let them have their little moment.

I had another thought. I figured suddenly that Mona hadn't really departed all that fast. Just not answering. Being difficult, herself. So I threw on some threads and ankled outside.

You ought to see the city that I emerged onto, as I came out of my skyscraper apartment building. Down here, a deserted sidewalk. Above, a hazy sky. Not too bad, really. What was bad was, it was hazy all the time.

The street itself was like death. Best comparison, those old pictures of European cities evacuated during wartime, with only patrol vehicles. I stood there; and of course it was hard to breathe now that I was away from my air conditioning. Hot, too. After five, late afternoon; and the temperature still over a hundred. Something to do with an excess of carbon dioxide in the atmosphere.

Suppressing an impulse to gasp, I hesitated. Was Mona really worth it? Quickly, I realized: —It's the principle. If you let one mistress get away, next thing another one will be slipping off. And before you know it, you're sleeping alone for a while.

So Mona had to be the object lesson. I needed to be in a position to say to Hettie, Adele and Zoe, "Okay, sister, take a look at what happens to a dame who had her little heart set on throwing over Art Atkins."

Where I had come out was a hundred yards from Crestmore Street, a main stem. So I went over there, and just for fun tried to thumb down one of the official tanks—which were all that cruised the streets these days. Ugly things. I suppose if you wanted to breathe a normal amount of oxygen you had to keep it sealed in. And the tanks were the simplest mass-produced machines, with their electric motors and rechargeable batteries and their closed-in front seats.

As usual, no one stopped merely to give a guy a free ride. Since my mind was made up, I held up a twenty-dollar bill to the next tank. He pulled over. I told him where I wanted to go, and he motioned me into his rear seat. No extra oxygen there, but still it was sitting down, and hardly any demands on the body.

For twenty dollars I often get a ride in the front seat; but I take these guys as they are. Once in, I mimed at him with the money. He indicated for me to put it into the ashtray; and then he had the usual trite thought and opened his intercom again. There was a tight-lipped smile on his face as he said, "If you wish, I'll take you over to the nearest tent entrance, and you can sign in."

As if anticipating an adverse reaction, he added quickly, "No amount of bravery is any good against what's coming."

I said patiently, "Look, I'm going to visit my girl. And if I ever decide to go into a tent, I'll use my private entrance."

He must have believed I was joking. In his rearview mirror, I saw the tight-lipped smile was back on his face. Still, he seemed to relax a little. He said in a conversational tone, "The kind of people we're running into this final month are a strange breed. Natural selection has given us another look at the human race. Huge crowds were camping at the tent gates a year ago. That's one group. When entrance was finally allowed three months ago, they went in; then came other categories—roughly divided by psychologists into about a hundred emotional types. But now we're down to a special type of male and the women this type associates with, over whom the man has an unusually dominant control." He hesitated, then: "May I ask one more question?"

I said, surprised, "You're doing me the courtesy and favor of giving me a ride. Sure, ask anything."

"Why isn't all this affecting you?" He waved with his free arm. It was a gesture that embraced half the horizon. "The no-oxygen condition. The big change that's coming. Why don't you try to get to a safe place?"

It's not easy to explain good sense. I didn't try. I merely said pityingly, "You don't look like a schoolteacher. But I feel I'm going to get a classroom lecture for elementary grades. That may be all right for kids, but I should tell you I graduated from high school fourteen years ago."

"Still," he persisted, after smiling that thin smile on his thin face, "you want to live." He didn't even wait for me to let that die a natural death. He added quickly, "Nature is bigger than Man; particularly, it's bigger than any one man. For once everybody *really* has to cooperate."

It was my turn to smile. "If everybody has to," I said, "then everybody will. So what's the problem?"

He looked at me uneasily. "The decision of what to do had to be made by qualified scientists," he said. "Some individuals are resisting that decision." He went on, half to himself, as if arguing with a doubting segment of his brain, "At this late stage there's nothing they can do. What do you think?"

"I've never given it a thought," I said—truthfully, because what I do in connection with all those conniving human beings is purely defensive. They start to move against me. My defenses come into view. That simple. I said, "Right now I'm visiting my girl."

He shook his head, wonderingly. "Mister," he said, "you're either a complete idiot, or a better man than I am. Good luck."

He let me off at Mona's street, waved at me from inside his mobile oxygen tent, and drove off. I walked along, slightly nettled by his final words, and mentally grappling with them.

—What I am, I told myself, is a man who confronts a problem long in advance. And then I don't pay any more attention to it until it actually happens . . . For Pete's sake, this oxygen shortage wouldn't be acute for another month. All right, so thirty days from now I'd finally confront it as a problem. When it began to rain fluorine I'd hold my hand out and let the drops fall on it, sniff them—that is, if the smell wasn't already permeating the whole damp universe around me. And then . . . well, that would be the time to get on my horse, or whatever, and canter over to my personal tent entrance.

By doing things like that, I'd made my first million before I was twenty-five—in a world that was coming to an end, when almost everybody else was sitting petrified. By age twenty-eight, I was one of those wealthy contractors; in case you wondered, that's where some of the big money is to be made, particularly if you find out early where the bodies are buried. Naturally, this past year things had been rough; not much planning ahead. Just bridge stuff. Details of helping people through the transformation. Once the tent was built, the details of what followed were out of my field. Mostly chemical, biological, medical—and thousands of bright-eyed jerks listening to lectures about how to give the injections that would convert the cells of an oxygen breather over to fluorine. And care and feeding of same while in transition.

Fine. It had to be done. But don't bother me with it.

I was riding up the elevator to Mona's floor by the time those thoughts completed. A minute later, I softly inserted my key into the door of 412-J.

I had myself braced. A quick bit of sweet talk to soothe her, and get her into bed. If that worked, it would be the end of it. But if it didn't—

I wouldn't really bash Mona up bad. Without her pretty face and curvy body, I wouldn't want her anyway. So there was no point being rough. Besides, I'm not one for violence except when it is needed. One good smash to the jaw to make her think, but break no bones. Maybe a little blood and after bruise as a reminder. Anyone who knows women will realize that I'd be leaning back practically horizontal in my desire to bring about a peaceful solution, if that's all I did.

The door swung open, as I manipulated the key; and I walked into the silence inside. I paused, taking it all in; and I've got to admit it, as always I was impressed by the absolutely delightful interior.

My current girls live like queens, and even my cast-offs have it pretty good. I give new mistresses *carte blanche* on how they fix up an apartment. You can be pretty sure that if you pick your girls carefully they'll create their own dream. Mona had been especially artistic.

So I gazed at sheer enchantment. But it felt empty. I walked through the glittering living room, glanced into the music and book room, examined the kitchen and then went into the glorious frilly bedroom. No one there, either.

She did it! I sat down on the gorgeous queen-sized bed, and let the madness of what she had done sink in. And right there, I got angry. It takes a lot to set me off. But I could feel the heat of that anger rise up into my cheeks, and the seethe of it was in my skin all the way down to the toes, like a shot of vitamin B complex. I could even taste the stuff, I was so teed off.

"—Okay, baby, you asked for it." I spoke the words softly but aloud.

. . . Once inside the tent, I put on my little badge—one of the ten-thousand series. And so I became a human molecule. People swarmed in all the corridors. To anyone but a person like myself (who had learned the pattern during the building stages) it must have seemed like total confusion.

Down to level H—for Henessey (Mona Henessey)—I forced my way, or rode, relieved, on one of the rolling sidewalks. My destination was the east section, where the He–s would be.

It took a while. A pigeon-faced stupe held me up at a checkpoint, while he studied my pass. But what I had was just the right level of authority. Not VIP—easily verifiable. But with just the proper amount of secondary eminence, more than anyone would be able to cancel out in this rush.

Sure enough, he let me by. Reluctantly. Some people just don't like the set of my beard. He had that look in his eyes. But—nothing he could do.

Since sectional computers had been built in to handle all room designations, when I came to the He– area I simply dialed her name on the first computer outlet I saw. Instantly, her room number flashed onto the plate in front of me.

I had brought a peep device with me. So I attached it to the wall of her apartment from the side corridor. The interior scene that came on to the little bright screen should have warned me. The apartment was a family-sized one. Mona did not have a family. But there she was, dressed as I had seen her on the phone viewplate that morning. A sleek-haired man was with her. Seeing him veered my attention from other suspicions.

A boyfriend? Yes—it turned out. As I watched, he took her in his arms and gave Mona one of those lingering lover's kisses. Observing the two of them, I could only shake my head in amazement at the nature of a woman. She didn't come here to breathe more oxygen. She came because she'd fallen for a pair of broad shoulders and striking black eyes.

I saw the eyes as he released her, and turned toward the door. Sizing him up quickly through the peep device, I placed him at twenty-seven or eight (Mona was twenty-two). The irony of it drilled deep into me, not for the first time in my adult years. Question in my mind: was this a marriage-to-be, or just a shack-up? A free man learns early to recognize that a woman gradually gets that got-to-be-married thing until she can't be reasoned with. I always tried to train my girls early to keep off that subject. No dice on marriage with Art Atkins.

The man turned at the door; and I had a full front view of him. The way he held himself gave me a new perspective. He radiated some level of purposefulness. An implication of authority—which I had learned to recognize in my career. Normally, I'd just go away until I checked his background. But that was not possible in this melee. I gave him two minutes after he went out the door. Then I went around and pushed the buzzer.

Mona opened the door.

When she saw me, she tried to shove it shut. But of course I had expected that. And so I had my foot in the jamb. As I pushed my way in, I said, "Don't worry. I just want to talk to you."

That was not exactly a truth; but it wasn't wholly a lie. Finding her with a man had transformed this situation, and my attitudes were modifying moment by moment as I considered the unpleasant reality of what level of man it might be.

She continued backing away from me, angling off toward the kitchen door. I pursued her unhurriedly. Fact was, I badly wanted information, but didn't know how to begin.

Before I could decide what to say, there was a diversion. A sound. Behind me. I swung around rapidly. Several men had come out of the hallway that led to the bedrooms. They carried those special electric-shock hand weapons used by the police. As I faced them, they stopped in a tight little cluster and regarded me.

There were five of them and one of me. I remained where I was, keeping my hands out where they could be seen. I had heard what a shock gun does to you, and didn't want any . . . A remote segment of my mind noted again the direction from which they had come, and reasoned that they had probably entered this apartment through a connecting door at the end of the hall from the adjoining apartment. It was a possibility I had failed to take into account.

I was not chagrined. One man can't think of everything. I had now—as I discovered—met a few of the conspirators, part of planet-wide resistance to what the authorities were planning. And although I had vaguely heard of such a conspiracy, it had never occurred to me that anyone involved had noticed me.

The surprise was that total.

Standing there, I was able to observe that two of my captors looked to be in their mid-twenties, two in their thirties and one probably forty-two or three. It was this oldest individual who summarized the situation for me. When he described how Mona had been the bait to catch my type of dominant male, my memory shot back instantly to the party where I had met her.

"But there were many beautiful girls there," I protested. "You mean, all?—" I paused, questioning.

My informant nodded. His companions continued to regard me unsmiling.

I remembered more now of the party. A political thing, given by a local bigwig. So he must be in on the scheme, and at this ultimate hour was prepared to have that information known to me. I had gone to the party because it was the commercial thing to do.

"It wouldn't have mattered," I was told, "which of the girls you were attracted to. They were all dedicated to the plan to save oxygen-breathing mankind."

"B-but—" I began.

What I intended to say was, "Why me?" I didn't say it. I was remembering something else. "Still," I said, "Mona must have been selected in advance. She arrived near the end of the party, and so she made an entrance, and bowled me over. That had to be planned."

No—was the headshake.

Her coming as she did was a consequence of a misunderstanding. She was not one of the original volunteers. What had happened was that she and her fiancé had an engagement to attend another affair, and Mona had arrived unexpectedly. Then, when I had been attracted to her, she made the best of her predicament and belatedly volunteered—which offer was immediately accepted by the desperate leaders of the conspiracy.

To say that I was thinking hard as I learned these details, was an understatement. I like to know where I'm going and what's next. I often had a purpose in a crisis the instant I became aware that there was one.

How should you act when you've been caught completely unprepared?

There was the room; family-size, but still damned small. And five people plus me and Mona were crowded into it. The five had me backed up against a wall by this time. No place to go but through five determined, armed men. Those were the kind of odds that I respected.

So getting away couldn't be my goal. Chance of success: zero.

It dawned on me I was in a spot tougher and different from any that I'd ever been in during my somewhat checkered career.

No purpose—except to find a purpose.

These people had swung a ringer in on me: Mona. There she stood, off to one side now. Her color was higher than I'd ever seen it . . . Embarrassed, I thought, she's ashamed.

That steadied me. Because it pointed up that these were amateurs. Sincere people. In my mind's calculator, I hastily counted the price she'd paid; and for a volunteer virgin—which is what I discovered she was, when we began our affair—it was colossal. I liked to get around to my girls four times every eight days. Divide that into six months. And the price leaves you gasping—if you examined it from the point of view of a fiancé off somewhere on the sidelines.

My instant feeling was that I'd better not let Black-eyed Broad-shoulders be alone with me while I was in a captured condition.

. . . All this did that lightning move through my brain. Which was the way things work inside me. And then, having again considered the improbability of the whole thing, I voiced my original thought.

"But why?" I asked breathlessly. "Why *me?*"

At this point the oldest of the men stepped forward. Funny, how people are. Until now he had stayed with the group, sort of identifying himself with the others, and not putting on any leadership airs. He could have continued that little game. Instead, he had a thought; and that thought, by God, triggered nervous energy, so that involuntarily he showed where his ego believed he really ought to be: up front.

You'll never catch Art Atkins going out of a role he has set himself to play. Where necessary, I can give a false signal until doomsday. Once more it proved . . . here were amateurs.

So I learned from the spokesman that people like me had been spotted as being capable of playing a decisive part in this crisis. And that, while several other men had also had an equivalent of Mona planted on them, the group had finally settled on me as being the one for our local tent.

All over the earth other versions of Art Atkins were getting this treatment today in connection with their tent as I in connection with mine. (The girl suddenly leaving, and they following her.)

"Look—" I protested at that point, "the only reason I came after Mona was—" My voice trailed off.

The group's lecturer smiled grimly. "A masculinity dominance thing," he said, "on a level of intensity comparable to a primitive Stone Age male."

I was still fumbling in my mind for something I could do. So I only shook my head over the analogy, rejecting it. After all, I only intended to give Mona a single hard punch.

What I did do was speak the basic puzzlement in my mind. "Okay, I'm the key guy in this crisis. *Key in what way?*"

Smiling grimly, the old guy told me . . . And, *of course,* I thought, almost blankly. Naturally, *that* would be it—

Pretty sharp of them to spot it.

Of course, they couldn't be sure . . . Suppose, I asked myself, I deny it?—

The spokesman must have deduced what was in my mind; so he smiled again, showing his teeth, "You might as well realize, Mr. Atkins, that we mean business. Naturally, we have no idea exactly what you did that places this tent at your mercy. But over in Peking the Art Atkins there was a minister in the government, and what he did was construct the principal oxygen converter beside a huge water reservoir; and so at the key hour that water will be released into the processing room, and if necessary will flood part of the tent itself. In Berlin, the Art Atkins there put in a tank of oxygen alternating with a tank of ammonia, and so at a key moment we will let the oxygen and ammonia intermix. Now, in New York, the story we have is—" He stopped, so he showed his teeth again, and said, "Need I go on?"

He added quickly, "In several instances, torture had to be used to obtain the information."

I sighed. I was never one of your super-brave types. All I ever wanted to do was protect myself from the schemers, so that I could go about my business.

"My method," I said, "was one of those chain reaction bombs, with a hundred fuses. Once it starts at any of those fuses it keeps going, flashing fire along a thousand exploding pathways.

"Why a bomb? Well, I like things simple and direct."

After the first stimulated excitement died down, they grew curious. What was my reason?

I could only shrug . . . "Think about it," I said. Here were those experts proposing that mankind endure a biologic transformation. Were they right? Maybe. But then again maybe not.

To me scientists were only people. We kept hearing the statement: *the scientists recommend*— Which scientists? Because there was usually another group of equally trained experts who said no; only they didn't happen to be the ones who had their lips close to the official ear.

I learned before I was twenty, it was a matter of personality, or sheer accident. The first great success with animal, then human, embryos nurtured on those moons of Jupiter and Saturn that had atmospheres; and finally by remote control on Jupiter itself—these were dazzling victories for what was called the cosmic school of biochemists. They became the kings of science. It was the bandwagon for a chemist to jump onto. And of course when a team developed serum d and its variations that could change an adult oxygen breather to a fluorine utilizer or—by another step—to chlorine gaspers (they actually did gasp, but they survived), just about all the hysteria that you ever wanted to see, hit the fan.

But long ago I met experts who said, "We're not giving this enough time. Fluorine-breathing human beings look great right now. But it's only been forty-two years since the first one. There may be side effects. Why not hold off another thirty years?"—which was about the time that (even the doubters agreed) would be about it for oxygen on earth.

My own feeling, after asking a few questions of astronomers: somewhere in space might be huge chunks of frozen oxygen similar in size to the fluorine meteorites that were now being maneuvered towards a close orbit around earth.

Why not allow the extra years for those to be discovered? At the time, that was just a thought. I wasn't obsessed. And yet—when I considered my usual type of advance precaution, the explosive was the possibility that I understood best. And it was a method that would actually control the situation. Cum see cum saw.

I *always* took such precautions. I remember once I had a contract to build a bank. Just for fun, in case I ever had a reason to enter the bank vault, I constructed a secret tunnel under it. You won't find that tunnel in the plans, and nowhere in my head was there intent to use it. But there it was waiting for me.

. . . I emerged from my private thoughts to learn that the time they wanted me to blow up the oxygen plant was the next day at 11 A.M.

I was startled. It had all happened so fast that I hadn't had time to consider the actuality. I protested, "With all those people near it?"

They did not reply; simply watched me. I watched back, baffled by my predicament.

In a way, there was no problem here. Nothing, really, to decide, or have a purpose, about. What I had to accomplish—what these conspirators wanted from me—was basically something I was in favor of. In my deepest being, I felt total—but total—resistance to being changed over from an oxygen to a fluorine breather.

Oh, I doubt if I'd have done anything about it on my own. And I quailed a little even now at the thought that people would die. But (I argued with myself) there were people dying every day either from oxygen deficiency, or from intense psychic disturbance, as the ultimate crisis approached.

Was I deciding, as I stood there?

It didn't seem like a decision.

I had no choice. There would be torture if I refused; I believed that. And they had all evening and all night to stick their needles into me.

Once more I looked them over; and they looked back, silently.

Pretty ridiculous (I thought) when a man had to be forced to do something to which he was not opposed.

Still—there were serious, unfavorable aspects that needed to be brought out into the open.

I returned their silent stares, questioningly now.

I could see from the expressions on their faces that they weren't planning to listen to any objections. So all I said, was, "They'll reconstruct it. And next time there'll be no implants possible."

The spokesman impatiently brushed that aside. That was a year, two, even three away. "By that time we'll figure something else."

I was silent.

They took that for agreement, and I had to admit to myself that it was.

While I listened, details were discussed. It seemed Mona's boyfriend had wormed his way high into the establishment. It was he who would guide me through the guard system that protected the oxygen.

When I heard that, I felt a queasy sensation in my stomach. I said finally, "May I talk to Mona?"

No one was against. I walked over to her. All the time I spoke to her, she avoided my eyes. But she answered each question.

"What is his name?"

"Terence O'Day."

It was a family name that I knew. High in local politics. But it was the father I had heard of, not the son.

"Was he jealous?"

"He said he'd had other girls before he met me, so there was nothing unfair for me to have another man, or even more than one." She added swiftly, "He was furious at me for having arrived early, but once it happened he was resigned."

She seemed in that simple way of girls and women, to believe that. Naturally, I rejected the explanation totally. But I did believe that the poor guy had had no choice, after her big blooper.

All I said was, "Will you see him before eleven A.M. tomorrow?"

"Tonight." She spoke reluctantly, face averted.

I fought instant jealousy. Because something in her face said that she would be spending the night with him.

(Onlookers have an idea that a man with four mistresses doesn't worry about what they do with their spare time. Boy, are they wrong.)

Mona was speaking. "You will be staying in this apartment tonight under guard," she said. "And I"—defiantly—"will be staying with Terence."

I had control of myself again. I said earnestly, "I want you to tell him that I regret the incident that brought you early to that party. That I never knowingly play around with other men's wives or girl friends—" That was not true. Who else was there? All the pretty girls had guys from the day they peaked over the edge of fourteen.

But it was an important lie to put over. "Will you tell him that?" I urged Mona.

"Yes, I'll tell him."

She seemed belatedly to realize the implication of my words. "I'm sure you can trust him," she said. "When you think of the sacrifice he made in letting me volunteer—" She stopped. She turned impulsively and placed her hand on my arm. "Good luck, Art. Please don't fail us."

But she still didn't look directly at me. And so when I turned to the five, I shrugged, and said simply, "What's your opinion?"

The oldest man was silent. One of the two middle thirties men said, "He's been with us since the beginning. He sacrificed his girl. What more can a man do to prove himself?"

I acknowledged that reluctantly. I said, "I've told you what my advance preparation was. When I did it, I had no particular plan in connection with it. But if I can't set off the trigger mechanism, that's it. There's nothing more in this tent that I know about."

For Terence, the next day, I did my clumsy routine. I kept bumping into people. I could see him gritting his teeth as, each time, he walked on as if he did not know me. That was the game we played at the beginning, at his suggestion. In case we ran into somebody important. Whenever I was delayed, and twice when I fell awkwardly, Terence went ahead about twenty feet, and then he stopped casually, and slowly turned around, and waited until I was ahead of him again.

I presently estimated that we were less than two hundred yards from the oxygen facility—only a short distance from where I had told them the trigger mechanism was located. And yet no sign of the guards that I had heard about. I was beginning to wonder if the security system wasn't a myth. A few seconds after that I rounded another corner.

As I did so, there were quick footsteps. Hands grabbed me from behind, and held me. Somebody reached around and grasped both my wrists. My arms were jerked back, and pulled together. But by that time I had relaxed from my initial automatic stiffening.

I felt the handcuffs, as they snapped around my wrists. But I was able by now to suppress my impulse to turn and see if Terence had also been seized. I suppressed it, because whether he was or not wouldn't change my conviction that this was a trap, and he had led me into it.

I had a sudden insight. Maybe across the world the score or so Art Atkins types were also being captured at this moment by other Terence-type counterspies. In all—so I had been told—twenty-three large tents were the targets for today. It was believed by the conspirators, if that many were knocked out (involving upward of thirty million people) that would end the threat of fluorine transformation for the time being.

Since I was being seized, and not instantly killed, I guessed there'd presently be a confrontation—I had to smile. Those poor goops. Thinking they could outwit Art Atkins with such an elementary tactic. Boy!

I had no time for additional thoughts. I was being hustled along the corridor at a run. I had a few quick glimpses of about a dozen men running with me.

As rapidly as we had started, we suddenly slowed. A door opened. The brightness from inside flooded the corridor. I was pushed through the doorway into a large, brilliantly lighted room; was vaguely aware the while of the dozen crowding in behind me.

—Somebody always lives better, I thought.

Now, that's not a complaint. I've lived like a king for years. But, still, here in the tent apartments were tiny, and in the big dormitories further down people occupied one unit in a tiered bunk system.

The room I was in looked lived in. There were settees and cunningly arranged tables, and on a dais to one side, carpeted floors and a combination music and book section. On this dais was an incongruity. A conference table had been squeezed onto it. Behind it, sitting at it, were four well-groomed older men.

I caught glimpses of other rooms through half-open doors; and for a moment in one of them a young woman's face. That door closed. But, yes, the place was lived in by somebody who was entitled to a living room over sixty feet long by forty wide, and bedrooms to match.

Still being held, I was led to the foot of the dais. And now, for the first time, I saw Terence again.

He was not handcuffed.

He stood just to my right, a faint, cynical smile on his face. His clothes were unruffled. Clearly, no one had shoved him around.

He said to the men behind the table, "I was with him every minute, and he didn't have a chance to do anything. Besides"—contemptuously—"he's yellow. I've seen fear before. This guy was so weak in the knees from terror, he could hardly stand up."

One of the seated men, a cold-faced individual, studied me with steely gray eyes. He was in civvies, but his bearing was military. I had never seen him before. He said in a resonant voice, "Mr. Atkins,

I'm General Peter Simonville. When I look at you, I see a cool, determined male about six feet tall. I see in your eyes the same kind of self-pitying expression that I used to observe in my oldest son. But women went for that boy, and I understand you're also a woman's he-man type. He was not afraid that I ever saw, and I don't see any fear in you. So my question is, did you have an opportunity during one of those moments of stumbling to trigger that bomb?"

"No!" I lied.

The general glanced at Terence O'Day. "It's now"—he looked down at his watch—"twenty-one minutes to eleven. You have five minutes to get the information out of him, and then we have sixteen minutes to undo the damage. Fair enough."

To me, he said, "I turn you over to your rival, Mr. Atkins. I should tell you that he has *carte blanche*."

Sharp man, General Simonville—I had to admit it. But I remained silent; simply watched as Terence climbed up the dais, went around to the rear of the table and seated himself. Those black eyes of his surveyed me.

He said, "You must have been out of your mind to set up a destruct system. Don't you realize you can't keep a secret like that? The authorities didn't know who put it there, but they knew about it three, four, years ago."

I simply stood there. Who do they think they're giving lessons to? I understood that kind of junk when I was sixteen. You can't keep a secret. Of course. What else is new? So you tell it yourself. Let it slip. Get it out there where the stupes can start gloating among themselves, and doing all those things like removing the fuses and the powder. Meanwhile, over where the real bomb was—

I had to smile, and shake my head.

I was aware of General Simonville's knowing gaze dissecting my thoughts. "Listen, Art," he said in a cajoling tone, "that is all there is to this, isn't it? We got it all three years ago. We didn't overreach ourselves, did we?"

When he said that, I knew something . . . For Pete's sake, I've got a decision to make.

The way I reasoned it, nobody could do anything. There wasn't enough time to torture me. Maybe six hundred, maybe seven hundred seconds. So they were out of luck, unless I did a switcharound inside my skull.

At that point, Terence O'Day said, "We've got Mona."

I shrugged. That little spy.

Belatedly, I realized who it was who had said that. "So?—" I reacted then.

Terence continued, "As soon as you and I left the apartment where you spent the night, troops went in and captured those five conspirators. At the same time Mona was picked up. All six of these criminals were rushed over to the oxygen process plant. If it blows up, they will blow up with it."

I let my mind's eye visualize Mona. Her golden hair would be hanging down, framing her face. In a few minutes the soft body that belonged to that beautiful face would be segmented into several thousand uneven chunks, and her blood everywhere.

I let my mind go slow-blank on that picture. No reason why it should bother me . . . what happened to a phony. It did a little. But all I said was, "She's your girl, not mine, Mr. O'Day."

His face was suddenly livid, "That stupid girl!" he snarled. "Let the little whore burn."

I stared at him, eyes widening, a large thought in my mind. Women who associated with the Art Atkins type were never satisfied with ordinary males afterward.

"Hey," I said, "I'll bet she wouldn't play last night."

It was a nasty thing to say. But if we weren't at the nasty stage in this situation, when do you get there?

I'm glad black-eyed glares don't kill. I'd've been dead in three seconds if they did.

I have to admit, looking at that handsome face twisted with hate and jealousy, I could feel the tight anger inside me start to ease up. Hastily, sensing that weakness might make my decision for me, I dredged up another possibility for Terence O'Day's severe reaction: Was this a game? Was he dramatizing against her as part of a scheme to delude me?

I couldn't—I realized—care less. In spite of my efforts, I was inwardly visualizing those golden curls burning in a fury of exploding flame, that beautiful face torn to shreds. And to hell with it. If that's the way they wanted to play, it was too rough for me.

"Listen!" I demanded. "Do the conspirators in this tent go free if I tell and show where everything is?"

Notice how badly I worded that. They used it against me later on: *I* was not one of the conspirators.

After I spoke, there were timeless seconds of emptiness in the room, as if everyone there stopped breathing. Then—

"*Yes!*" General Simonville's voice hit across that silence like a blow.

I accepted his promise. Because there was no time to get proof, or read the fine print. And in fact it was later carried out *to the letter*.

No time to waste. A couple of engineers and I made a dead run for one of the places in the corridor, where I had stumbled against the wall. When the trigger system that was there, was back in its safety position again; and for two days after while, with my help, they stripped the explosive from the real bomb, they seemed to take it for granted that I would be treated like the others. Then—

The job was done.

I was handed a paper with official seals, which began:

The unified governments of earth hereby command, and it shall be, that . . .

My property was confiscated, all my possessions ordered seized, no human being was to have consort with me again, ever.

Clutching this paper, I was kicked out into the street.

I was the S.O.B. who had planned four years ago to destroy the human race.

"Look," I protested, "that isn't why I set up that destruct system. I set it up because I *always* do things like that—"

Nobody listened. Or cared. To hell with Art Atkins. There was a universal rage at the narrowness of the world's "escape."

I gathered that the twenty-two guys like me in other tents were given the same brush-off treatment.

They had told me when they shoved me out, "Don't think you'll find your private entrance to the tent available a second time."

—Okay, boobs, take a good last look. You'll never see me again, nor locate my body.

Hell, I'd been expecting the world to turn against me since I came up out of the mists of childhood. Somehow, I always knew those so-and-sos didn't like me.

Soon as I was old enough I began getting another identity polished up for the day when they came after me. Why do you think I started growing a beard, practically over my mother's dead body, when I was sixteen? I didn't want anyone, not even her, to remember what I would look like if I ever had to go smooth face.

. . . Two years have gone by.

They say the fluorine rain has stopped.

Deep in the bowels of the big oxygen tent, a knock comes on my door. I guess who it is, and I say to Mona, "You answer it."

She opens the door. General Simonville stands there. His cold face has a forced smile on it. He says in a somewhat over-hearty voice, "The people in this apartment have been selected by lottery to be the first in this tent for the fluorine shots."

I take that with a straight face. The rest of the selections will—I imagine—actually be by lottery. But my being number one had to be arranged.

The general steps aside, and a trio of girls wheel in the equipment: a metal table with a large transparent jar on it with liquid in it. The liquid is the serum (I deduce). And there are a host of connecting tubes and needles.

As I lie there, and the girls are busy with my exposed thigh, my eyes turn and meet the gaze of General Simonville. "Everything okay?" he asks.

His question has a double meaning, and I consider before I answer. After I had shaved off my whiskers and altered my fingerprints, the problem was to get into the tent.

Well—I figured that a man with a private entry into a bank vault might have, say, a hundred thousand dollars available as a starter. That much cash, it seemed to me, might persuade a general who had not hesitated to accept a super-sized apartment for his own living quarters, to open a gate for me, and find a lower level place where I could live away from it all, and bring Mona over there. With that combo I figured I could sit out the rainstorms in relative comfort. In handing over the down payment, I also stipulated that I would be the first to be changed over.

I promised him a second hundred thousand if I got through alive—My gaze flicked down to the needle that was being shoved into me. The question in my mind is, will I wake up?

Have I offered him enough?

I've got a whole bank to draw on. Since the government has guaranteed losses suffered from looting during the transition, the bank will be repaid . . . My plan is to filch exactly what was expropriated from me.

I look up. I say, "Everything okay, General—on my side."

"On mine, also," he says.

People are hoping that changing mankind to fluorine breathing may alter human nature for the better. My suggestion is, they'd better not hold their breath while they wait for these peculiar two-legged beings to alter their behavior.

Believing that, I'm guessing as I sink into unconsciousness that the general's words mean what I think. And that I will wake up. I will. I will.

And I will be the first fluorine breathing son of a bitch on the new earth.

Robert Silverberg's is yet another name which has been so pre-eminent in the field of speculative fiction for so long that it defies introduction. It may be interesting, if not useful, to remark on the fact that he is (by recent adoption, anyhow) the seventh or eighth Californian to appear in these pages; at least half of those people are among those who have *fled* to California. A dismaying statistic.

Let a colleague and friend of Silverberg's, a writer of even longer standing within the field, supply the final word; *l'envoi* to these introductions; striking a somber note all his own.

DIES IRAE

Flense the rock of our race.
It seethes with us. Let it be hard.
Nothing we will gives reason to
what we do; at the heart's core
is the word.
We are the globe's disease; our
ulcer is ouns,
and our hoard.

The rock will carry, but it will not know
the scintillations of our
wisdom. Then, it will not.
It will boil with joy
when we quit it; but our
joy, not
any joy of the rock,
thought, wound, paprika wine, vermin or bird.

—James Blish

Robert Silverberg
THE WIND AND THE RAIN

The planet cleanses itself. That is the important thing to remember, at moments when we become too pleased with ourselves. The healing process is a natural and inevitable one. The action of the wind and the rain, the ebbing and flowing of the tides, the vigorous rivers flushing out the choked and stinking lakes—these are all natural rhythms, all healthy manifestations of universal harmony. Of course, we are here too. We do our best to hurry the process along. But we are only auxiliaries, and we know it. We must not exaggerate the value of our work. False pride is worse than a sin: it is a foolishness. We do not deceive ourselves into thinking we are important. If we were not here at all, the planet would repair itself anyway within twenty to fifty million years. It is estimated that our presence cuts that time down by somewhat more than half.

The uncontrolled release of methane into the atmosphere was one of the most serious problems. Methane is a colorless, odorless gas, sometimes known as "swamp gas." Its components are carbon and hydrogen. Much of the atmosphere of Jupiter and Saturn consists of methane. (Jupiter and Saturn have never been habitable by human beings.) A small amount of methane was always normally present in the atmosphere of Earth. However, the growth of human population produced a consequent increase in the supply of methane. Much of the methane released into the atmosphere came from swamps and coal mines. A great deal of it came from Asian rice fields fertilized with human or animal waste; methane is a by-product of the digestive process.

The surplus methane escaped into the lower stratosphere, from ten to thirty miles above the surface of the planet, where a layer of ozone molecules once existed. Ozone, formed of three oxygen atoms, absorbs the harmful ultraviolet radiation that the sun emits. By reacting with free oxygen atoms in the stratosphere, the intrusive methane reduced the quantity available for ozone formation. Moreover, methane reactions in the stratosphere yielded water vapor that further depleted the ozone. This methane-induced exhaustion of the ozone content of the stratosphere permitted the unchecked ultraviolet bombardment of the Earth, with a consequent rise in the incidence of skin cancer.

A major contributor to the methane increase was the flatulence of domesticated cattle. According to the U. S. Department of Agriculture, domesticated ruminants in the late twentieth century were generating more than eighty-five million tons of methane a year. Yet nothing was done to check the activities of these dangerous creatures. Are you amused by the idea of a world destroyed by herds of farting cows? It must not have been amusing to the people of the late twentieth century. However, the extinction of domesticated ruminants shortly helped to reduce the impact of this process.

Today we must inject colored fluids into a major river. Edith, Bruce, Paul, Elaine, Oliver, Ronald and I have been assigned to this task. Most members of the team believe the river is the Mississippi, although there is some evidence that it may be the Nile. Oliver, Bruce and Edith believe it is more likely to be the Nile than the Mississippi, but they defer to the opinion of the majority. The river is wide and deep and its color is black in some places and dark green in others. The fluids are computer-mixed on the east bank of the river in a large factory erected by a previous reclamation team. We supervise their passage into the river. First we inject the red fluid, then the blue, then the yellow; they have different densities and form parallel stripes running for many hundreds of kilometers in the water. We are not certain whether these fluids are active healing agents—that is, substances which dissolve the solid pollutants lining the riverbed—or merely serve as markers permitting further chemical analysis of the river by the orbiting satellite system. It is not necessary for us to understand what we are doing, so long as we follow instructions explicitly. Elaine jokes about going swimming. Bruce says, "How absurd. This river is famous for deadly fish that will strip the flesh from your bones." We all laugh at that. *Fish?* Here? What fish could be as deadly as the river itself? This water would consume our flesh if we entered it, and probably dissolve our bones as well. I scribbled a poem yesterday and dropped it in, and the paper vanished instantly.

In the evenings we walk along the beach and have philosophical discussions. The sunsets on this coast are embellished by rich tones of purple, green, crimson and yellow. Sometimes we cheer when a particularly beautiful combination of atmospheric gases transforms the sunlight. Our mood is always optimistic and gay. We are never depressed by the things we find on this planet. Even devastation can be an art form, can it not? Perhaps it is one of the greatest of all art forms, since an art of destruction *consumes* its medium, it *devours* its own epistemological foundations, and in this sublimely nullifying doubling-back upon its origins it far exceeds in moral complexity those forms which are merely productive. That is, I place a higher value on transformative art than on generative art. Is my meaning clear? In any event, since art ennobles and exalts the spirits of those who perceive it, we are exalted and ennobled by the conditions on Earth. We envy those who collaborated to create those extraordinary conditions. We know ourselves to be small-souled folk of a minor latter-day epoch; we lack the dynamic grandeur of energy that enabled our ancestors to commit such depredations. This world is a symphony. Naturally you might argue that to restore a planet takes more energy than to destroy it, but you would be wrong. Nevertheless, though our daily tasks leave us weary and drained, we also feel stimulated and excited, because by restoring this world, the mother-world of mankind, we are in a sense participating in the original splendid process of its destruction. I mean in the sense that the resolution of a dissonant chord participates in the dissonance of that chord.

Now we have come to Tokyo, the capital of the island empire of Japan. See how small the skeletons of the citizens are? That is one way we have of identifying this place as Japan. The Japanese are known to have been people of small stature. Edward's ancestors were Japanese. He is of small stature. (Edith says his skin should be yellow as well. His skin is just like ours. Why is his skin not yellow?) "See?" Edward cries. "There is Mount Fuji!" It is an extraordinarily beautiful mountain, mantled in white snow. On its slopes one of our archaeological teams is at work, tunneling under the snow to collect samples from the twentieth-century strata of chemical residues, dust and ashes. "Once there were over seventy-five thousand industrial smokestacks around Tokyo," says Edward proudly, "from which were released hundreds of tons of sulfur, nitrous oxides, ammonia and carbon gases every day. We should not forget that this city had more than one and a half million automobiles as well." Many of the automobiles are still visible, but they are very fragile, worn to threads by the action of the atmosphere. When we touch them they collapse in puffs of gray smoke. Edward, who has studied his heritage well, tells us, "It was not uncommon for the density of carbon monoxide in the air here to exceed the permissible levels by factors of two hundred and fifty per cent on mild summer days. Owing to atmospheric conditions, Mount Fuji was visible only one day of every nine. Yet no one showed dismay." He conjures up for us a picture of his small, industrious yellow ancestors toiling cheerfully and unremittingly in their poisonous environment. The Japanese, he insists, were able to maintain and even increase their gross national product at a time when other nationalities had already begun to lose ground in the global economic struggle because of diminished population owing to unfavorable ecological factors. And so on and so on. After a time we grow bored with Edward's incessant boasting. "Stop boasting," Oliver tells him, "or we will expose you to the atmosphere." We have much dreary work to do here. Paul and I guide the huge trenching machines; Oliver and Ronald follow, planting seeds. Almost immediately, strange angular shrubs spring up. They have shiny bluish leaves and long crooked branches. One of them seized Elaine by the throat yesterday and might have hurt her seriously had Bruce not uprooted it. We were not upset. This is merely one phase in the long, slow process of repair. There will be many such incidents. Some day cherry trees will blossom in this place.

This is the poem that the river ate:

DESTRUCTION. I. *Nouns.* Destruction, desolation, wreck, wreckage, ruin, ruination, rack and ruin, smash, smashup, demolition, demolishment, ravagement, havoc, ravage, dilapidation, decimation, blight, breakdown, consumption, dissolution, obliteration, overthrow, spoilage; mutilation, disintegration, undoing, pulverization; sabotage, vandalism; annulment, damnation, extinguishment, extinction, invalidation, nullification, shatterment, shipwreck; annihilation, disannulment, discreation, extermination, extirpation, obliteration, perdition, subversion.

II. *Verbs*. Destroy, wreck, ruin, ruinate, smash, demolish, raze, ravage, gut, dilapidate, decimate, blast, blight, break down, consume, dissolve, overthrow; mutilate, disintegrate, unmake, pulverize; sabotage, vandalize; annul, blast, blight, damn, dash, extinguish, invalidate, nullify, quell, quench, scuttle, shatter, shipwreck, torpedo, smash, spoil, undo, void; annihilate, devour, disannul, discreate, exterminate, obliterate, extirpate, subvert; corrode, erode, sap, undermine, waste, waste away, whittle away (*or* down); eat away, canker, gnaw; wear away, abrade, batter, excoriate, rust.

III. *Adjectives*. Destructive, ruinous, vandalistic, baneful, cutthroat, fell, lethiferous, pernicious, slaughterous, predatory, sinistrous, nihilistic; corrosive, erosive, cankerous, caustic, abrasive.

"I validate," says Ethel.
"I unravage," says Oliver.
"I integrate," says Paul.
"I devandalize," says Elaine.
"I unshatter," says Bruce.
"I unscuttle," says Edward.
"I discorrode," says Ronald.
"I undesolate," says Edith.
"I create," say I.

We reconstitute. We renew. We repair. We reclaim. We refurbish. We restore. We renovate. We rebuild. We reproduce. We redeem. We reintegrate. We replace. We reconstruct. We retrieve. We revivify. We resurrect. We fix, overhaul, mend, put in repair, retouch, tinker, cobble, patch, darn, staunch, calk, splice. We celebrate our successes by energetic and lusty singing. Some of us copulate.

Here is an outstanding example of the dark humor of the ancients.

At a place called Richland, Washington, there was an installation that manufactured plutonium for use in nuclear weapons. This was done in the name of "national security," that is, to enhance and strengthen the safety of the United States of America and render its inhabitants carefree and hopeful. In a relatively short span of time these activities produced approximately fifty-five million gallons of concentrated radioactive waste. This material was so intensely hot that it would boil spontaneously for decades, and would retain a virulently toxic character for many thousands of years. The presence of so much dangerous waste posed a severe environmental threat to a large area of the United States. How, then, to dispose of this waste? An appropriately comic solution was devised. The plutonium installation was situated in a seismically unstable area located along the earthquake belt that rings the Pacific Ocean. A storage site was chosen nearby, directly above a fault line that had produced a violent earthquake half a century earlier. Here one hundred and forty steel and concrete tanks were constructed just below the surface of the ground and some two hundred and forty feet above the water table of the Columbia River, from which a densely populated region derived its water supply. Into these tanks the boiling radioactive wastes were poured: a magnificent gift to future generations. Within a few years the true subtlety of the jest became apparent when the first small leaks were detected in the tanks. Some observers predicted that no more than ten to twenty years would pass before the great heat caused the seams of the tanks to burst, releasing radioactive gases into the atmosphere or permitting radioactive fluids to escape into the river. The designers of the tanks maintained, though, that they were sturdy enough to last at least a century. It will be noted that this was something less than 1 per cent of the known half-life of the materials placed in the tanks. Because of discontinuities in the records, we are unable to determine which estimate was more nearly correct. It should be possible for our decontamination squads to enter the affected regions in 800 to 1,300 years. This episode arouses tremendous admiration in me. How much gusto, how much robust wit, those old ones must have had!

We are granted a holiday so we may go to the mountains of Uruguay to visit the site of one of the last human settlements, perhaps the very last. It was discovered by a reclamation team several hundred years ago and has been set aside, in its original state, as a museum for the tourists who one day will wish to view the mother-world. One enters through a lengthy tunnel of glossy pink brick. A series of air-locks prevents the outside air from penetrating. The village itself, nestling between two craggy spires, is shielded by a clear shining dome. Automatic controls maintain its temperature at a constant mild level. There were a thousand inhabitants. We can view them in the spacious plazas, in the taverns, and in places of recreation. Family groups remain together, often with their pets. A few carry umbrellas. Everyone is in an unusually fine state of preservation. Many of them are smiling. It is not yet known why these people perished. Some died in the act of speaking, and scholars have devoted much effort, so far without success, to the task of determining and translating the last words still frozen on their lips. We are not allowed to touch anyone, but we may enter their homes and inspect their possessions and toilet furnishings. I am moved almost to tears, as are several of the others. "Perhaps these are our very ancestors," Ronald exclaims. But Bruce declares scornfully, "You say ridiculous things. Our ancestors must have escaped from here long before the time these people lived." Just outside the settlement I find a tiny glistening bone, possibly the shinbone of a child, possibly part of a dog's tail. "May I keep it?" I ask our leader. But he compels me to donate it to the museum.

The archives yield much that is fascinating. For example, this fine example of ironic distance in ecological management. In the ocean off a place named California were tremendous forests of a giant sea-weed called kelp, housing a vast and intricate community of maritime creatures. Sea urchins lived on the ocean floor, one hundred feet down, amid the holdfasts that anchored the kelp. Furry aquatic mammals known as sea otters fed on the urchins. The Earth people removed the otters because they had some use for their fur. Later, the kelp began to die. Forests many square miles in diameter vanished.

This had serious commercial consequences, for the kelp was valuable and so were many of the animal forms that lived in it. Investigation of the ocean floor showed a great increase in sea urchins. Not only had their natural enemies, the otters, been removed, but the urchins were taking nourishment from the immense quantities of organic matter in the sewage discharges dumped into the ocean by the Earth people. Millions of urchins were nibbling at the holdfasts of the kelp, uprooting the huge plants and killing them. When an oil tanker accidentally released its cargo into the sea, many urchins were killed and the kelp began to re-establish itself. But this proved to be an impractical means of controlling the urchins. Encouraging the otters to return was suggested, but there was not a sufficient supply of living otters. The kelp foresters of California solved their problem by dumping quicklime into the sea from barges. This was fatal to the urchins; once they were dead, healthy kelp plants were brought from other parts of the sea and embedded to become the nucleus of a new forest. After a while the urchins returned and began to eat the kelp again. More quicklime was dumped. The urchins died and new kelp was planted. Later, it was discovered that the quicklime was having harmful effects on the ocean floor itself, and other chemicals were dumped to counteract those effects. All of this required great ingenuity and a considerable outlay of energy and resources. Edward thinks there was something very Japanese about these maneuvers. Ethel points out that the kelp trouble would never have happened if the Earth people had not originally removed the otters. How naïve Ethel is! She has no understanding of the principles of irony. Poetry bewilders her also. Edward refuses to sleep with Ethel now.

In the final centuries of their era the people of Earth succeeded in paving the surface of their planet almost entirely with a skin of concrete and metal. We must pry much of this up so that the planet may start to breathe again. It would be easy and efficient to use explosives or acids, but we are not overly concerned with ease and efficiency; besides there is great concern that explosives or acids may do further ecological harm here. Therefore we employ large machines that insert prongs in the great cracks that have developed in the concrete. Once we have lifted the paved slabs they usually crumble quickly. Clouds of concrete dust blow freely through the streets of these cities, covering the stumps of the buildings with a fine, pure coating of grayish-white powder. The effect is delicate and refreshing. Paul suggested yesterday that we may be doing ecological harm by setting free this dust. I became frightened at the idea and reported him to the leader of our team. Paul will be transferred to another group.

Toward the end here they all wore breathing-suits, similar to ours but even more comprehensive. We find these suits lying around everywhere like the discarded shells of giant insects. The most advanced models were complete individual housing units. Apparently it was not necessary to leave one's suit except to perform such vital functions as sexual intercourse and childbirth. We understand that the reluctance of the Earth people to leave their suits even for those functions, near the close, immensely hastened the decrease in population.

Our philosophical discussions. God created this planet. We all agree on that, in a manner of speaking, ignoring for the moment definitions of such concepts as "God" and "created." Why did He go to so much trouble to bring Earth into being, if it was His intention merely to have it rendered uninhabitable? Did He create mankind especially for this purpose, or did they exercise free will in doing what they did here? Was mankind God's way of taking vengeance against His own creation? Why would He want to take vengeance against his own creation? Perhaps it is a mistake to approach the destruction of Earth from the moral or ethical standpoint. I think we must see it in purely esthetic terms, i.e., a self-contained artistic achievement, like a *fouetté en tournant* or an *entrechat-dix,* performed for its own sake and requiring no explanations. Only in this way can we understand how the Earth people were able to collaborate so joyfully in their own asphyxiation.

My tour of duty is almost over. It has been an overwhelming experience; I will never be the same. I must express my gratitude for this opportunity to have seen Earth almost as its people knew it. Its rusted streams, its corroded meadows, its purpled skies, its bluish puddles. The debris, the barren hillsides, the blazing rivers. Soon, thanks to the dedicated work of reclamation teams such as ours, these superficial but beautiful emblems of death will have disappeared. This will be just another world for tourists, of sentimental curiosity but no unique value to the sensibility. How dull that will be: a green and pleasant Earth once more, why, why? The universe has enough habitable planets; at present it has only one Earth. Has all our labor here been an error, then? I sometimes do think it was misguided of us to have undertaken this project. But on the other hand I remind myself of our fundamental irrelevance. The healing process is a natural and inevitable one. With us or without us, the planet cleanses itself. The wind, the rain, the tides. We merely help things along.

A rumor reaches us that a colony of live Earthmen has been found on the Tibetan plateau. We travel there to see if this is true. Hovering above a vast red empty plain, we see large dark figures moving slowly about. Are these Earthmen, inside breathing-suits of a strange design? We descend. Members of other reclamation teams are already on hand. They have surrounded one of the large creatures. It travels in a wobbly circle, uttering indistinct cries and grunts. Then it comes to a halt, confronting us blankly as if defying us to embrace it. We tip it over; it moves its massive limbs dumbly but is unable to arise. After a brief conference we decide to dissect it. The outer plates lift easily. Inside we find nothing but gears and coils of gleaming wire. The limbs no longer move, although things click and hum within it for quite some time. We are favorably impressed by the durability and resilience of these machines. Perhaps in the distant future such entities will wholly replace the softer and more fragile life-forms on all worlds, as they seem to have done on Earth.

The wind. The rain. The tides. All sadnesses flow to the sea.

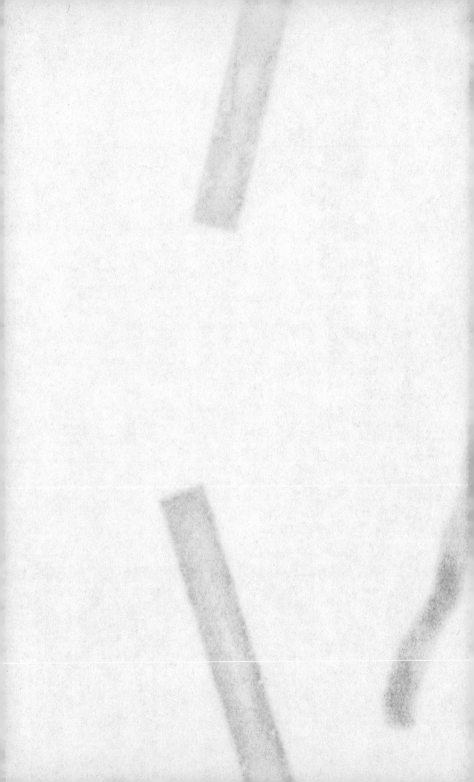